BLURRED REALITIES

[TWO STORIES]

DAVID A. OAS

LUMINARE PRESS
WWW.LUMINAREPRESS.COM

Blurred Realities: Two Stories
© 2018 David Oas

All rights reserved. This book or any portion thereof may not be reproduced or used in any manner whatsoever without the express written permission of the publisher, except for the use of brief quotations in a book review.

Printed in the United States of America

Cover Design: Claire Flint Last

Luminare Press
438 Charnelton St., Suite 101
Eugene, OR 97401
www.luminarepress.com

ISBN: 978-1-944733-79-7

*To all the dreamers who create
art for themselves and others.*

BLURRED REALITIES

My imagination makes me human and makes me a fool; it gives me all the world and exiles me from it."

Ursula K. Le Guin

Maybe each human being lives in a unique world, a private world different from those inhabited and experienced by all other humans… If reality differs from person to person, can we speak of reality singular, or shouldn't we really be talking about plural realities? And if there are plural realities, are some more true (more real) than others? What about the world of a schizophrenic? Maybe it's as real as our world. Maybe we cannot say that we are in touch with reality and he is not, but should instead say, His reality is so different from ours that he can't explain his to us, and we can't explain ours to him. The problem, then, is that if subjective worlds are experienced too differently, there occurs a breakdown in communication…and there is the real illness.

Philip K. Dick

INTRODUCTION

I thought I was pretty normal. Twenty-eight-years old, married, three children, and starting my doctoral internship as a clinical psychologist at a VA hospital. I had always been rebellious and defiant growing up, but now I was embarking on a lifetime career. I needed to behave.

I switched from soft-hearted Solipsism (I am my own world, all I got is me) to Scientific Empiricism. Reality became Consensual Reality; i.e., statistical calculations and validity studies of what I observed in life. Yes, the relativity of human perception could be scrutinized and quantified.

Events and happenings became scientific events and facts out there. We had confidence levels where things were true enough until further notice. Did I get my PhD in Clinical Psychology or a PhD in Consciousness? That was 1965.

At the Veteran's Administration Hospital, psychiatrists and clinical psychologists were mentors who also sat in judgment of my interactions with patients—grading me. There were pools of schizophrenics, paranoids, catatonics, psychopaths, depressives, druggies, ex-military servicemen with PTSD from WWII, Korea, and Vietnam. Others with a mix of undiagnosed disorders. Messed up humans you were supposed to help, not experiment on or fool around with.

And then there was *King Leo*, a mostly true first case study that left me bewildered. I mean, how could he? That was when I learned I still had a pathological need to create my own reality with patients and clients.

Boundaries were lost, and my ethics were questionable. They were puppets for my fantasy life. They belonged to me. They fulfilled me.

I hadn't completely lost my mind yet with King Leo. So what follows is a synopsis for a screenplay. I kept file notes separate from my fantasy notes that began to fill boxes by the time I attended film school at USC in Los Angeles in 1973.

THE ORIGINS OF KING LEO

Prelude: Fall 1965

During my doctoral clinical psychology internship at the Minneapolis VA Hospital, I made a presentation to the staff of psychologists and psychiatrists, psychiatric nurses, and fellow clinical interns. Title: (Something like the following) "The merits of complete behavioral control over a patient's day-to-day activities as the ultimate prescription for therapeutic progress and change in patient populations with severe psychopathology."

I was laughed at. Eventually the chief psychiatrist responded, "King Leo just came back again off skid row. Why don't we give Leo to intern Oas as his primary case for a year, and see how he feels about his confidence in changing behavior when he reports to us at the end of his internship?"

So said the chief psychiatrist to the smirking, nodding heads of the rest of the psychiatrists, clinical psychologists, clinical interns, and psychiatric nurses at the staff meeting. Other psychology interns looked at me for a reaction. They seemed embarrassed on my behalf.

Over the next week, I read the case files on Leo, and observed him as he was "drying out." At the next staff meeting I had to decide: Was I willing to take on Leo as my year's primary case study with attempts to conduct a therapeutic intervention throughout the year?

The staff had concluded Leo was a failed experiment during the last ten years that he was in and out of the mental health unit at the VA. I asked if I could do anything that I wanted with Leo. I was told yes, as long as

I didn't break any rules or regulations as stated in the hospital and department manuals on patient care.

I broke a few rules. After all, I had always broken a few rules, I was an "adrenalin junkie."

KING LEO

(based on a mostly true story)

Logline: David Olson, a young psychologist-in-training at a Midwest VA hospital, attempts to rehabilitate an alcoholic psychopath called King Leo.

Synopsis: Psychologist intern David Olson, age 28, married, with three children, is introduced along with a half-dozen other interns at the staff meeting in the mental health wing of a VA Hospital. The interns are charged with making a presentation to the staff on their approach to psychotherapy based on their theoretical framework developed through their education and training in graduate school. Each intern is assigned to meet with inpatients throughout the following week and decide on their case study patient selections at the next staff meeting.

When the interns, including Olson, visit King Leo's room, they see a 38-year-old, disheveled, grotesquely ugly, drying-out alcoholic staring unblinking at them. He stands out among the "crazies" with an, "I-dare-you-to-try-to-do-anything-with-me" look.

After the stare down, he offers a toothless grin exposing the few rotting, stained teeth that remain. His lower jaw is broken and projects out. Numerous old scars and recent black and blue marks add to what the other interns see as a "bum" who came from a circus sideshow. At the end of the rounds after visiting all the other inpatients, intern Olson goes back to Leo.

Olson says he is going to be Leo's counselor and what could he do to help him? Leo laughs and says, "I need teeth and a new jaw, but that's not your bailiwick." Bailiwick? *This guy might have a brain.*

Interns offer their patient choices the following week at the staff meeting. Intern Olson surprises the staff by stating he has chosen King Leo as his primary case study.

King Leo's story and Olson's relationship with Leo begins. The first week his teeth come out and his jaw is broken and rotated. His mouth is wired shut for six weeks. His meals are sipped through a straw and his communication with Olson comes through Olson's assigned writings and responses written by Leo.

Back story: Leo was a high school valedictorian from a St. Paul Catholic school. As the first born from a large Irish Catholic family, he was groomed for and received a scholarship to Notre Dame. The summer before leaving for Notre Dame, he began drinking and realized alcohol and women were his first loves. He "bagged" education and joined the Navy.

After a short stint in the Navy, and an early discharge after AWOL drunken binges, he married. The next ten years included five children, dozens of prostitutes, other sexual liaisons, and a wife who kicked him out of the house and onto the street. King Leo recalls coming home to visit his children and finding his ex-wife in bed with another man. He states that he went to his pickup, got his shotgun and "was going to shoot the guy's sorry ass, and maybe my ex-wife too." His oldest daughter and favored child entered the scene and managed to calm him down. He hasn't seen his ex-wife or any of his children except one, since.

While intern Olson counsels Leo, Olson does doctoral research and goes on weekly rounds in the Neurology Unit. He is validating a memory test he developed and uses it to test patients throughout the hospital. (See online: www.screeningformemoryloss.com)

Olson tests and retests Leo with every intelligence and neuropsychological test Olson can get his hands on to see if Leo's brain is getting well and whether he is getting smarter. Leo challenges Olson with his divergent creative test responses. Olson observes Leo at the unit library reading books and newspapers. Other days when Olson comes looking for Leo, Leo behaves as a social butterfly in the mental health unit. He knows all the other patients on the unit by name. Leo questions them on their health, counsels them, and advises them. He explains in detail to Olson things he observes, has read, or thought about.

Olson is suspicious Leo has secrets that he is keeping from him. Olson discovers activities are going on behind closed doors that Leo hides.

Meanwhile, intern Olson is receiving compliments from the professional staff and intern supervisors for what they see as a miraculous change in Leo. Olson is given permission to take Leo off the hospital grounds to purchase clothing. They behave like best buddies. Olson helps Leo get his driver's license, loaning him his 1957 Bel Air Chevrolet.

Olson becomes aware that something isn't right. First, Leo has female visitors during visiting hours. Olson asks Leo if he could meet his visitors. Leo responds with a smile, "It wouldn't be prudent." One night, Olson comes back to the VA to work on data he's gathered from his research. He walks down the unit hall to go to the bathroom. The door to Leo's bedroom is closed. Olson listens, hears Leo getting it on sexually with a woman. Olson walks away, hears more sex going on in the next room. Olson strikes up a conversation with the station psychiatric nurse located nearby. She reminds him it's still visiting hours. A woman comes out of Leo's room, walks to the next bedroom, taps on the door, and waits. Another woman comes out, straightening and buttoning her skirt.

Olson questions Leo the next day about the nighttime visits. Leo says his cousins are frequent evening visitors.

Olson continues spying on Leo. The next time the women come, Olson follows the women when they leave the VA. When the women get on a bus, Olson gets on the bus with them. The women get off on St. Paul's skid row. A number of the homeless from the street welcome the two women. They share welcoming hugs and from what Olson can see, they exchange contraband. The women are taking "stuff" from their purses and getting cash in return from some of the homeless. Olson is convinced the women are getting the contraband from Leo. Leo's name is frequently mentioned in animated conversations. Olson tries to get closer to hear more, but a couple of the homeless come begging. He leaves before the women notice.

Leo has his new teeth, new clothes, and a new look to his face with his new jaw. He's drug- and alcohol-free, and his brain is healing. Leo is shaving every day. When Olson comes to work in the morning, he drops by Leo's bedroom, watches Leo scrutinizing his face in the mirror. Leo and Olson drop by the weight room and lift weights while Leo informs Olson on local politics. Leo gives his strong opinions about the poor, the need for health care, and why humans fall through the cracks in life. The conversation changes to Leo going off the unit to look for a job. Leo envisions a possible reconnection with his children and other relatives.

The conversations often end with Leo making a joke that Olson is his hero in the hospital, but outside there is a jungle that will not allow Leo to escape his history. Leo accuses Olson of a privileged background too distant from Leo's world of reality.

Spring is in the air and Leo is "antsy." The staff and Olson's supervisor tell Olson it's time for Leo to become an outpatient. They also tell Olson to plan the termination of Leo's therapy. Olson resists by challenging the staff to prove to him that resources are available to help Leo transition out of the hospital. The staff backs off. They challenge Olson to do the research on where he thinks Leo should go instead of going back to skid row.

Meanwhile, Leo has permission to leave the VA during the day. Leo tells Olson on his return to the Unit he has visited various employment agencies. Olson doesn't believe Leo is telling the truth after demanding details. He catches Leo in a lie. Leo tells Olson employment is impossible due to his criminal past. Leo says, "You find me any job. I'll gladly take it."

One night while working late at the Unit, Olson observes Leo leaving the VA. Leo is carrying a shoebox from the shoes they purchased together from an earlier clothes-shopping trip. Olson decides to follow Leo. Leo catches the same bus the women rode earlier. Olson, in his station wagon, follows Leo. Leo gets off the bus on skid row. Olson observes from his parked wagon. The women and at least a dozen other now familiar homeless people welcome Leo. Leo opens the shoebox and hands out what appears to be pill bottles.

King Leo appears to be back in his element counseling the homeless.

Olson observes Leo tapping shoulders, hugging, gesturing as he hands out his supplies. Leo is offered alcohol and cigarettes. He takes a cigarette, smokes, shakes his head on the alcohol. Leo goes inside one of the run-down buildings with one of the women. Olson drives away.

The next day Olson confronts Leo. He asks Leo what he was doing away from the unit at night. Leo states he had received permission to leave the hospital to visit a cousin. Olson doesn't have the courage to admit he followed Leo. Olson changes the subject, says it's time to talk about what to do to keep Leo from going back to the streets.

Olson asks Leo if he is willing to move away from the Twin Cities. Leo responds, "Get me a job and I'll go anywhere." Olson tells Leo the results from all the different psychological, intelligence, and interest tests taken over the last several months.

"Your brain is healing. You could go to a trade school, a college. I will help you get a place to live, a job, and loans to attend night classes."

Leo is surprised by Olson's confidence. "You can really do that?"

Olson says both VA and GI money are there if Leo demonstrates he can stay clean. Olson tells Leo the supervising staff wants Leo to be a newsworthy example of a successful rehabilitation program that will give recognition to the effectiveness of the VA mental health units outreach to the community around the Twin Cities.

Meanwhile, it is time for Olson to leave the VA. He tells Leo he lucked out and got a teaching job at a West Coast college in a dream city.

Olson and Leo visit a job site and apartment a few miles away from the Twin Cities. The VA doesn't know Olson drives Leo to Olson's home. They rehabilitate an old trailer to carry the Olson family's personal belongings west. Leo is irritated when Olson talks about the importance of AA and developing new, healthy friendships to keep him from going back to a former self-defeating life style.

Leo states he wants to get rid of the restraining order keeping him from visiting family members that has been hanging over his head the last ten years. His oldest daughter will graduate from high school in a couple weeks and he wants to attend her graduation. He knows where his ex-wife lives.

Can intern Olson pull off a few more coups before he goes West? Olson does. The job at a Coca Cola bottling company in a nearby city comes through with funds from the VA to move and house Leo until his first paycheck. Intern Olson gets Leo connected with the local college to start night school. Olson is so invested in Leo that he goes with Leo to his daughter's graduation. Olson choreographs an emotional meeting between the two.

And that is not all that Olson does. He helps Leo move into his new rental. He allows Leo to drive his '57 Bel Air with Leo's sparse belongings. Olson follows Leo to his new home in his old station wagon. It is an emotional goodbye for intern Olson. Leo asks Olson what he was going to do with the Bel Air?

Olson says to Leo, "I'd sell it to you."

Leo says, "I have no money."

Olson takes the title of the car out and says, "How about $5 a month."

To which Leo puts out his hand and says, "Deal."

Olson gives Leo the car and his forwarding address. They finish their promises, hugs, and goodbyes.

Intern Olson returns home to his family and continues packing for departure the next day. Goodbyes are said to relatives and friends. The family retires for the night.

At 4 a.m. the next morning Olson receives a phone call from Leo. Loud laughter and other raucous sounds come from drunken partiers.

"Who is this?" asks Olson.

"Dave, it's your friend Leo. We're having a party."

Olson is angry. "You've been drinking."

Leo slurs, "It's a great party. Why don't you come down before you leave? All my friends are here."

Olson never hears from Leo again.

Postscript: Thirty years later Dr. Olson sees Leo's uncommon last name in a local newspaper. Curious, Olson does some research and catches up with Leo's oldest daughter back in the Midwest by phone. He asks her about Leo.

Leo's daughter, surprised and somewhat hesitant, says to Dr. Olson, "Leo died fifteen years ago. Who are you?"

Olson responds. "I was his therapist at the Minneapolis VA hospital in the 1960s."

Leo's daughter hesitates again. "Leo never talked about any of his therapists. He only talked about a young intern who helped him get a new face and gave him a car."

Olson said, "What about his problems with alcohol?"

"That? He quit drinking and became a volunteer with the homeless in St. Paul. They called him King Leo. It was the biggest funeral ever. Who are you again?"

THE ORIGINS OF PEACE THAT KILLS

I was into my career teaching and counseling at Southern Oregon University. I consulted with and trained staff at mental health clinics. I had my small clinical practice. I looked pretty good professionally on the outside.

The joke in my family was that I was somewhere else in my head half the time, not paying attention to the immediacy of life in the moment.

We had foster children. I was brought up as a "preacher's kid" to do good, to help the needy. In 1968, along came five-year-old D——, a Native American child from the Klamath tribe who became a foster sister to my daughter. Our family met D——'s mother when she wasn't away in prison. More often, we met D——'s grandmother. I asked both D——'s mother and grandmother who and where was the father? Both said he wasn't from the Klamath tribe, but rather a descendent from a Rogue River tribe who used to inhabit the Rogue Valley of southern Oregon. I hadn't heard about this tribe and was told they were swallowed up in a "trail of tears" to a reservation on the Oregon coast. Curious, I began reading and found that this little valley I lived in had basically annihilated the Rogue River Indians. Disease, racism, and forced evacuation to reservations from their land by government land grants to pioneers hastened the Native Americans' demise.

My fantasies took over and I began to walk in moccasins. In my 30s, I became Adam, son of Indian Chief Tecumtum (Chief John to the white eyes). Later, in my late 40s and early 50s, as I became more nearsighted, I became Chief Tecumtum. The result of my musings is my favorite screenplay, *PEACE THAT KILLS* (period piece covering the Rogue River Indian Wars, 1853-1856). The screenplay has strong historical roots with fictional coloring. It's inappropriate for a white man telling stories and writing a screenplay about Native Americans. But why not? We have dozens of westerns and other movies with Native American themes that don't tell the story from a Native American perspective.

PEACE THAT KILLS (2018 Revision)

Southern Oregon Rogue River Indian Wars

1853-1856

BLACK

"The ethnic cleansing that befell the western Indians made for a tragedy so ghastly that it cannot be dismissed as merely the inevitable consequence of the clash of competing ways of life."

                Bureau of Indian Affairs, September 2000

FADE IN:

EXT. OREGON COAST - SUMMER DAY

The ocean, coastline, clouds and fog, rock cliffs, land and trees. The Rogue River. ADAM, son of Tecumtum, famous southern Oregon war chief, NARRATES OFF SCREEN.

Begin with an IMITATION OF A LOST NATIVE AMERICAN language (Athabaskan).

          ADAM (V.O.)
    My ancestors say all of this land was
    water. One day, when it was light out,
    our Father, the Creator, came out of his
    sweathouse. Our Father blew the fog

          (MORE)

> ADAM (V.O. CONT'D)
> away.... He saw trees and rocks and a mother that they clung to. Our Father, and our Earth Mother, they smoked the pipe together. Their smoke crept across the land and created the birds and animals.

EXT. SOUTHERN OREGON CREEK - SUMMER 1853 - DAY

ADAM, 17, a lithe, alert Rogue River Indian brave, is on a Spirit Quest. He wears nothing but a deerskin loincloth and moccasins.

> ADAM (V.O.)
> Here by the river, were Coyote, Grizzly Bear, Mountain Lion, Deer, Owl, Salmon, Beaver, and Eagle... Our spiritual parents... When humans first came there was Skunk Man and Bear Woman... After many seasons, came my father, Tecumtum, and my mother, River Maiden.

In his altered state of consciousness, Adam scoops up mud from creek-side, smears his body and face. He PLUNGES INTO THE CREEK, submerging himself. He rises from the water, hands raised.

He walks upstream through the water, rounds a bend. A buck and doe drink from the creek. Adam sees something move along the opposite bank of the creek. He sinks down low.

FOUR WARRIORS with facial markings, similar to Adam, wearing a mix of native American and white man's clothing, creep along the creek. Two natives raise their bows. A GUNSHOT. The buck's legs buckle as he falls to the water. The doe leaps - runs into the forest.

>   WHITE HUNTER (O.S.)
>   I got it.

TWO HUNTERS dressed in miner's clothing run to the water's edge, drop their guns, and wade in. The first hunter cuts the dying buck's throat, guts him.

>   FIRST HUNTER
>   Hold the legs.

Blood flows into the river, followed by bloody entrails.

They start to drag the deer out when an ARROW PENETRATES the chest of one of the hunters. They drop the deer.

The first hunter dives for his gun - rolls into the brush.

He crawls toward the horses, leaving his moribund partner GURGLING BLOOD. Two arrows barely miss the first hunter as he mounts his horse and RIDES AWAY.

The four Warriors APPEAR from the brush. One takes the horse.

Two take the deer and throw it across the back of the horse. One STABS and SCALPS the Miner. They pick up the musket - SLIP AWAY. Adam remains low in the water as the bloody entrails of the buck float by.

EXT. TECUMTUM'S VILLAGE - DAY

INDIAN CHILDREN and YOUNG ADULTS between 8 and 25 years of age PLAY a field-hockey-like game called Shinny in a grass field.

The spirited, 18-year-old KITTY, Tecumtum's daughter, is doing battle with DANIEL GILES, a 16-year-old white friend. Giles trades pots and pans with the Indians for leather, stone pipes, and tobacco pouches.

Many ELDERS, WOMEN, and CHILDREN of the village watch, CHEER and continue to work while the game is played. Kitty breaks toward the goal. She slips around a couple defenders, scores. Giles, exhausted, looks to the sidelines.

Kitty's father, TECUMTUM, the headman of the village (called Chief John to the whites), steps in to take Giles' place.

Very skilled, the wiry warrior of over 60 years goes up against his daughter. This gets everyone's attention.

CHEERS, LAUGHTER, CLAPPING, CHANTING is heard.

ELDERS GAMBLE on the next goal using dentalia (strings of exotic sea-shells, valued as money), tobacco pouches, stone pipes, and obsidian blades.

Neither Kitty nor Giles, who has come back in, can defend against Tecumtum as long as he is close to the puck.

Kitty knows that her father is very nearsighted. She shoots the puck to another warrior. She breaks toward the goal - stops. Tecumtum has lost sight of the puck. When his back is turned, the warrior shoots the puck back to Kitty, who puts it behind her foot. She stands looking at Tecumtum.

EXT. TECUMTUM'S POV

A BLURRY SCREEN. The CAMERA PANS to see who has the puck. Kitty has a smile on her face.

END POV

Kitty pushes the puck out - runs. Tecumtum pushes his stick against hers and takes the puck away to the CHEERS of those who watch. He passes the puck.

Suddenly the cheering and laughter stop. THE FOUR WARRIORS seen earlier enter the village leading pack mules laden with contraband including pots, pans, hoes, spades, and a quarter of beef.

The miner's horse and dead deer follow. The bloody scalp is tied to the saddle. Family members and the other villagers quickly gather around.

CULTUS JIM, mid-30s, (who did the scalping of the miner) is the subchief and the powerful warrior son of Tecumtum. He leads the warriors. His face is painted with tribal markings. He hands the musket to an elder and approaches his father.

> CULTUS JIM
> See what I have.

The village people excitedly explore the contraband.

> TECUMTUM
> (visibly upset)
> How long until the whites with guns come?

CULTUS JIM

They were at the creek crossing. Two men with guns and horses.

Tecumtum walks to the horse - looks at the scalp.

TECUMTUM

They will come to the village. Why do you not follow your father's wishes?

CULTUS JIM

I will fight the white eyes.

TECUMTUM

No! We will go to the high country.

CULTUS JIM

Warriors from the other villages are already fighting the white eyes.

Your brother waits for you to join him.

TECUMTUM

I will fight no more battles. I will speak with my brother.

Cultus Jim walks back to the contraband - locates a leather flask filled with whiskey. He gives the flask to the warriors - gestures to them to go to the sweat lodge.

He turns to his wife, THISTLE DOWN, and his TWO SMALL CHILDREN. Picking up the youngest, he goes into his plank house.

Tecumtum gives a hand gesture to all watching that it's time to move to the mountains. Kitty, Giles, and all the rest of the family nearby, prepare to move. Kitty walks towards the creek. Giles follows. Kitty turns.

>KITTY
>
>You have to leave. It's not safe here.

Giles looks at warriors entering the sweat lodge.

>GILES
>
>They want to make good trades.

Cultus Jim COMES RUNNING out of the plank house, ENTERS the sweat lodge. Giles looks back at Kitty, who watches her older brother.

>KITTY
>
>No more.

Giles turns to go over to OTHER WARRIORS. Kitty grabs his arm.

>KITTY
>
>I told you before. The Klamaths, the Cow Creek, and the Umpqua... Many warriors are coming.

Tecumtum walks toward the sweat lodge. He gestures to the villagers to speed up their preparation for leaving.

The SIGHT and SOUND of steam on the rocks. The GRUNTS, TALK, and LAUGHTER from warriors can be heard from inside.

EXT. KITTY AND GILES - CONTINUOUS

Giles hesitates, comes back to Kitty. Kitty walks to the creek to gather fishing nets. ELDERS help while CHILDREN spear and trap fish.

WALKING BEAR, an orphaned boy, 11 years of age, spears a fish.

He excitedly runs to Kitty and then to an ELDER, who hands Walking Bear his cane. The elder takes the fish off the spear. He gives the boy an affectionate hug. Walking Bear helps the elder get out of the creek.

> GILES
>
> Tell Tecumtum to have Cultus Jim and the other warriors stop stealing and killing the whites. You can't stop the settlers and miners from wanting to live here. More are coming.

Kitty gathers the younger children. Elders gather the nets.

> KITTY
>
> You have your way, we have ours.

Kitty steps away from Giles as she gets the children away from the creek. Giles looks to his mules and trading goods.

> GILES
>
> I will never do anything to harm your family. Tell your father that, too.

Walking Bear runs by Kitty and Giles towards the creek. Other children follow.

                    WALKING BEAR
    Adam! Adam!

Adam ENTERS, walking along the creek. The children gather around. Adam is unresponsive.

                    WALKING BEAR
    See the fish I caught.

Kitty approaches Adam, Giles following. Giles moves forward to greet Adam. Kitty takes Giles's arm and pushes him back - shakes her head. She turns to Adam.

                       KITTY
    My brother. You came back before the
    Great Spirit gave you his power.

Adam ignores all - walks on. Adam walks towards the plank house. His mother RIVER MAIDEN and OTHERS stop gathering/packing belongings to greet Adam.

                       ADAM
    Where's Father?

Kitty points to the sweat lodge.

EXT. SWEAT LODGE - CONTINUOUS

Cultus Jim and other naked warriors ERUPT OUT of the sweat lodge - leap into the creek. Some children dive in after them. Tecumtum EXITS from the plank house - sees Adam. Cultus Jim comes out of the water.

                     CULTUS JIM
    Adam! Come!

Adam directs his attention to his father. Tecumtum looks at the sun - looks long and hard at Adam.

>   TECUMTUM
>   Is this not a good day?

>   ADAM
>   White hunters came to the river.

>   TECUMTUM
>   Go high in the mountains.

>   ADAM
>   I want to join my people in the battle
>   against the white man.

Adam's words carry to the warriors in the water. CHEERS. Tecumtum angrily turns - gestures all to be still.

>   TECUMTUM
>   Come! You are not ready. You're not to
>   be a warrior.

Tecumtum beckons a life-long friend, the ELDERLY SHAMAN. Tecumtum, Adam, and the Shaman ENTER the plank house.

INT. PLANK HOUSE

>   TECUMTUM
>   (visibly upset)
>   You are not done with the sacred
>   journey.

ADAM

I am.

Tecumtum looks at the Shaman.

TECUMTUM

I have warriors... Your heart is soft.

ADAM

My power came to me at the sacred place.

Tecumtum is disbelieving. He shakes his head.

TECUMTUM

You're not listening. Go to the sweat lodge. Purify yourself. Then go back to the mountains.

ADAM

The Great Spirit gave me a sign.

SHAMAN

Sign? What sign?

ADAM

To fight and die by the white man's gun.

TECUMTUM

That's crazy talk. Your brother wants to make war. You are my son who has to make peace.

ADAM

I can shoot squirrels, rabbits, deer with Giles's gun.

I will teach our people to shoot better than the white man. I will show you.

Tecumtum still frustrated, looks to the Shaman for support.

TECUMTUM

You see what the white eyes do to our people with their guns and greed?

Tecumtum shakes his head.

TECUMTUM

The white man has taken the spirit away from my son.

ADAM

Father, my journey is done.

TECUMTUM

Your path is to be the path of peace. You are to be a healer.

Tecumtum points to the Shaman.

TECUMTUM

Have you not been taught by my brother?

Adam looks at the Shaman, hoping for a response. A long pause as the Shaman looks into Adam's soul.

Finally, the Shaman pulls out a tubular pipe and tobacco pouch from his pack. Tecumtum waves the Shaman away.

> SHAMAN
> (persisting)
> What is this power? You do not always take the first power that comes.

> ADAM
> (with resolve)
> I have the eyes of the eagle.

Adam looks at his father.

> ADAM
> I can see all that my father cannot see. We will not survive without my father to lead in the great war to take back our land.

Tecumtum remains frustrated. He stands up and faces Adam.

> TECUMTUM
> No!

The Shaman puts his hand up to Tecumtum. The Chief refuses to sit down.

> SHAMAN
> Where will you be when your father is at war?

Adam gets up, walks over and stands by his father.

                          ADAM

At his side. My eyes will become his
eyes. I will help our people to shoot
guns better than the white man.

The Shaman LIGHTS the pipe - draws deeply.

                        SHAMAN

Your eyes shall penetrate all the dark
and evil places of the earth.

Shaman gestures to Tecumtum and Adam to sit down.
They sit. The Shaman passes the pipe to Adam. Adam
draws from the pipe - COUGHS - draws again. The
Shaman gives the pipe to Tecumtum. The chief hesitates.

                        SHAMAN

Your eyes grow old. This is good medicine for you.

Tecumtum looks long at the Shaman - trusting him, he
takes the pipe and draws on it. He looks at his son. He
passes the pipe back to Adam.

EXT. TECUMTUM'S VILLAGE - NIGHT

Kitty PLAYS a MELODY on her reed flute. The FAMILIES of 30 to 40 people of Tecumtum's village gather
around the FIRE. The CHILDREN SLUMBER.

                         GILES

Will we hunt again?

                    ADAM

When the white man stops telling us how to live. Tomorrow, early, you leave. Warriors here will soon kill you. There is no more peace between the white man and Indian.

                    GILES

I have brothers from other villages who trade with me.

                    ADAM

You are a fool. Hear my warning.

Giles gets up - walks to Kitty. Adam turns to RIDGE RUNNER, a messenger scout who looks like a decathlete. Ridge Runner often wears a deer head when on a hunt or to avoid detection.

                    ADAM

Watch him until he is safely away.

Kitty, Tecumtum, River Maiden, Cultus Jim and family, and the rest of the Indian village settle in before the trip to the high mountains. Kitty CONTINUES the MOURNFUL MELODY.

EXT. FOREST TRAIL - DAY

GENERAL LANE (mid-40s, future territorial governor of Oregon), robust, wearing dirty gray breeches and a forage cap. He bears the cuts, dirt, and smudges that go with living in the field of battle.

JOEL PALMER (mid-40s, sympathetic Indian Agent to southern Oregon Indian tribes), a lifelong friend of

Lane, he is unpretentious and practical. They survey the damages to settlers' homes along their ride to Jacksonville.

CAPTAIN SMITH, early 30s, is a meticulously dressed officer, with a variety of nervous facial twitches. Newly dispatched from the East, he leads a DETACHMENT OF YOUNG UNIFORMED DRAGOONS.

Smoke comes from mountain tops and from burning cabins of settlers throughout the Rogue Valley. General Lane, agent Palmer, and the military detachment stop at a smoldering cabin. Chickens, pigs, cows, and domesticated ducks forage nearby.

A figure EMERGES from behind a thicket. It is GILES on foot. He walks through the ruins.

General Lane and Joel Palmer observe as Giles picks up a stuffed doll and puts it in a pack on one of the mules. He walks by a couple cows that have been butchered, part of their carcasses missing. He looks up as the entourage approaches.

> GILES
>
> Looks like they all went to Jacksonville, or been killed.

> JOEL PALMER
>
> Where you headed, son?

> GILES
>
> Goin' to town to get the rest of my mules, then head north.

> JOEL PALMER
>
> Where you coming from?

GILES

Chief John's village. They've left for the mountains.

JOEL PALMER

When?

GILES

This morning.

JOEL PALMER

What about the warriors?

GILES

Don't rightly know. They're itching for a fight. I heard the Cow Creeks and Klamath are coming.

GENERAL LANE

And the Umpqua. There's going to be a battle, son. Volunteers are signing up. We could use those mules.

JOEL PALMER

Go easy, Joe. The boy's no older than your son.

GENERAL LANE
(ignoring Palmer)

The government will pay good wages for you and your mules.

GILES

I ain't gonna be no part of no war. Chief John's family are my friends.

Lane looks at Palmer - nods his head to Captain Smith. The DETACHMENT RIDES on. Ridge Runner, WEARING DEER HEAD, watches from the trees. Ridge Runner turns - DISAPPEARS into the forest.

As Palmer, Lane, and the detachment ride, smoke surrounds them from the hills.

GENERAL LANE

Look at the smoke. Chief John and his brother Joe are in those hills gathering a thousand Indians... I smoked the pipe with John and his brother - gave their families Christian names. Now they're killing as many of us as they can. And you think you can stop it?

JOEL PALMER

I was hoping to have Chief John appeal to the other chiefs for peace.

It's no use now. We best get back to Jacksonville to get the volunteers organized before they go out and get themselves killed.

Palmer, Lane, et al ride by a couple of dead Indians on the trail. They ride on - DISAPPEAR in the trees.

FIVE INDIAN WARRIORS ENTER from the trees riding a couple of mustang horses pulling litters. On one litter contraband, including a beef quarter, pots and pans, etc. They pick up the dead Indians and DEPART.

EXT. JACKSONVILLE - CROWDED TOWN CENTER - DAY

SETTLERS, SETTLERS' FAMILIES, MINERS, GUNSLINGERS, MERCHANTS, AND OTHER TOWNSFOLK mill around the crowded street. BANNERS hang from store windows: "EXTERMINATE THE INDIANS."

TWO DEAD INDIANS in war paint hang from a scaffold for all to see. Animated CONVERSATIONS carry news about cabin burnings, animal slaughter, and missing settlers.

A SETTLER'S FAMILY, GEORGE AND MARY HARRIS, WITH CHILDREN, SOPHIE, 11, AND DAVID, 9, AND AN INDIAN BOY, 9, maneuver their horse and flatbed through the crowd to HOLMAN'S STORE.

A COMMOTION arises when the crowd sees the Indian boy. The family gets off the wagon, the father gripping the boy's hand tightly. Mary Harris keeps the other two children close to her. With difficulty, they work their way through the crowd to the general store entrance.

A half-dozen RAUCOUS DRUNKEN MINERS see the boy.

SHORTY, 35, a seasoned Indian killer, miner, and psychopath, and CHARLIE, his cowardly, avaricious sidekick push SETTLERS aside and grab the boy.

> SHORTY
> Another savage to hang

George Harris fights back. A COUPLE SETTLERS step in to help.

All attention is on the confrontation. The drunk miners force George and the settlers away.

Shorty and Charlie drag the boy toward the scaffold. The crowd chants, "HANG HIM, HANG HIM."

ANOTHER TWO MALE SETTLERS barge in and break the grasp of Shorty and Charlie on the boy.

> SETTLER
> Have you lost your minds? He's a boy.

> SHORTY
> (snarling)
> Nits breed lice!

Shorty pulls a knife, flashes it. Charlie cowers from the husky settlers and quickly drops his grip on the Indian boy. MORE MINERS crush in to help Shorty.

B.B. GRIFFIN, a powerful, rough-looking miner bolts through, grabs the boy, lifts him over his head and walks to the scaffold.

George and Mary Harris and their two children are pushed back into the crowd.

EXT. DETACHMENT - LANE - CONTINUOUS

The SOUNDS of JACKSONVILLE'S CROWD is heard in the distance as they ride along. Giles follows close behind with his mules. Lane puts his hand up. All stop. Giles rides on by.

GENERAL LANE
You think you can control those people?

Palmer looks towards Jacksonville and the crowd.

JOEL PALMER
Not with what's behind us.

(glances back at
Captain Smith)

The settlers want protection. The gold in the valley is gone. The miners are out of control with no place to go. Volunteer militias are springing up all over.

GENERAL LANE
Joel, it's progress. Back East our parents shoved the redskins to the other side of the Mississippi. Now the miners here see the redskins as an irritation, and the pioneers coming over the—

PALMER
To you it's all politics and progress. I don't want to hear it.

General Lane shakes his head at Palmer.

JOEL PALMER
(irritated)
The miners ruined the rivers with all the dredging. The pioneers come in and

(MORE)

                    JOEL PALMER (CONT'D)
settle on the fertile areas and plunder
their growing season.

Quit thinking about politics and help
me solve the problems in this valley.

                    GENERAL LANE
                    (wanting to change
                    the subject)
Let's go see what the ruckus is about.

                    PALMER
                    (mystified)
You mean you don't know?

Lane waves the detachment on. The CROWD HAS GROWN SILENT.

EXT. JACKSONVILLE - DOWN THE STREET - CONTINUOUS

LINES OF VOLUNTEERS sign up to join the military campaign against the Indians. B.B. Griffin ENTERS - joins MAJOR LUPTON at the table. Lupton, barely in his twenties, wearing a military jacket, exudes bravado.

Observing are two WELL-DRESSED MERCHANTS, CHARLES BRAY AND BENJAMIN DIRKSON intent on profiting from the war with the Indians.

In line are smatterings of settlers and miners hoping to get a chunk of government money and a few scalps.

BEN WRIGHT, a dark-skinned Indian scout of indeterminate race stands nearby. He wears a holstered revolver, long Bowie knife in a buckskin sheath, buckskin leggings, moccasins, black broad-brimmed hat covering long black hair, and a black shirt with a strand of dentalia.

Shorty and Charlie ARRIVE. They come to the head of the line. Shorty extends his hand to Major Lupton.

> SHORTY
>
> At camp they call me Shorty. By the looks of that jacket, you've been in a few skirmishes with the savages.

> MAJOR LUPTON
>
> Can you use that gun?

> SHORTY
>
> I got me some scalps when I was mining at Humbug Creek.
>
> I rode with Ben Wright over there
> > (pointing)
>
> against the Modocs.

B.B. Griffin and the Major look at Wright, who is wrapping and lighting his cigarette. Not in the line, he observes those in line.

> GRIFFIN
>
> Ben Wright. The greatest Indian fighter ever lived in these here parts.

Major Lupton jumps up to take Wright's hand. Wright doesn't offer it.

>					MAJOR LUPTON
>					(to Wright)
>		You signing up?

Ben doesn't respond. Lupton looks back at Shorty. Shorty looks over at the merchants.

>					SHORTY
>		He's already employed.

Major Lupton sits down - waves Charlie up.

>					CHARLIE
>					(speaking to
>					the crowd)
>		I hear tell the city of Jacksonville is offering ten dollars a scalp.

CHEERS go up from those that are close. B.B. Griffin looks at the two merchants.

>					GRIFFIN
>		Don't know about that. The government will get you that for sure. Sign up.

>					CHARLIE
>		Ain't no gold left out there on Deer Creek. May as well.

EXT. SCAFFOLD - CONTINUOUS

The CROWD gathered around the scaffold is slowly departing. The Indian boy hangs next to the other two Indians. Giles RIDES BY. He hurries his mules along.

Palmer and Lane ENTER. Lane signals the detachment to stop. Palmer quickly gets off his horse climbs on the scaffold. The crowd gathers again.

To the BOOS of some of the crowd, Palmer climbs the ladder - cuts down the Indians. He waves to the dragoons. Captain Smith points to a COUPLE DRAGOONS to assist Palmer.

EXT. STREET - CONTINUOUS

Wright walks with the merchants, Bray and Dirkson.

> DIRKSON
> How's it going with the volunteers over there?

> WRIGHT
> You saw.

They walk on. Wright stops outside a bar. MANY MINERS and GUNSLINGERS are WALKING IN.

> DIRKSON
> You come by my office next week. I have another job for you.

Wright nods - ENTERS the bar.

> BRAY
> Doesn't talk much does he?

> DIRKSON
>
> We don't need him for talking.

They walk on slowly through the crowded street.

> BRAY
>
> We need a thousand volunteers and cold hearted killers like him to stir the pot. I'm going to get me a paper and some tobacco.

Bray WALKS IN the general store. Giles ties his mules to a hitching post.

INT. GENERAL STORE

Bray picks up a copy of *The Oregonian*. Giles ENTERS. He picks out supplies. HOLMAN, the BALDING PROPRIETOR listens and waits ON CUSTOMERS at the same time. Bray READS.

> BRAY
>
> "...another treaty of peace has been made with the thieving murderous bands of Indians.

Joel Palmer ENTERS.

> BRAY (CONT'D)
>
> ...who under former treaties have continued to steal and destroy property whenever opportunity is offered, to murder the defenseless and unprotected."

JOEL PALMER

That paper is out of date. It was that young boy out there who was defenseless and unprotected.

Holman helps Giles. Bray looks at Palmer.

BRAY

I see you're back with that tin army of milk-fed pups.

JOEL PALMER

Did you sign up out there? I don't see your gun.

BRAY

I'll sign up as soon as General Lane goes back to Washington and gets the government to back the volunteers.

JOEL PALMER

He's on his way. He's going to be the new territorial governor.

BRAY

So I heard. Now you're thinking that new West Point Lieutenant or whatever he is will protect us from Chief John and his brother? You can't ride anywhere in this valley without taking your life in your hands.

GILES
(facing Bray)
It's the same for the Indians.

Bray looks at Giles, who is picking up supplies.

BRAY
(walking up to Giles)
You still friendly with that renegade chief? Let's see, Tecum...

GILES
Tecumtum. Chief John to most people.

Bray turns to Holman, Palmer, and other store visitors.

BRAY
This boy knows all those ignorant savage's names.

Palmer is looking at the *Oregonian.* Holman wants to change the subject.

HOLMAN
Giles, where do you think you're going?

GILES
I'm thinking about getting out of here, maybe go north. I'm taking my mules.

HOLMAN
You best stick around. I heard the redskins down river are stealing horses, mules too.

Bray picks up some tobacco. He approaches the counter. Holman takes his money. Bray turns to Palmer.

> BRAY
>
> You best keep that boy around. Giles here is one of our Indian lovers.

> GILES
>
> I'm going north, Mr. Bray, before they get your scalp. Maybe mine too.

Palmer looks at Bray.

> JOEL PALMER
>
> Have you thought about the fact that you're on their land?

> BRAY
>
> (mockingly)
>
> Their land? Their land? Whose land are you on? Did you buy it from the Indians? This land was given to us by the government for settling here. Now you want to pay them for it, after the government said we could get it for free.
>
> Watch your back, Mr. Palmer. The savages out there still think you stole it from them.

Bray LAUGHS - WALKS OUT of the store.

> GILES
>
> I hate that man, Mr. Palmer. Ever since
>
> (MORE)

                    GILES (CONT'D)
I've known him, he and that other guy,
Mr. Dirkson, have been trying to make a
buck off the Indians.

Holman looks at Palmer.

                    HOLMAN
You think there will be war?

                    JOEL PALMER
We're in a war now.

                    GILES
I know the chiefs. They're getting guns.
They'll never leave their land.

                    JOEL PALMER
You better stick around. I may need
you.

EXT. BELOW TABLE ROCK - POWWOW - DAY

MANY WARRIORS, painted in different patterns of war paint, battle each other in shinny. OTHER WARRIORS shoot arrows at a stuffed miner wearing wool trousers and shirt, a floppy hat, and a red bandanna around its grass-filled neck.

The MANY WOMEN provide containers of dried meats, Camus cakes, berries, and water to OTHER VISITING WARRIORS waiting to participate.

Tecumtum, Cultus Jim, and Adam RIDE IN and ENTER the powwow. Tecumtum and sons are wearing woodpecker feathers that identify their family and village.

Cultus Jim has the facial markings of a warrior ready for battle.

Tecumtum and Adam do not. They stop - watch. They all have new and improved guns attached to their horses.

> ADAM
>
> The warriors are using bows and arrows. They're not shooting guns.

Tecumtum turns to Cultus Jim.

> TECUMTUM
>
> Go with Adam.

> CULTUS JIM
>
> (resisting)
>
> Adam can teach them about guns. I will go with you to learn about how to win the battle against the whites.

> ADAM
>
> Give me your guns.

Cultus Jim and Tecumtum give their guns to Adam. Adam looks at his father.

> ADAM
>
> What if they don't want to learn from me?

> TECUMTUM
>
> Go play games with them. They have pride. Let them respect you. Then they will learn from you.

OTHER SUBCHIEFS and ELDERS nod greetings to Tecumtum and Cultus Jim.

Adam splits off - rides over to the shinny game - dismounts.

An ELDER greets Adam, takes his horse and guns. A number of warriors watching shinny notice the guns. They come and look, then look at Adam.

> ONE WARRIOR
>
> He's not to fight?

ANOTHER WARRIOR shrugs his shoulders.

Adam looks for a stick. He stands out as the only unpainted brave. He removes his regalia - gives it to the elder.

ONE WARRIOR closely watches Adam. He hands his stick to Adam, then yells at the players. They stop. Neither team wants Adam. A stick goes up and falls and points to the team that gets Adam.

Adam joins the reluctant team. The game is played. Adam has all the athletic agility, intelligence, and unselfish play to get everybody's attention. Soon PLAYERS CHEER his skilled passing and scoring.

EXT. HEADMEN AND SUBCHIEFS - CONTINUOUS

Besides Tecumtum and Cultus Jim, there's Tecumtum's younger Brother, CHIEF APSERKAHAR, named CHIEF JOE, after General Joe Lane. He's tall, intelligent, and resplendent in embroidered apparel.

His daughter, MARY, a strong and very striking woman of 21 years comes frequently to listen and serve the headmen. She is invited to remain and sit with them under the lean-to at Apserkahar's gestured request. She is respectfully accepted by all.

>TECUMTUM
>
>You don't have guns. How many horses?

>APSERKAHAR
>
>Horses are no good in the mountains.

>TECUMTUM
>
>I know. But the warriors cannot fight with supplies on their backs.

>APSERKAHAR
>
>Our strong women will bring food and supplies.

Tecumtum shakes his head. The mood is intense. They share food and drink except for Cultus Jim, who carries his own food and miner's flask (whiskey) from a saddle bag.

>TECUMTUM
>
>There are too many white eyes. I want no war. The Bostons leave me alone, I leave the Bostons alone.

>APSERKAHAR
>
>Your son attacks the wagons passing through. He breaks the treaty.

> CULTUS JIM
>
> Not my treaty. Your treaty? If the white Chief wants a treaty with our village, let him come to me. I will tell the Chief to find a path around our land.

> TECUMTUM
>
> You see, I am at war with my own sons, who want to fight.

Periodic CHEERING from the shinny game brings a smile to Tecumtum. The LOUDNESS OF THE CHEERING disrupts the flow of the conversation.

EXT. ADAM - MANY WARRIORS - CONTINUOUS

Adam is third in line. The stuffed miner is pulled on a rope pulley between two trees. A crowd, including Mary, watches the warriors.

Mary walks on - gets more water. AN ELDER uses a long stick to push the miner out from behind the tree. A warrior stretches his bow - lets go. The arrow flies and hits the miner in the torso. Many CHEERS. The next warrior hits the tree with his arrow - gets a second chance. He tries again - hits the miner's leg. CHEERS.

Adam next, lets his arrow fly. A perfect hit to the floppy hat. CHEERS. Adam signals the elder to bring the guns and pouch of ammunition. Adam takes one gun - gives the other two to warriors. All the warriors follow him.

Mary WALKS BY going the other way. She stops when she sees Adam. Their eyes meet. She walks directly to him. She offers him a drink. Adam takes a drink.

>MARY
>You are my cousin, Adam.

Adam returns the container.

>ADAM
>Yes.

Adam is pulled away by a warrior.

EXT. HEADMEN - CONTINUOUS

>APSERKAHAR
>My brother, you will not fight beside us?

Tecumtum stands.

>TECUMTUM
>No.

>APSERKAHAR
>I fought the Klamath with you.

Tecumtum paces.

>APSERKAHAR
>We have warriors from Cow Creek, Umpqua, Klamath, and the great water.
>
>Our brothers Toquahear, Chocultah, and Lympe send warriors. Let us fight the white eyes together.

Mary ENTERS. She offers Tecumtum the container of water. He drinks. SHOOTING is heard.

> MARY
> The warriors are having a contest with guns.

The headmen and Cultus get up - walk to look.

EXT. ADAM - CONTINUOUS

The stuffed miner is pulled quickly on a rope pulley between two trees. Three warriors take turns SHOOTING at the miner. No one hits it. Other warriors have a few muskets. They pass the muskets back and forth making awkward efforts at loading them.

It's Adam's turn. With the new and improved gun, Adam BLOWS THE STUFFING from the moving miner. He quickly reloads his gun, takes aim, and FIRES AGAIN - blowing the head off the miner. CHEERS and active movement by warriors and others to get in line to get closer looks at the action.

Mary stands next to the chiefs - watches. Cultus Jim walks over, takes his turn on the half-blown away miner. He SHOOTS - misses. He stokes his gun, puts lead in, aims, FIRES and blows off a leg.

Adam steps up and SHOOTS - blows the miner in half. He gives his gun to another warrior.

Cultus Jim stares at his brother - takes his gun and walks back to Tecumtum.

TECUMTUM

My son Adam has the eyes of an eagle. I have chosen him to be our village's spiritual leader. He has promised to never use the gun.

APSERKAHAR

I will find guns. He will teach us.

CULTUS JIM

Uncle, I will fight beside you.

Apserkahar clasps Cultus Jim's hand. The chiefs return to the erected lean-to and sit down. Mary follows and offers food. All are silent as they look at Tecumtum.

TECUMTUM

We need many guns, better guns and many horses for a great war to save our sacred land.

APSERKAHAR

We cannot wait, my brother. Soon it is winter. By summer another thousand white families will come unless we chase them away.

Apserkahar COUGHS. Mary quickly reaches for a container of water. Apserkahar waves her back.

APSERKAHAR

We had the treaty with the great white chief, Joe Lane. It did not stop the white people on Indian land digging up Mother Earth with their plows... They kill our rivers... They dig up our sacred grounds where ancestors rest.

Another COUGHING SPELL. Apserkahar accepts water from Mary.

          TECUMTUM
    There are many whites with guns in Jacksonville. They want to fight.

Another SHOT. A GREAT ROAR. Cultus Jim rises.

          CULTUS JIM
    Father, let me lead the battle against the white man.

Apserkahar rises, stands beside Cultus Jim.

Apserkahar faces Tecumtum.

          APSERKAHAR
    You have given me great honor by hearing my plea. We are still one family. Will you give your sons your blessing to stand beside me against the whites?

          TECUMTUM
    My son Cultus will fight. You cannot have my son, Adam.

          APSERKAHAR
    Let us eat and celebrate in preparation for war.

EXT. ADAM - CONTINUOUS

The warriors are practicing with another stuffed miner.

Adam stands behind them. It's a melee of arrows, tomahawks, knives. Warriors step aside when others FIRE muskets. Cultus Jim joins them.

WAR CRIES fill the air. Mary walks up to Adam.

> MARY
> Teach me to shoot.

Mary is pushed aside as Adam is dragged back into the fracas by warriors ready to go on the warpath. Adam looks back. Mary is left standing there.

EXT. BATTLE MOUNTAIN - DAY

The air is filled with SMOKE. Indians burn dry brush along the trail behind them. From his horse, Cultus Jim directs warriors to fall trees across the trail.

Through the trees ahead of the burning brush, Indians unpack blankets, guns, and ammunition from mules. Apserkahar and Mary RIDE UP to Cultus Jim.

> APSERKAHAR
> (worriedly)
> They come on horses and mules with many guns.

> CULTUS JIM
> When the horses cannot climb over the rocks and trees, we attack.

MOTHERS AND WIVES provide food to the braves and help lead the mules and horses that pull litters. Cultus Jim looks at his uncle. Apserkahar COUGHS.

> CULTUS JIM
> Are you losing your courage, Uncle?

> APSERKAHAR
> I fear more will come and take the place of the whites we kill.

> CULTUS JIM
> There will be no surrender to this pack of wolves.

Apserkahar nods to Mary. They ride up the trail. Mary dismounts - separates to help other women. Adam, Ridge Runner, and a half dozen warriors on horseback EMERGE from the trees. Adam and Apserkahar dismount.

Apserkahar clasps arms with Adam. Ridge Runner and the other warriors RIDE ON to Cultus Jim.

> APSERKAHAR
> Both of my brother's sons come to fight... What is the message from your father?

> ADAM
> Father will not come. He sends me to see who wins the battle.

Apserkahar looks at Adam, who is without war paint.

                        APSERKAHAR
You will not fight with your brother?

                           ADAM
No. I will help with the guns.

They walk close to those preparing for battle.

Mary helps women unload supplies from mules. Mary watches Adam and Cultus Jim.

Mary stops - approaches them with a container of water and Camus cakes. She gives Adam a Camus cake and Cultus Jim the container of water. She takes the water container from Cultus Jim - passes it to Adam. She watches Adam drink.

                           MARY
You are not a warrior?

                           ADAM
I am to be a teacher, healer, and guide
to my people.

                           MARY
You are afraid?

                           ADAM
                   (not liking what
                      Mary said)
I am not afraid.

Adam hands her the container and gives the Camus cake back. He turns his attention to his brother.

EXT. BATTLE MOUNTAIN - DAY

Over a HUNDRED VOLUNTEERS are congregated in different groups waiting to go to war. The miners, settlers/farmers, and businessmen are dressed appropriately for their usual roles. While waiting, they play cards, eat and drink, tell stories, polish their guns, carve wood, and sleep.

INT./EXT. TENT - CONTINUOUS

In a separate area, an open tent houses Major Lupton, B.B. Griffin, Ben Wright, and Captain Smith. They are looking over a map. The same TEN or so very green-looking DRAGOONS/SOLDIERS from earlier scenes mill about outside.

> CAPTAIN SMITH
> General Lane is arriving any minute.
>
> If I know the general, we'll be heading out of here in the morning, if not sooner. Mr. Griffin, you can follow the infantry with—
>
> GRIFFIN
> My men will not be following you or any of your pups in uniform.

Griffin glances at Wright, who stands to the side rolling a cigarette.

> GRIFFIN
> We have leaders for every fifteen men. They will answer to me and Major

Lupton. Ben Wright there leads the California volunteers.

CAPTAIN SMITH

I don't want to have absolute chaos here. Some of those volunteers will end up shooting out the backsides of my men.

GRIFFIN

Captain, you can fight your own little war when General Lane arrives.

I'm going to take some of my men and get around behind them. We got Indians to kill.

Griffin and Major Lupton EXIT. Captain Smith, uncomfortable, twitching, looks at Wright.

CAPTAIN SMITH

I understand you fought beside General Lane against the Modocs.

Wright, without emotion, stares at Smith. The SOUND of HORSES outside breaks the silence. A SOLDIER ENTERS - walks up to Captain Smith.

SOLDIER

General Lane and Indian Agent Joel Palmer are approaching camp, Sir.

Captain Smith and the soldier EXIT. Wright lights his cigarette FOLLOWS.

EXT. BATTLE MOUNTAIN - CONTINUOUS

GENERAL LANE, JOEL PALMER, and A DOZEN SOLDIERS RIDE INTO camp.

> CAPTAIN SMITH
> Soldiers, ATTENTION!

General Lane dismounts - approaches Captain Smith.

They shake hands and the no-nonsense General scans the dozen soldiers and hillside of ragtag volunteers, most of whom slouch and lounge rather than come to attention.

ADDITIONAL VOLUNTEERS join the volunteers already present. Exhausted, they stumble into the gathering.

Griffin and his group of 20 volunteers are on their horses.

General Lane trots down towards them. Palmer and Smith follow. Griffin, Major Lupton, and excited volunteers RIDE off into the trees.

> GENERAL LANE
> Where are those men going?

> CAPTAIN SMITH
> Around the flank, Sir. To come in behind them, Sir.

Lane shakes his head.

> GENERAL LANE
> There is no behind them. They'll be back.

JOEL PALMER

Look at those ragtag volunteers. You're crazy to lead them into all that brush and trees.

GENERAL LANE

God damn it, Joel. I'll make the military decisions here. Your job is not to get yourself shot. Do what you're hired to do.

Lane, Palmer, and Captain Smith walk back up to the tent.

Soldiers remain at attention. Wright stands near a tree, observing.

GENERAL LANE

Captain. You or those boys over there ever been in a war?

CAPTAIN SMITH

No, Sir. My men are trained and ready, Sir.

GENERAL LANE

Well, the first thing you do is get a couple of your men to tether those horses. Leave soldiers to guard them. Otherwise they'll be gone when we come back down the hill.

CAPTAIN SMITH

Sir. We're ready to ride into battle.

GENERAL LANE

Captain, you will walk into battle behind Ben Wright's California volunteers, Mr. Palmer, and me. You can't ride and shoot in this brush.

Hearing his name, Wright stomps his cigarette - waits for Lane to notice him. He doesn't move. Lane immediately notices Wright - goes up and shakes his hand.

GENERAL LANE

There you are. Come over here, Joel. Meet a great Indian fighter.

Palmer and Wright shake hands.

JOEL PALMER

It's good to know someone who knows the Indian's ways in battle.

Lane signals Wright and Smith to follow him into the tent.

GENERAL LANE

Let's set out a line of attack.

EXT. BATTLE MOUNTAIN - LATER

General Lane, Ben Wright, and Joel Palmer walk through the smoke filled trees followed by the more organized volunteers, including Shorty, Charlie, and other TOUGH LOOKING GUNSLINGERS. Captain Smith has the soldiers follow him two by two.

The nearly 100 ragtag volunteers, every age, with every kind of weapon follow the more organized volunteers, who are behind the soldiers.

                    WRIGHT
    Over the hill.

Lane glances up at the hill, turns, looks back behind him.

Some volunteers behind the soldiers are straggling a long way back - doing more resting than marching.

EXT. BACK TIER - CONTINUOUS

A lot of COUGHING AND GRUMBLING from UNSEASONED VOLUNTEERS about the smoke and trail.

EXT. BACK TO FRONT - GENERAL LANE

                GENERAL LANE
    We have to hold up here until we get
    those volunteers caught up.

                JOEL PALMER
    They're not going to hurry unless you
    kick 'em in the ass.

SPORADIC GUNFIRE is heard. The men look ahead. Lane looks at Wright.

                GENERAL LANE
    You and your men head straight up that
    hill.

    I'm going back to pull those volunteers
    together and tell the Captain how to
    fight.

Lane turns to Palmer.

GENERAL LANE
You coming?

JOEL PALMER
I'm staying.

GENERAL LANE
I'll be back to lead the attack.

Lane runs down the hill through brush, trees, and smoke. When he reaches the majority of the volunteers, he mounts a rock.

GENERAL LANE
All right, men. We are engaging the enemy over that hill. Stay close to your leaders.

PORTLY BUSINESS MAN
My men are ready.

A group of BUSINESS MEN/MERCHANTS mixed with a FEW FARMERS gather around the PORTLY BUSINESS MAN.

Lane looks out over the other volunteers.

GENERAL LANE
Stay in sight of me and those up ahead. When we see the Indians, spread out, use trees and rocks to protect yourselves. They are using guns as well as bows and arrows.

They're going to come at you with knives while you're reloading. Find a partner to cover you and—

Shorty spits and walks up to Lane.

SHORTY

We know, we know. You better hurry your ass on up there or we'll fight this war without you.

A barrage of GUNFIRE. Lane turns - runs. One of the soldiers ahead approaches Lane.

SOLDIER

Sir, one of the volunteers has been shot.

The soldier points ahead. Two volunteers aid a third volunteer who is sitting down with an arrow through his jaw. In front of crouched soldiers, Lane reaches down and BREAKS THE ARROW - pulls the arrow out.

The volunteer CRIES OUT.

Lane rushes on through the trees and brush - finds WRIGHT and PALMER.

GUNFIRE, SMOKE from powder fill the air. YELLING volunteers, HOWLING DOGS, WAILING Indian women, SOUNDS FROM FLYING ARROWS, and the WAR CRIES of the warriors bring the battle home to Lane and company.

An arrow enters a nearby volunteer's chest. Other arrows narrowly miss Lane and company.

Captain Smith crawls up.

CAPTAIN SMITH

They have many more guns than we thought, Sir. They're hard to spot, except for the smoke from their guns.

EXT. SHORTY AND CHARLIE - CONTINUOUS

Next to Shorty and Charlie, a second volunteer is brought down by an arrow. He falls next to Charlie.

SHORTY FIRES at a warrior WHO APPEARS OUT OF NOWHERE, then DUCKS into a thicket.

Charlie is too frightened to stick his head up. Another volunteer kneels down low to help the wounded volunteer. Charlie stares at the blood and arrow in the man's chest.

CHARLIE

I think he's going to die.

SHORTY

That's what fightin's all about. Get your head up there and take a peek.

You ain't shot that gun of yours yet.

Another warrior COMES OUT of a trough in the ground. An arrow barely misses Shorty.

Shorty jumps up and SHOOTS AGAIN. A couple arrows barely miss him, one digging into the ground next to Charlie.

Warriors imbedded in the natural environment of trees, brush, rocks, and ravines startle soldiers and volunteers as they attack. This continues through INTERCUTS.

EXT. LANE - CONTINUOUS

Lane crawls next to Wright and Palmer - turns to Smith.

> GENERAL LANE
> I'll take command here. Have your soldiers move the wounded down the hill...
>
> Smell that powder, Captain? I want the air filled with smoke and dead Indians. Get on with it.

Captain Smith EXITS. General Lane signals Wright and Palmer to follow him. He rushes through the trees to get closer to the enemy. He looks at Wright.

> GENERAL LANE
> This isn't Tule Lake. At least we could see them there, even in the lava beds.

Lane tries to ascertain where the arrows and gun shots are coming from. He looks at Wright.

> GENERAL LANE
> Take some of your men and follow me.
>
> (to Palmer)
> You ready, Joel? I'm going right at them.

Both Lane and Palmer are sweating.

                    JOEL PALMER
        I've always covered your backside, Joe.
        Make sure you cover mine. Now, and
        later.

                    GENERAL LANE
        Let's go.

They rush ahead into the brush and trees. They crawl over a fallen tree.

WARRIORS RISE OUT OF NOWHERE WITH MUSKETS FIRING and bows drawn at point blank range. HOWLING SOUNDS ECHO THROUGH the forest. Lane gets off a round, then drops down. A volunteer clutches his chest, blood oozing from a gaping hole.

                    SHOT VOLUNTEER
        Dead center shot.

The volunteer collapses to the ground. Palmer hoists him over the fallen tree and lays him down on the protected side. With a final DEATH RATTLE, the volunteer is gone.

Wright leads on. Lane and Palmer, side by side, creep ahead. Lane SHOOTS an Indian. Wright SHOOTS a couple Indians.

HOWLING WOMEN EXPOSE THEMSELVES in the line of fire to pull WOUNDED WARRIORS BEHIND COVER. Wright SHOOTS one woman down with his gun. Palmer turns, YELLS.

                    JOEL PALMER

We're not shooting women here unless they have guns or arrows pointing straight at you, you hear?

Wright LAUGHS.

                      WRIGHT

Better not let the squaws get behind you, Palmer. You'll likely get a knife in your back.

                   GENERAL LANE

Forward, Men. Split them down the middle.

Wright, Lane, Palmer, volunteers, and soldiers forge ahead, climbing over fallen trees, SHOOTING, reloading, SHOOTING. The three men synchronize their shooting. One gets a shot off while another reloads. Palmer SHOOTS another Indian.

                   GENERAL LANE

I see drawing up treaties hasn't destroyed your marksmanship.

                    JOEL PALMER

Tell that to the folks in Jacksonville.

EXT. BATTLE MOUNTAIN - INDIANS -CONTINUOUS

Mary helps with the wounded. Apserkahar observes from a hill crest. A SWEATING WARRIOR APPROACHES.

                    WARRIOR

We are behind them. We have their horses. Many white eyes are coming back from the river's edge.

                    APSERKAHAR

Move the warriors higher into the mountains. They will tire and go home after another sunset.

The warrior QUICKLY LEAVES. Mary walks up to Apserkahar. Apserkahar is nervous.

                    APSERKAHAR

The farmers of the Valley will tire. But Joe Lane will not tire or give up until we kill him or make peace with him.

                    MARY

Father, you made peace with him. Smoked the pipe with him.

Now it's time to kill him... I'm going to get Cultus Jim.

EXT. CULTUS JIM AND ADAM - CONTINUOUS

Adam crouches low next to Cultus Jim and other warriors.

Cultus Jim SHOOTS at volunteers. Skillfully, Adam reloads a second gun.

Very close and camouflaged, they see WRIGHT, LANE, and PALMER slowly move towards them.

EXT. MARY - CONTINUOUS

Mary and ANOTHER WOMAN slide on their bellies through a trough. Another Woman assists a warrior away from the battle. Mary crawls/slides on ahead. She slides in next to Cultus Jim and Adam.

EXT. CULTUS JIM AND ADAM - CONTINUOUS

Lane EXPOSES HIMSELF as he signals others to follow him. Mary looks at Cultus Jim.

> MARY
>
> That's Joe Lane. Shoot him!

> ADAM
>
> No! Wait until he stands to shoot so we don't miss.

> MARY
>
> He's not going to stand and shoot.

Adam ignores Mary - turns to Cultus Jim.

> ADAM
>
> When I wave my knife, you shoot him.

Adam gives an WAR CRY - waves the knife. Lane rises to shoot at the exposed Adam, who mounts a frontal attack with a raised knife. Lane aims.

Lane is SHOT by Cultus Jim from point blank range. Lane falls. Adam quickly falls - ducks back into the thicket. Lane grabs at his shoulder. Palmer YELLS.

> JOEL PALMER
>
> General Lane is hit! General Lane is hit! We need some help here.

> ADAM
>
> Did you hear? We kill the leaders first.

He turns to Mary.

> MARY
>
> Your father will want to know.

Mary looks at Adam and smiles. Mary turns to crawl away from a barrage of GUNFIRE coming their way. Other warriors counterattack.

Adam and Cultus CRAWL WITH MARY until safe. They stand, run - DISAPPEAR THROUGH THE TREES. Ridge Runner RUNS PAST. Cultus Jim YELLS - points.

> CULTUS JIM
>
> Back up over the hill!

Cultus Jim turns - FOLLOWS Ridge Runner. Adam hesitates, turns and follows Mary.

> ADAM
>
> Apserkahar may want to give a message to the white eyes with Joe Lane wounded or dead.

EXT. LANE - CONTINUOUS

Lane rises, looks ahead - YELLS.

GENERAL LANE

Keep moving forward! Stay with me, Joel.

With blood dripping from his shoulder, Lane moves ahead. He drops his musket and pulls a pistol from his belt. The volunteers YELL and pass along that General Lane is hit. Two soldiers and Captain Smith crawl next to the General as he falters. Palmer and Wright move on ahead.

SOLDIER ONE

Sir, we're here to assist you down the hill.

GENERAL LANE

The hell you are, Son. Get your gun, follow Palmer and engage the enemy.

CAPTAIN SMITH

Palmer's not a soldier, Sir.

GENERAL LANE

I don't give a damn. He's fought more Indians than you'll see here today. You and your boys get up there beside him, y'hear!

CAPTAIN SMITH

Yes, Sir.

A GROWING SILENCE from the Indian front. General Lane signals the volunteers and soldiers to move forward. Lane slowly gets up to watch Palmer - tries to follow. He steps over a dead Indian.

> GENERAL LANE
> They're in retreat. Forward.

There is a PAN to Wright and Palmer - other volunteers - moving targets. Wright LAUGHS.

> WRIGHT
> Better look under a rock, first.

> JOEL PALMER
> Careful, men. The scoundrels are always in retreat until they have you where they want you. Go slowly.

Suddenly a VOLLEY OF SHOTS AND ARROWS. A couple volunteers are shot down. Lane fades. He rises to climb over another fallen tree, Palmer turns to assist Lane.

As Palmer lifts Lane, Lane pushes him back.

> GENERAL LANE
> Use your gun, Joel. Use your gun.

An arrow buries into the tree next to Lane. Palmer sees Lane slowly sinking back - unable to proceed. Again there is silence from the Indian front lines.

> JOEL PALMER
> Soldiers! Soldiers!

Palmer looks at Lane. Lane tries to rise. He's too weak.

> JOEL PALMER
> I'll take command here.

Captain Smith crawls next to Lane. Two soldiers lift him. Lane protests.

> CAPTAIN SMITH
> No one commands my soldiers but me.

Agent Palmer, you go back down the hill with General Lane.

> JOEL PALMER
> The hell I will!

> GENERAL LANE
> (faintly)
> Joel, don't give them a chance. Move forward.

Lane grabs his gun away from one soldier. He slowly gets up.

> GENERAL LANE
> I can get down the goddamned hill. You boys get back to the front.

Lane WALKS OUT OF SIGHT. The soldiers crawl back, mixing in with Wright's California volunteers. Wright and Palmer slowly move forward. Smith, close behind, waves his frightened soldiers on behind him.

SILENCE. No arrows fly. Every now and then a volunteer SHOOTS at an unseen noise or target. Wright signals the men to hold their fire.

Wright moves forward - stops - listens.

A SOUND ECHOES through the woods, "JOE LANE." "JOE LANE." Wright holds up his hand for quiet. The eerie SOUND OF SOMEONE CALLING "JOE LANE" echoes again through the forest.

EXT. LANE - CONTINUOUS

Lane reclines by a log. A soldier checks his wound. Other wounded men sit or lie next to him. One volunteer is dead. The wounded volunteers get minimal care.

The haunting sound, "JOE LANE." Everyone stops - listens. A SOLDIER COMES RUNNING down the hill.

     SOLDIER
 Sir, they are calling your name.

     GENERAL LANE
 I hear it. Who?

     SOLDIER
 Indians, Sir.

ANOTHER SOLDIER COMES RUNNING.

     ANOTHER SOLDIER
 Two Indians, one a squaw, are coming down the mountain. The young brave keeps calling, "Joe Lane."

Lane hoists himself to a standing position. He pulls his coat around his wounded, bloody shoulder.

Griffin and Major Lupton and the small group of volunteers all look exhausted, ENTER on horseback.

     GENERAL LANE
 Get me Palmer.

One of the soldiers RUNS UP the hill. Griffin, Major Lupton, and the volunteers dismount. Palmer and Wright WALK UP with Mary and Adam. Palmer approaches Lane.

> JOEL PALMER
>
> They've sent this boy and young woman here. He's the one who's calling your name.

Lane immediately recognizes Mary. He reaches out to her, takes her hand with his left hand.

> GENERAL LANE
>
> Mary.
>
> (to Palmer)
> This is Mary, the daughter of Chief Joe.
>
> (turns to Mary)
> What does your father want?

Mary looks at Adam.

> ADAM
>
> Great Chief Apserkahar wants to speak with Joe Lane.

> GENERAL LANE
>
> Why does he send a boy?

> MARY
>
> My father says you will not kill our warriors if we stop for a powwow.

Lane waits - thinks.

Wright walks over to Griffin. They whisper on the sidelines. Then look at Lane. Lane is silent.

> GENERAL LANE
> I will come and speak with him.

Palmer begins to speak but is interrupted by Wright.

> WRIGHT
> (facing Lane)
> A stalling tactic. Remember the Modocs...

Lane raises his hand to silence Wright.

> GENERAL LANE
> I'm in command here. This is the chief's daughter. Apserkahar will not attack us while she's in our camp.

> JOEL PALMER
> Let's go.

Mary and Adam lead, Palmer assists Lane up the hill. Lane puts his hand up - turns back to Wright.

> GENERAL LANE
> Mary remains here while we go have a powwow with the chief.

Wright runs up and grabs Mary.

> JOEL PALMER
> You don't have to do that. Let her go.

Wright reluctantly lets Mary go. Mary, who understands, spots a shaded spot on the ground - goes over to it. She sits down. Lane, Palmer, and Adam walk up the hill.

Captain Smith escorted by two soldiers, ENTER.

> GENERAL LANE
>
> Ben Wright is in command here until I return.
>
> Get back up to your men. Hold the line.
>
> (Lane points)
> Put Mary under the protection of those two soldiers.
>
> CAPTAIN SMITH
>
> With all due respect, Sir, you may not be able to carry on.
>
> GENERAL LANE
>
> I'll decide when I can't carry on.

Lane turns again. LEAVES with Palmer and Adam.

EXT. WRIGHT - CONTINUOUS

Griffin and a number of volunteers gather around Wright. Shorty and Charlie COME out of the trees and join Wright and Griffin.

They look over at Mary. Smith turns - HEADS back up the hill. Two soldiers remain with Mary.

EXT. APSERKAHAR - CONTINUOUS

Apserkahar stands with Cultus Jim and many warriors who hold guns and bows. General Lane, Palmer, and Adam slowly APPROACH.

WEEPING women put wood on the fires. A half dozen Indian bodies get incinerated.

> CULTUS JIM
> They hold Mary hostage.

> APSERKAHAR
> The Great Chief Joe Lane is wise. We will hold Agent Palmer hostage in return.
>
> But let us speak first. Let the great General Lane see we are strong.

Cultus Jim signals Ridge Runner and a number of warriors to surround Lane and Palmer. Lane looks around carefully as he approaches Apserkahar.

> GENERAL LANE
> I see they are burning their dead. They're afraid we'd take scalps.

> JOEL PALMER
> Well, General. Isn't that what you were going to do?

> GENERAL LANE
> There's still a chance of winning this battle.

Lane looks around at the terrain.

>JOEL PALMER
>
>No, Joe. This will go on for days.
>
>Once the volunteers realize this may drag on, we're going to see a thinning of the ranks. Many will be out of food.
>
>GENERAL LANE
>
>We have soldiers coming from the north and the coast.
>
>Take heart, Joel. The Indians have nowhere to go except higher into the mountains. They're no better off.
>
>JOEL PALMER
>
>Let's look for alternatives.

Lane and Palmer walk directly to Apserkahar. Adam goes to Cultus Jim. Lane grasps Apserkahar's arm in greeting.

Apserkahar immediately speaks without taking Palmer's arm.

>APSERKAHAR
>
>We are weary of war with the whites.

Apserkahar looks at Palmer.

>APSERKAHAR
>
>We have a treaty with you. That treaty is broken. Then I make treaty with you,
>
>(MORE)

APSERKAHAR (CONT'D)

General Lane. Your people break that treaty. Why?

GENERAL LANE

Many white people who have traveled through this land have had horses and cattle stolen. You promised safe passage.

APSERKAHAR

The white men take food from our sacred earth. Our women cannot find food for the children.

Lane, feeling the loss of blood, struggles to respond. Palmer waits for Lane to answer. Apserkahar signals to a woman to bring water to Lane.

APSERKAHAR

When I hear the great General Joe Lane is here, a white man I respect, who gave me my name Joe, gave my family the names Sally, Mary, Ben, names we wear proudly in our village... I ask you. Come speak of peace between our people.

Lane looks at Palmer. Palmer takes Lane aside.

JOEL PALMER

Ask Chief Joe about a meeting place where all the chiefs of the valley will come and negotiate a treaty of peace.

> GENERAL LANE
>
> We're not there yet. We have men who want to finish this battle.

Feeling faint, Lane walks over - sits down on a fallen tree. Palmer ignores Lane, he walks back to Apserkahar.

> JOEL PALMER
>
> General Lane wishes to know where we can meet for a peace council with all the chiefs.

Apserkahar points at Table Rock. Cultus Jim looks at Adam. Adam nods.

> APSERKAHAR
>
> By the river, at the sacred cliff.

Palmer looks at Lane, who is not able to protest. He turns back to Apserkahar.

> JOEL PALMER
>
> General Lane will speak with his sub-chiefs. He will send a messenger with his decision.

Palmer goes back to Lane.

> GENERAL LANE
>
> What are you doing? The volunteers aren't going to want the council.

> JOEL PALMER
>
> It's in our hands. Or I should say your hands. I want you to do it.

> GENERAL LANE
>
> I'll need some time.

Apserkahar nods his head to Cultus Jim and Ridge Runner. They walk over and grab Palmer.

> APSERKAHAR
>
> (facing Palmer)
>
> I will keep the Agent Palmer as protection until a decision comes from the white subchiefs. Go back.

Lane is upset by what is happening. Lane struggles to get on his feet. Falls back.

> APSERKAHAR
>
> Adam, you are learning the ways of the peacemaker. Go back with General Lane.

> ADAM
>
> I will stay.

Adam goes to Cultus Jim's side.

> CULTUS JIM
>
> Father would want you to go.

Cultus Jim grabs Ridge Runner.

> CULTUS JIM
>
> Go quickly to my father.

Ridge Runner DISAPPEARS into the trees.

EXT. GRIFFIN AND MAJOR LUPTON - CONTINUOUS

HEATED ARGUMENTS between settler volunteers, Jacksonville business men, gunslingers, and miners. Mocking remarks are made to those who are leaving.

GRIFFIN

You ain't even fired your guns.

SETTLER

We hear more soldiers are coming. We have crops to tend.

GUNSLINGER

Go back to Ohio.

SETTLER

Missouri.

GRIFFIN

Wherever you're from.

Mary tends to some of the wounded volunteers and soldiers.

WOUNDED VOLUNTEER

We came to help you farmers.

SETTLER

You came from the gold fields. They dried up. Now you're like the rest of us, broke, and wanting government money.

Griffin appeals to those who are leaving.

                    GRIFFIN

Wait for General Lane. He's going to finish this fight.

                    ANOTHER SETTLER

No, he's not. He's wounded.

He's going to wait for the troops. He don't need us.

A COUPLE SOLDIERS ARRIVE pulling Lane on a litter. Adam follows. All are silent. Adam separates and goes to Mary. She hands him a container - points to one of the wounded. Both attend the wounded. Adam keeps his distance from Mary.

                    GRIFFIN

I say we stay here until we have reinforcements. A defeat now will take away the Indians' will to fight later.

                    SETTLER

I want to hear from General Lane.

General Lane glances at the wounded and the half dozen dead volunteers. Exhausted, he gets off the litter - goes over to them - sits down on a tree log near Mary and Adam.

                    GENERAL LANE

I have seen their fortifications. We can win, but it will be a protracted war taking weeks.

                    (MORE)

GENERAL LANE (CONT'D)

We can't encircle them, even with a thousand soldiers and volunteers.

It will be a war of attrition. Two of them, one of us; then two of us, one of them.

Griffin steps forward.

GRIFFIN

Unless we annihilate them, we'll never be safe in this valley. I'm telling you, murder's in their blood.

There are CHEERS for Griffin. Many can be heard saying, "FIGHT THEM NOW!", "WE WANT A VOTE!"

Mary gives Lane a container of water. Lane pushes himself up.

A THIRD SETTLER

We can't cultivate our land without fear of an Indian attack. When our backs are turned, they come on our property and steal our mules, cut off the heads of our cattle.

I'm not gonna live like this anymore. It's either we chase them out of this valley, or we might as well leave.

SETTLER

My family has lived peacefully next to the Indians on Anderson Creek the last two years.

More GRUMBLING and DEBATE.

                GENERAL LANE

We have an opportunity today to formulate a treaty that will put the Indians on separate land...where they can have protected hunting and fishing grounds.

                A THIRD SETTLER

No! No Indian has ever kept a treaty. I say they have a choice - leave or get killed.

                GRIFFIN

They don't want to leave.

Lane gets up, slowly walks away from the wounded.

                GENERAL LANE

I want to find out what the chiefs have to say. There may still be room for all of us on this land.

Wright steps forward.

                WRIGHT

Let's finish this battle, General.

After CHEERS, there's a pause as those within hearing distance wait for Lane's response. Lane looks at the wounded, then at Adam and Mary.

                GENERAL LANE

Mr. Palmer and I need to hear what the chiefs have to say.

                (MORE)

GENERAL LANE (CONT'D)
Prepare to fall back. We have many wounded who need care. We have dead to bury.

Lane waves to two soldiers to come to him.

GENERAL LANE
Get Captain Smith down here.

The two soldiers RUN UP THE HILL. There are MANY BOOS, and A FEW CHEERS among those who can hear Lane. Word is quickly passed on to the volunteers who are at the front.

Exhausted, Lane staggers over - sits down by Mary. Mary opens Lane's jacket.

GENERAL LANE
Adam, go back to Chief Joe. Take Captain Smith with you.

Mary tends to Lane's wound.

EXT. BATTLE MOUNTAIN - DAY (LATER)

INTERCUT SCENE

Palmer and Adam ARRIVE, FOLLOWED by Apserkahar, a couple braves, and a half dozen Indian women. The women and braves carry baskets of food and their possessions. The volunteers congregate and follow Apserkahar and company until they reach Lane.

Apserkahar immediately goes to his daughter, then turns to Lane. Lane tries to stand. Apserkahar motions him to stay seated. Mary turns to Adam.

MARY

Come help.

The two go to Lane. Mary reaches down, begins to take off Lane's coat. Adam looks at the makeshift bandage, begins removing it. Lane resists, Apserkahar shakes his head.

APSERKAHAR

You are brave. Do not be foolish. Your people have many wounds. Our people have many wounds. We want you and Palmer at the peace council.

Apserkahar motions to Adam to continue. Adam looks at Mary.

ADAM

I need your water.

Adam reaches into his pack and pulls out a packet for making a poultice. Other Indian women clean wounds and apply poultices to the wounded soldiers and volunteers.

Captain Smith, his soldiers, a hundred warriors - many wounded - and more women ENTER. The Indians pull their supplies and wounded on litters.

Dumbfounded, Wright, Major Lupton, soldiers, and volunteers watch the parade. Soon, Cultus Jim and Indians on horses pulling empty litters, APPEAR.

CAPTAIN SMITH

Those are our horses.

Apserkahar signals one brave to lead a horse and litter over to Lane. Lane looks around at what is happening. Wright, Griffin, Major Lupton are disgusted and WALK AWAY - Shorty and Charlie FOLLOW.

A GUNSLINGER brings a horse to Wright. He mounts and RIDES OFF alone. Palmer looks at General Lane - smiles as he watches Adam and Mary tend to him while the other women clean and put poultices on the wounded. Mary watches Adam. Adam avoids eye contact.

Griffin, Major Lupton, Shorty, and Charlie hurriedly come together. Griffin signals to the volunteers to follow. Only a few of the more disgusted volunteers LEAVE WITH THEM.

> JOEL PALMER
> Looks like a new way to conduct a war, Joe.

General Lane doesn't respond. He looks at Adam and Mary.

EXT. BATTLE MOUNTAIN – DAY - (LATER)

INTERCUT SCENE

A procession of wounded warriors, volunteers and soldiers help each other down the mountain.

Mary, Apserkahar, and Palmer walk beside the litter carrying General Lane. Adam helps other women with the wounded.

NEXT COMES Captain Smith with his soldiers, followed by Cultus Jim and the warriors from Tecumtum's village. All pass by a HALF DOZEN INDIANS and TWO

BOUND SOLDIERS and the rest of the Indians left behind.

Apserkahar waits for Captain Smith. He motions to the Indians to unbind the soldiers and release the horses.

Captain Smith walks up - orders soldiers to retrieve their horses. One unbound soldier looks at Captain Smith.

> UNBOUND SOLDIER
> Sir? Who won the battle?

Captain Smith doesn't know what to say. Joel Palmer overhears.

> JOEL PALMER
> Sanity, son, sanity.

EXT. TECUMTUM'S VILLAGE - DAY

INTERCUT SCENE

Ridge Runner, wearing the deer head, EMERGES from the trees.

Tecumtum and many tribal members gather around Ridge Runner to hear news of the battle.

> ELDER
> Where are our sons?

> RIDGE RUNNER
> They are coming.

Ridge Runner points. Cultus Jim, Adam, and warriors ENTER the camp pulling the wounded on litters. The members of the tribe separate and gather around the warriors. Tecumtum takes Ridge Runner's arm.

> TECUMTUM
>
> Ridge Runner runs like the wind over the hills. He makes the horses look slow.

Ridge Runner smiles. The two clasp arms. The warriors dismount. Horses are corralled. Women and elders bring food and drink.

Kitty brings a container of water to Cultus Jim, who is already chewing ravenously on jerky and berries.

The Shaman and Adam are to the side in a heated conversation. Cultus Jim takes drinks from his flask of whiskey. He joins Tecumtum and Ridge Runner.

> TECUMTUM
>
> My son, did you fight? I see no horses. No new guns.

> CULTUS JIM
>
> Adam's right. We need many more guns.

Adam and the Shaman JOIN them.

> ADAM
>
> More warriors than whites were wounded and killed. Apserkahar stopped the fight.

Kitty and other family members join Tecumtum and Cultus Jim.

TECUMTUM
Why did the battle stop?

CULTUS JIM
I shot Joe Lane.

TECUMTUM
Joe Lane?

ADAM
Agent Joel Palmer was fighting beside Joe Lane. They stopped the fight.

Apserkahar wants a council.

TECUMTUM
Council? What is this council?

Tecumtum turns to the Shaman.

SHAMAN
General Lane has a treaty with Apserkahar.

TECUMTUM
I know the treaty. Both the white man and red man break the treaty.

What did the general say?

EXT. TECUMTUM'S VILLAGE - NIGHT

Tecumtum, Adam, the Shaman, Cultus Jim, Kitty, mothers, and elders sit around a fire. The fire sends embers into the sky as younger boys and girls poke it with sticks.

ADAM

Father, I think you should go to the council. Your voice will be strong for all our people.

TECUMTUM

Why? Our ancestors found peace when warring villages became weary of fighting.

ADAM

My heart says General Joe Lane wants a trade agreement with the Indians.

TECUMTUM

Trade is good. We trade if what they have is good. We don't trade if what they have is bad. They can choose to do the same with us. Isn't that the way with all people?

We don't need a council for that.

ADAM

The general wants a written guarantee.

Tecumtum is getting edgy.

TECUMTUM

Where did you learn this white man's word? What is this word "guarantee"?

Kitty enters the fray.

> **KITTY**
> Daniel Giles used the word. He would say to Cultus, "I give you good whiskey. No water in it. That is my guarantee."

Cultus Jim raises his flask. Then slumbers.

Tecumtum is thinking as his family waits.

> **TECUMTUM**
> If I give a white man bad fish for a gun, the white man will come back... take his gun back or demand good fish. Why do we need a guarantee?

> **KITTY**
> Father, a guarantee is a promise not to give bad fish in the first place.

> **TECUMTUM**
> That is not our way. If I give bad fish to another Indian village, they come steal buckskins, baskets, good fish from my village.

> **KITTY**
> But Father—

Tecumtum puts up his hand.

> **TECUMTUM**
> If they take more than what is rightfully

> (MORE)

TECUMTUM (CONT'D)

theirs, I will steal back the buckskins and baskets, but leave the fish. Now both villages are happy.

ADAM

Why not give them good fish the first time?

Tecumtum gets up and begins to pace from the pressure he is getting from his children.

SHAMAN

Your father is testing the strength of the other village.

Tecumtum puts his hand up to silence the Shaman.

TECUMTUM

Yes. If the village with bad fish does not make me pay for the wrong, that village is weak. I would not want my sons and daughters to marry into such a village.

Tecumtum looks at his family waiting for their approval.

Adam and Kitty LAUGH at their father's serious demeanor. Shaman decides to enter the conversation to help Tecumtum.

SHAMAN

Your father, the Great Elk Hunter speaks with wisdom. The white man's greed leaves the red man only bad fish to trade. Soon other white men and red men die from the bad fish.

> KITTY
>
> But no one dies if Joel Palmer and Joe Lane give a guarantee to the Indians.

Tecumtum looks at the Shaman and all of his children. He shrugs his shoulders. He speaks to the mothers.

> TECUMTUM
>
> We raise wise children. I will go see about the "guarantee."

After hugging the mothers, TECUMTUM embraces Adam and Kitty.

He glances over to Cultus Jim, who's sound asleep.

> TECUMTUM
>
> My eldest is dreaming about war and General Lane's scalp... It is good that his aim was not true.

Kitty has her reed flute out - PLAYS.

EXT. BELOW TABLE ROCK - DAY

General Lane wears a red wool shirt, baggy gray military pants, and boots. He favors a wounded shoulder. He walks next to Palmer, along with Captain Smith and A COUPLE of SOLDIERS and HALF DOZEN OFFICIAL-LOOKING CIVILIANS carrying leather briefcases.

Smith is in his best uniform. He remains overly meticulous, still with his nervous twitches.

Behind Smith, on a knoll, a LINE OF DRAGOONS sit statue-like on their horses. They wear white belts and carry burnished scabbards and musketoons. Lane engages in a heated discussion with Palmer.

The CAMERA PANS the scene.

> GENERAL LANE (V.O.)
>
> And how do you plan to keep the Indians and the settlements separate?
>
> It's not in their blood to get along.
>
> JOEL PALMER (V.O.)
>
> Let the Indians do their hunting and fishing or whatever else suits them. If they don't want to raise wheat or vegetables, you can't force them.
>
> They have been living here a thousand years without us. Maybe more.
>
> GENERAL LANE (V.O.)
>
> There are still renegades out there trying to trade bad meat for beef. Killing settlers when they don't get what they want.
>
> JOEL PALMER (V.O)
>
> They're starving, Joe.
>
> GENERAL LANE (V.O.)
>
> It's cultivation. Can't they learn cultivation? They steal potatoes and cabbages.
>
> (MORE)

                    GENERAL LANE (V.O. CONT'D)
          It's your job to get those rogues to use
          tools for farming.

Captain Smith WALKS up beside them.

                    CAPTAIN SMITH
          The soldiers will remain ready if you
          decide to call them into action.

General Lane glances ahead. He puts his hand up.

                    GENERAL LANE
          We have an agreement to be unarmed.
          Leave your weapons here. Soldiers here
          will stay with the weapons.

Lane and Palmer look up ahead. The rest of the entourage follow Lane, Palmer, and Smith.

EXT. TABLE ROCK TREATY SITE - DAY

HUNDREDS OF INDIANS in war paint sit below Table Rock. They hold guns or bows and arrows across their laps. General Lane spots Apserkahar, Mary, and OTHER HEADMEN who are seated on the ground. The Chiefs do not get up to welcome Lane and Palmer. Lane approaches, extending his hand to Apserkahar and Mary. Neither responds.

Lane signals his entourage to sit on the ground. Smith, with a nervous twitch in his face and upper body, looks in the distance at the line of dragoons. The headmen wait for Joel Palmer or General Lane to speak.

GENERAL LANE
I do not see all the great chiefs here. Where are Tecumtum and Tipsu Tyee?

Apserkahar points to Tecumtum. Not far behind the Chiefs, Tecumtum, Adam, and Cultus Jim sit with other SUBCHIEFS.

APSERKAHAR
Speak!

Lane gets up. He gestures to Palmer to stand.

GENERAL LANE
Our Great White Father has appointed Joel Palmer as the Superintendent of Indian Affairs for all the Northwest.

He will now speak.

APSERKAHAR
We are here. Why is the great white father not here?

JOEL PALMER
I will speak for him.

Palmer signals to other entourage members to pull maps from large leather cases.

EXT. APPLEGATE RIVER - DAY

Griffin, Shorty, Charlie, and a COUPLE GUNSLINGERS ride along the Applegate River. They come through trees and SPOT the Lame Elder and Walking Bear from Tecumtum's village trapping fish.

The gunslingers pull their revolvers and attack, with the rest following. Walking Bear runs through the water to the other side and climbs through some rocks.

The men on horses gallop across the creek and spread out. The Elder is cut off from Walking Bear. The Elder turns - throws a rock at one of the gunslingers.

The horse rears and the gunslinger falls in the water. The distraction allows Walking Bear to escape over rocks and DISAPPEAR into thick brush.

Griffin catches up to the Elder, who tries to fight him off with his crutch.

> GUNSLINGER
> (shouting)
> Don't shoot the son of a bitch.

Griffin strikes the Elder with his revolver as the other gunslinger puts a lasso over his head. He turns his horse and drags him across the river to the other side.

EXT. SHORTY - CONTINUOUS

Shorty rides along the rocks - looks into the thicket to try to spot Walking Bear. He tries riding in but his horse balks at the bramble bushes.

> SHORTY
> Damn you, Nellie.

Shorty rides back across the creek. Walking Bear peers out from the bushes.

EXT. APPLEGATE RIVER - CONTINUOUS

The Elder is tied to a tree. Shorty RIDES by the gunslinger who limps - pulls his horse behind him out of the creek.

GUNSLINGER
Lost my pistol in there.

SHORTY
You can use mine.

Shorty and the Gunslinger approach the rest of the men.

Griffin looks at the wet, limping gunslinger.

GRIFFIN
What d'ya want to do with him?

GUNSLINGER
Put Charlie ten paces back and see how many shots he needs to kill him.

They all LAUGH as Charlie takes ten short paces.

SHORTY
You're cheating, Charlie. I only counted nine. Bet you a gold piece you can't hit him first shot.

Charlie takes his first SHOT. He misses. He aims again. SHOOTS. The frightened elder jerks, blood oozing from his shoulder.

CHARLIE
Got him.

Charlie aims again.

EXT. WALKING BEAR - CONTINUOUS

Walking Bear watches as a third SHOT RINGS through the forest. He turns, runs through the thick brush and bushes.

His loincloth gets caught on the blackberry bushes - gets almost torn off. He RUNS INTO the forest.

EXT. TABLE ROCK TREATY NEGOTATIONS – DAY (LATER)

Palmer stands - READS from an official looking document.

Mary brings water, which is passed among the seated entourage and headmen.

                JOEL PALMER
       The land ceded to the settlers for cultivation and farming shall be thirty-five hundred square miles.

Lane, also standing, slowly moves his extended arm from east to west, then takes the map from Palmer and shows the map to the Chiefs. The map is passed around to the Chiefs, who show minimal interest.

                JOEL PALMER
       The land north of Table Rock shall be one hundred square miles and will be reserved only for the Indians. No settlers shall live there.

Palmer hands Lane another map, which Lane passes on to Apserkahar as Palmer speaks.

JOEL PALMER
(pointing)

This land belongs only to the Indians. No settlers will live here.

Again the chiefs show little interest in the maps. Apserkahar rises to speak. He wears a long black robe adorned with dentalia.

APSERKAHAR

What will the Great White Father give us who allow the white man to live on Indian land?

Palmer signals another member of the entourage who gets up. He pulls out a document from his leather case. Palmer looks at it - looks at Lane - steps close to him.

JOEL PALMER

All these documents are for the government. They won't understand them.

GENERAL LANE

You and I both know what will make this work. Spare them the details.

Palmer thinks - gives the document back to the entourage member.

JOEL PALMER

All the villages will have blankets and

(MORE)

JOEL PALMER (CONT'D)

clothing for the cold winters. Farm tools...tools for building houses, raising wheat and vegetables. Houses will be built for the Chiefs.

The Great White Father will give sixty thousand dollars to the Chiefs here today over the next five years, of which—

GENERAL LANE

Of which fifteen thousand will be kept back for damages by the Indians on settlers" property.

Lane turns to the entourage and smiles. Lane and Palmer walk away from the headmen.

GENERAL LANE

My idea.

Palmer looks back - turns to Lane.

JOEL PALMER

(sarcastically)

Of course the Chiefs will accept the damage claims.

Many in the entourage overhear and LAUGH at the humor of the whole situation. Palmer and Lane come back to the headmen. Palmer points to the Indians on the hill.

                    JOEL PALMER

Each of the warriors will get some United States currency to spend in Jacksonville.

The headmen get angry as the ENTOURAGE TALKS BACK and FORTH among themselves.

Palmer looks at the headmen.

                    JOEL PALMER

As I said, the Great White Father will send blankets and clothing for winter. Houses for Chiefs. Every Indian family will...

A LOUD INCESSANT SCREAMING is heard. Walking Bear ENTERS from the trees. He runs past the group, on up the hill toward Tecumtum, Adam, Cultus Jim, and Ridge Runner. He is sweating profusely. His body is covered with deep scratches and dried blood mixed with sweat and dirt.

EXT. ADAM - CONTINUOUS

Adam and Ridge Runner recognize Walking Bear at the same time. They leap up and run toward the SCREAMING, CRYING boy. He throws himself into Adam's arms. Tecumtum and Cultus Jim surround Walking Bear. Mary joins them.

                    WALKING BEAR
                    (sobbing)

White men came to the river and killed Crooked Foot. They tied him to a tree and shot him.

His words are heard and understood by Indians seated nearby. The story spreads like wildfire. Hundreds on the hill rise and EXCITEDLY TALK to each other.

EXT. LANE AND PALMER WITH HEADMEN - CONTINUOUS

Lane urges Palmer to continue to speak. He is DROWNED OUT by the SHOUTS. Mary RETURNS - tells Apserkahar of the tragedy. Apserkahar is ENRAGED. He SPEAKS to the rest of the headmen. They all stand up. Tecumtum joins the headmen.

>TECUMTUM
>(SHOUTING)
>
>Walking Bear is from my village. Crooked Foot, who raised him with my family, was killed by white men. I will avenge his death.
>
>I want no treaty. Joe Lane and Joel Palmer cannot guarantee the protection of our people.

INTERCUT SCENE

Cultus Jim signals a half dozen warriors from his village to follow him. They RUN down the hill, past the group, INTO THE TREES. Mary hesitates - returns to her father. Apserkahar faces Palmer and Lane.

Some Indians point their weapons at the assembled whites. Others surround them.

Captain Smith turns to signal the dragoons. Palmer QUICKLY TRIPS Captain Smith, bringing him to the ground.

> JOEL PALMER
>
> Are you trying to get us all killed?

Smith rises, dusting himself off. Tecumtum stands beside Apserkahar.

> TECUMTUM
> (bitterly)
>
> First I learn the white man's word "guarantee." Now I know the white man's word "betrayal." Joe Lane, you betrayed our people.

> APSERKAHAR
> (to the warriors surrounding the entourage)
>
> Tie them and hang them.

Warriors locate lassos. Palmer and Lane are close together, standing back to back, preparing for the worst.

> JOEL PALMER
>
> Think fast. I'll speak to Apserkahar about his son. You better come up with something!

> GENERAL LANE
>
> Start talking.

Palmer rushes to Apserkahar, warriors grab him. Lane forces his way next to Tecumtum, his eyes flashing fire. He SHOUTS.

                    GENERAL LANE

The men who killed this boy's father are bad men. They broke the treaty. They are not soldiers. I will catch them and punish them.

While General Lane SPEAKS, Palmer stands close to Apserkahar and Mary.

                    JOEL PALMER

Your son Ben is with white soldiers as a guarantee that no Indians will attack us here. If any of us die, he will be killed for revenge.

                    APSERKAHAR

How did you get my son?

                    JOEL PALMER

Soldiers were sent to your village.

Apserkahar hastily puts his hand up to stop the Indians from attacking. General Lane's BOOMING VOICE carries over the DIN. Lane looks directly at the headmen, who have lifted their arms to quiet the members of their villages.

                    GENERAL LANE

Apserkahar and Tecumtum are not cowardly dogs who would kill unarmed men. What good will our blood do you? You and your people will be hunted down and exterminated.

                        (MORE)

GENERAL LANE (CONT'D)

We are here for peace. Let us be calm and proceed with our treaty.

Lane points at Walking Bear. Adam and Ridge Runner are comforting him. Lane turns - faces Tecumtum.

GENERAL LANE

I'll give Walking Bear blankets and shirts. I'll catch the evil white men and punish them.

TECUMTUM

(angrily)

Blankets and shirts? You killed one of my people. You go to Walking Bear. Tell Walking Bear you will give a blanket and shirt for Crooked Foot. See what he says.

Lane turns to Palmer. Palmer's RAISED VOICE carries through the DIMINISHING NOISE.

JOEL PALMER

(shouting)

Let us proceed. Let us proceed.

Lane gestures to the headmen to be seated. He looks directly at Tecumtum, who decides to sit with the other headmen. Warriors slowly return to the hillside.

Apserkahar sends Mary to Adam, Ridge Runner, and Walking Bear. Mary removes a basket on her back - opens a container of water. Adam is plucking thorns from the boy's arms and back. Adam looks at Ridge Runner.

> ADAM
>
> My father has chosen to sit with the headmen. Can you take Walking Bear back to the village?

Ridge Runner looks at the exhausted boy - looks around - begins to build a litter with the help of a couple other warriors.

Mary touches Adam on the shoulder. She gently removes his hand from the boy's back. She hands Adam a cloth from her basket. She pours water on the cloth. Adam's eyes meet Mary's - he quickly looks away.

Mary keeps her eyes fastened on Adam. He sneaks another look, then averts his eyes. Mary smiles. The two work together tending to Walking Bear's wounds. Ridge Runner ENTERS with a litter.

> MARY
>
> I want Walking Bear to stay. He's too hungry and weak to travel.

Adam wrings out the cloth and hands it to Mary, who slowly and tenderly cleans the boy's skin. She hands the basket to Adam. Adam looks inside, finds a wrapped Camus cake - hands it to Walking Bear.

Joel Palmer WALKS UP. He hands Walking Bear his canteen.

Walking Bear hesitates. Palmer LEAVES. Walking Bear drinks from the canteen - takes a bite of Camus cake.

> ADAM
>
> Walking Bear has no mother or father.

Mary looks compassionately at Walking Bear.

> MARY
>
> Many of us now have lost mothers and fathers.

Mary looks back at the headmen. LANE'S VOICE CARRIES over to them.

EXT. GENERAL LANE - CONTINUOUS

> GENERAL LANE
>
> All weapons shall be surrendered.

The headmen PROTEST IN UNISON. Apserkahar requests a drink as he begins COUGHING again, suggesting a developing illness. Tecumtum speaks for him.

> TECUMTUM
>
> White hunters kill many deer, squirrels, rabbits. Now braves have to go high in the mountains to find meat. We will not surrender guns.

Lane looks at Palmer and other members of the entourage. He looks up at all the guns among the warriors who sit along the mountainside. He also looks at the braves surrounding his entourage. Palmer WHISPERS to Lane.

> JOEL PALMER
>
> How about a token number for each village?

All is quiet again as the expectant headmen wait for Lane's response.

> GENERAL LANE
>
> Three guns in each village for hunting. If Indians trade with white men for guns, the Indians will be punished. If white men sell guns to the Indians, the white men will be punished with one hundred lashes and put in prison.

EXT. MARY AND ADAM - DAY (LATER)

Walking Bear is in a deep sleep. Mary periodically glances over towards the treaty negotiations as she speaks.

> MARY
> (pointing to her head)
> My father is old in his body, but young in his mind. Last summer he grew white man's vegetables, potatoes, pumpkins, squash.

Mary forms a circle with her arms, showing size.

> MARY
>
> He's learned to use the white man's tools. He's learning to read their books. Before the white man broke the treaty, he saw how the white man builds houses.
>
> He wants to live beside the white man. He wants the children of our villages to go to their schools.

Mary looks at the sleeping boy and smiles. Mary is aware she has talked a lot. She looks at Adam expectantly - waits for a response. Adam is silent. He is aware she is waiting for him to speak. Adam points to the headmen.

EXT. HEADMEN - CONTINUOUS

INTERCUT

The headmen stand next to Palmer and Lane. The entourage also stands for the signing of the treaty.

BACK TO MARY AND ADAM

                MARY
  My father is signing the peace treaty.

Adam gets up. Mary follows suit. They watch the historical event.

BACK TO LANE AND PALMER

Lane holds the treaty against a firm leather saddle bag held by Palmer. Palmer shows the headmen where to sign. He has written the names of the chiefs on the document. It reads "Joe," a blank space and "Apserkahar."

Each of the headmen sign with an X next to the names given them by Lane and Palmer, Last to sign is Tecumtum. John X Tecumtum.

EXT. JACKSONVILLE – DAY

MONTAGE

MONTHS LATER: Buildings are erected in Jacksonville. Fences and barns are built in the country. Livestock and fowl, mature gardens surround farms. CHILDREN play outside near WORKING MOTHERS, FATHERS, AND OLDER SIBLINGS. Fields are plowed for planting winter wheat. NEW WAGON TRAINS enter the valley, GREETED BY OTHERS. Winter sets in.

END OF MONTAGE

EXT. TABLE ROCK RESERVATION - TECUMTUM'S PEOPLE - WINTER - DAY

Makeshift shelters and partially-built plank houses. Indian elders and children shiver around burning campfires. The younger and able-bodied work to improve the shelters. It's bitter cold. Some have blankets wrapped around them. Others are draped with animal hides and wear fur hats.

There is COUGHING. A closer view of various families reveal children, elders, and others are sick with dysentery and typhoid fever.

Adam and Mary assist the ill and dying people. Walking Bear runs to the trees and squats. A LOW WAIL comes from around the camp. Tribal members gather around their sick.

Bear Woman and Kitty try to get Thistle Down to drink water as she battles a fever. TWO CHILDREN cling together - watch GRANDMOTHER wipe away vomit. Walking Bear RETURNS.

Adam and Mary wash and dry his feverish body. Adam gives him a broth - puts different clothes on him. Mary cuddles him. Adam goes and attends to Thistle Down.

EXT. TABLE ROCK RESERVATION - APSERKAHAR'S PLANKHOUSE - DAY

Tools for cultivation lean against a pile of lumber, falling snow gathers on them. Six saddled horses stand next to the large plank house. Outside the plank house three soldiers pace, clapping their hands to fight off the cold and snow storm.

INT. APSERKAHAR'S PLANK HOUSE - DAY

Apserkahar, and Tecumtum stare across at Palmer, a COUPLE CARPENTERS and a SOLDIER. Palmer is defensive about the lack of supplies and foods.

JOEL PALMER
Supplies for building houses for the other headmen will soon come.

TECUMTUM
Too late. Many are sick from the cold and bad food. We are going back to our village.

Apserkahar begins COUGHING, gets up, starts to pace.

APSERKAHAR
Many of our people have no shelter or blankets. You have broken your promises again.

JOEL PALMER
Tipsu's warriors keep attacking the wagons coming into the valley from the East.

APSERKAHAR

We cannot control Tipsu. Do not use him as an excuse for breaking your promises.

Palmer, visibly angry, looks at the carpenters.

JOEL PALMER
(to carpenters)

What about the houses promised?

WHITE CARPENTER

I don't get no cooperation from these heathens. Let them build their own houses.

JOEL PALMER

With what? Boards, hoes, plows are missing.

Palmer looks at Tecumtum.

JOEL PALMER

I can't keep you here. The white people of the valley will be angry. The great white chief will be angry. Joe Lane will be angry. You come back in the spring.

TECUMTUM

You keep your promises, we keep our promises.

EXT. - FOREST TRAIL - TECUMTUM'S PEOPLE - DAY

Snow is falling. Tecumtum, Cultus Jim, Adam, Kitty, and Tecumtum's people travel slowly through harsh winter conditions. A number of travois and litters carry belongings and the many dead.

Kitty, River Maiden, and Bear Woman ride horses next to Cultus Jim. His horse pulls a fur-lined litter.

The travelers create a stark silhouette against the grey sky and leafless oak trees.

A lone man on a horse-drawn wagon RIDES BY. He is one of the white carpenters seen earlier at Apserkahar's plank house. As he passes by Tecumtum, he waves. No one waves back.

Tecumtum takes a close look at the wagon. It carries hoes, shovels, a plow, and boards.

Tecumtum speaks to Adam and the Shaman as they ride.

> TECUMTUM
> The white chiefs Palmer and Lane tell us stop stealing from the white man. That white man steals from the reservation.

EXT. DRAGOONS - CONTINUOUS

In the distance TWO MOUNTED DRAGOONS in military uniform watch Tecumtum's people pass.

EXT. FORT LANE - DAY

INTERCUT SCENE

AN INFANTRY MAN, looking through binoculars, perches atop a high point in the almost completed fort. He watches the passing tribe of Indians.

Below, between the buildings, MILITARY EXERCISES with INFANTRY are in progress. General Lane, the least well-dressed military man at the fort, walks with Palmer and Captain Smith.

> GENERAL LANE
>
> Company E over there doesn't seem to be out of sorts after building the Fort. I must say, it is magnificent.

> CAPTAIN SMITH
> (proudly)
> In a little less than four months!

Palmer turns to General Lane.

> JOEL PALMER
>
> And you, my friend, can't get Congress to approve the use of infantry for building houses for the Indians over by Table Rock?

The three walk past barracks, officers' housing, and other buildings.

About 20 MOUNTED DRAGOONS ENTER, LIEUTENANT CROOK leads. He's a broad-shouldered West Point rebel who wears a slouch hat and braids his whiskers. He has an unkempt sloppy look. He separates from the dragoons. He enters a corral, dismounts - unsaddles his own horse.

>   GENERAL LANE (O.S.)
> Let them build their own houses.

>   JOEL PALMER (O.S.)
> With what? The carpenters steal. The men have to leave to forage for food. Half of them are dying from our diseases.
>
> I'm not going to stop them from going back to their villages.

INT. FORT LANE HEADQUARTERS - CONTINUOUS

>   GENERAL LANE
> I hear talk in Jacksonville about extermination again.

>   JOEL PALMER
> There's a killer mentality out there. I want to move the Indians out of this valley.

Lt. Crook ENTERS. Captain Smith separates from Lane and Palmer and confronts Lt. Crook.

>   CAPTAIN SMITH
> Do you always have to look like you're still at the bottom of your West Point class?

                    LT. CROOK

If it's good enough for the General, it's good enough for me, Captain.

The two approach General Lane and Palmer. Palmer is intense.

                    JOEL PALMER

I told you, Joe, we can't bring them back to the reservation without food or housing. I'll try to bring them back in the spring.

                    GENERAL LANE

I want them back on the reservation, now.

Lane looks at Captain Smith.

                    GENERAL LANE

Captain, you hear me.

                    CAPTAIN SMITH

Yes, Sir.

General Lane looks fondly at Lt. Crook.

                    GENERAL LANE

Lieutenant, what did you find out there?

                    LT. CROOK

Chief John is on his way back to his village. I believe, Sir, his people need med-

                    (MORE)

LT. CROOK (CONT'D)

ical assistance. Many have died. Some of Chief Joe's village have settled out on Little Butte Creek.

GENERAL LANE

Get them back on the reservation.

LT. CROOK

No, Sir. That is as inhumane as you can get. All the diseases have come from the carpenters. Chief Joe is going to die.

GENERAL LANE

Chief Joe? I'm sorry to hear that. He had my respect for bringing peace to the valley.

JOEL PALMER

(exasperated)

Peace? Peace? While they die from our diseases! The government, through your efforts, is prepared to pay volunteers to exterminate the Indians?

GENERAL LANE

It's in your hands, Joel. Now it all depends on who or what gets them first, doesn't it?

EXT. TECUMTUM'S VILLAGE - NIGHT

A winter storm. Most Villagers are in their plank houses. A few GUARDS wrapped in furs sit/stand around fires. Others are WAILING at the burial ground.

Cultus Jim walks from the burial ground in swirling snow to Tecumtum's plank house. The sounds of WAILING for dead village members penetrates from plank houses.

INT. TECUMTUM'S PLANK HOUSE

A fire burns in the fire pit. The Shaman paces back and forth. The WIND HOWLS outside. Kitty has children cuddled against her. Cultus Jim ENTERS - sits next to Tecumtum and Bear Woman. Adam and Walking Bear sit by River Maiden.

Tecumtum's other children sit together on the other side of the fire next to Ridge Runner, RUNNING DOE, and their children. A couple children play STRING GAMES.

The Shaman's coyote story unfolds, accompanied by the EERIE SOUNDS OF WIND outside. Children stop the string games and sidle over next to Adam and their mothers. The Shaman creates theater with sweeping gestures.

As the following story is told, a MONTAGE OF DREAMY IMAGES, corresponding with the content of the story, are INTERCUT with INTERIOR SHOTS of the story-teller and his audience. Begin with an IMITATION OF THE LOST LANGUAGE.

SHAMAN

In the beginning of the world, there was no such thing as death. Everyone lived until there were so many people that Mother Earth had no room for any more. All the great headmen came together to decide what to do. They smoked the pipe until one headman stood up and said, "I think when people die, they go away for a while, then come back." As soon as he sat down, Coyote, who came to listen, jumped up and said....

Kitty moves to center stage - gets on her knees - pantomimes a coyote.

KITTY

"I think people die forever. This little world is not large enough to hold all people. If people who die come back to life, there will not be enough food."

Kitty crawls over to the side.

SHAMAN

All the headmen jumped up and said to Coyote, "No, no." We don't want our mothers and fathers, our brothers and sisters, our grandparents and friends gone forever."

The Shaman looks at the children.

> SHAMAN
>
> Why is that so?

> CHILDREN
>
> They cry and be unhappy.

> SHAMAN
>
> Yes, no happiness in the world.
>
> So all the headmen decided they did not like Coyote's idea. They tried to chase Coyote away.

Adam and Cultus Jim get up and chase Kitty around the fire.

> SHAMAN
>
> The headmen decided when people die, people go away for a little while, then come back again.

Adam and Cultus Jim sit down.

> CHILD
>
> How long is a little while?

> SHAMAN
>
> Two moons... The headmen asked the medicine men to build a large grass house facing east.

EXT. GRASS HOUSE - DAY

BLURRED SURREAL IMAGES OF A GRASS HOUSE WITH MANY PEOPLE AROUND IT.

> SHAMAN (V.O.)
> The medicine man in each village gathered all the people of the village outside the grass house. The medicine man said to the sad people, "Sing songs to call the spirit of the dead to the grass house."

A MOURNFUL INDIAN CHANT.

> SHAMAN (O.S.)
> "When the spirit comes, all the dead inside the house will come back to life. Then everyone can be happy again."

> When the first man died, everyone came to the grass house to sing. Coyote was there too... Before the medicine man went into the house, a whirlwind blew in from the west.

INT. PLANK HOUSE

The adults and some of the older children BLOW SOUNDS of WIND.

> SHAMAN
> It circled the grass house. When the wind came to the door, Coyote jumped over the wind, and slammed the door shut.

Kitty leaps - OPENS and SLAMS THE DOOR of the plank house.

> SHAMAN
>
> When the wind found the door closed, it whirled on by. So Coyote made death last forever. Now all the people of the village cry and are unhappy when anyone dies.

EXT. FOREST TRAIL - DAY

Adam and Kitty ride horses through BLOWING SNOW.

> SHAMAN (V.O.)
>
> When the wind howls people of the village say, "Someone comes, someone comes." The whirlwind is the spirit of the dead trying to find a place to go. The spirit wanders over the earth trying to find a place to rest.

EXT. RESERVATION - APSERKAHAR'S PLANK HOUSE - DAY

Adam and Kitty ride to Apserkahar's plank house. They dismount. An ELDER takes the horses. Lt. Crook and TWO OTHER SOLDIERS shaking from the cold, warm their hands around a fire.

> SHAMAN (V.O.)
>
> The Coyote ran away and never came back. When Coyote saw what he had done, he was afraid. Now Coyote runs from one place to another.
>
> He's forever looking back, first over one shoulder, then over the other shoulder,

to see if anyone is chasing him. Now Coyote is forever hungry because no one will feed him.

INT. APSERKAHAR'S PLANK HOUSE - DAY

Palmer leans over Apserkahar, who is BREATHING LABORIOUSLY. Mary sits close.

> JOEL PALMER
> You ask, why do the whites come? It doesn't matter why. You cannot stop them. Our great chief cannot stop them. I cannot stop them.

Adam and Kitty ENTER and quietly APPROACH. Apserkahar reaches out to them. Each takes his hand.

Apserkahar looks back at Palmer. Adam and Kitty seat themselves on each side of Mary. Tearful, Mary turns - gives each a kiss on the cheek. Adam puts his arm around Mary. Mary buries her head into Adam's shoulder. 12-YEAR-OLD BEN slides over next to Kitty. Kitty wraps her arms around him. Apserkahar has tears in his eyes.

> APSERKAHAR
> My wife, two of my daughters, and one adopted son have all gone to the Great Spirit. It is time for me to join them.

Apserkahar begins COUGHING again. Palmer touches his shoulder.

JOEL PALMER

Your family and my family could live together in peace and respect each other's ways. The earth, this land, was not made only for the red man.

The air we breathe, the water we drink, the animals we hunt are made for all men, white and red. Who can say this is mine, that is yours?

God made...

Apserkahar puts up his hand.

APSERKAHAR

White missionaries came to us, bringing their Bible and prayer to "bring the red man out of darkness."

We have our own Sun God who comes in the spring, cleansing the earth with rain. Can he not cleanse our souls?

We give prayers and dance to the Great Spirit in the sky. Your eyes and my eyes tell us all life comes from the Great Spirit, what you call "God," who makes the trees bud and grasses grow. My whole life I have danced a holy dance for the return of the dead.

Go now, Palmer. I will die with my family.

Palmer, sad, looks around at the family. He is a stranger. He EXITS.

EXT. PLANK HOUSE - DAY

Lt. Crook brings Palmer his horse. Many of Apserkahar's tribe stand outside. The WIND begins to BLUSTER and Palmer pulls his coat tight around him. A MOURNFUL SONG from Kitty's reed flute comes from within the lodge.

The women and men outside begin their WAIL as they grieve for the great Apserkahar. The sounds of the flute float with WHIRLWINDS PASSING BY THE MYTHICAL GRASS HOUSE as Palmer rides off. The COYOTE'S hungry and MOURNFUL YIPS AND HOWLS are heard in the distance.

EXT. JACKSONVILLE - DAY

It's a beautiful Spring Sunday in Jacksonville. In the background an ORGAN PLAYS a HYMN. Many new houses and buildings have been built. Horses and carriages wait outside the Methodist church.

Tecumtum, Cultus Jim, Adam, Kitty, and Mary ENTER Jacksonville on horseback. Tecumtum and Cultus Jim wear a mixture of white men's clothing and Indian apparel. Adam, Kitty, and Mary are dressed in their finest traditional Native American dress.

As they ride by the church, Tecumtum stops the entourage. They listen to the music. A REFRAIN TO THE HYMN is repeated after each verse.

Kitty rides up to Tecumtum and the two HUM the refrain after the third verse. When the refrain comes for the fourth time, they HUM MORE LOUDLY, urging the others to hum along.

> KITTY
> They sing words from a book. I'm going to learn to play the white man's songs on my flute.

> TECUMTUM
> Come Adam, sing.

Adam shakes his head. They all dismount, lead their horses slowly down main street. They tether them to a hitching post. SETTLER'S FAMILIES and MINERS watch. Mary takes Adam's and Kitty's hands as they look in the store windows. Kitty drops their hands - bravely decides to go back to the church.

Tecumtum and Cultus Jim walk by the new clapboard buildings where Tecumtum inspects the details of construction. Cultus surveys the RAUCOUS bar. He watches Miners ENTER AND EXIT. He separates from Tecumtum. Tecumtum grabs his arm. Cultus jerks away and ENTERS the bar.

Adam and Mary stop at Holman's store - look in the window, then ENTER. Tecumtum FOLLOWS.

INT. GENERAL STORE - CONTINUOUS

Adam, Mary, and Tecumtum browse in awe at what has been brought in from the East. OTHER PATRONS are in stop-motion as they observe the Indian family.

Adam spots eyeglasses in a box. He drags Tecumtum over to them. Tecumtum tries a number on - finds a pair. The chief goes to the door - looks outside. He comes back to the counter, takes out a pouch, pulls out a gold nugget. It's fairly large. Holman shakes his head. Returns the nugget.

Adam watches, figures it out - takes Tecumtum's pouch and pours out the other gold nuggets. Holman sorts through - takes a much smaller one. He looks at Tecumtum. The chief smiles - acknowledges that it is a good trade. Adam scoops up the nuggets and returns the pouch to Tecumtum.

EXT. METHODIST CHURCH - CONTINUOUS

INTERCUT SCENE

Kitty stands outside the church.

Across the street another FAMILY OF HUNGRY IMPOVERISHED LOOKING INDIANS INCLUDING A MOTHER, GRANDMOTHER, AND 3 CHILDREN stop/listen to the music. They slowly walk by. Inside, a FLUTE AND VIOLIN DUET flows beautifully through the air. Kitty is enchanted.

Tecumtum, followed some distance back by Mary and Adam who carry bags with purchases, APPROACHES Kitty. Tecumtum proudly wears his glasses. The FLUTE AND VIOLIN DUET STOPS. There is silence.

Kitty notices Tecumtum - runs to him - tries the glasses on, shakes her head and gives them back.

TECUMTUM
(pointing to the sky)
I see everything. I see birds, trees, sky.

The CHURCH BELL RINGS. WORSHIPERS EXIT.

WORSHIPERS intermixed with Joel Palmer, Benjamin Dirkson, Charles Bray with WIFE, EXIT and mingle with FRIENDS. The METHODIST MINISTER EXITS - shakes hands with WORSHIPERS. Giles WALKS OUT.

A FEW WOMEN separate from the men - hasten to set out tables and chairs for a potluck. Small groups form.

CHATTER fills the air. They notice the Indians, both next to church property and the other impoverished family walking/watching from across the street.

Giles runs over to Tecumtum's family - starts a conversation with Kitty.

> GILES
>
> You came from Deer Creek?
>
> KITTY
>
> Agent Palmer helped us.
>
> GILES
>
> You are brave to come to Jacksonville.
>
> KITTY
>
> Why? The treaty gives us freedom.
>
> GILES
>
> Where's Adam?
>
> KITTY
>
> Over there.

Kitty points to Adam and Mary, who APPROACH. Giles runs to greet Adam.

Palmer notices Tecumtum and Kitty. He comes over, shakes hands.

>   JOEL PALMER
> Beautiful day.

Tecumtum looks around.

>   TECUMTUM
> Beautiful day.

>   JOEL PALMER
> Glasses are good?

>   TECUMTUM
> I see everything.

>   JOEL PALMER
> Have you planted seeds on the reservation?

>   TECUMTUM
> The seeds are in the ground at my village.

>   JOEL PALMER
> You plow the ground?

>   TECUMTUM
> There are no plows. We hoe the ground.

Tecumtum moves his hands in a hoeing motion.

JOEL PALMER

It is time to plant seeds on the reservation so you will have food for horses and cattle at the end of the growing season.

Tecumtum does not respond. Palmer, not wanting to start anything, glances around at the SOUND OF A FLUTE. He separates from Tecumtum - walks over to the rest of the church members.

MARY HARRIS is showing her flute to an ADOLESCENT GIRL. Several people surround Mary Harris, her husband GEORGE HARRIS, and their TWO CHILDREN. Kitty ENTERS - gets close to watch.

MARY HARRIS

See. Place these fingers here, and these fingers here. Now blow.

The girl struggles - begins to make DISCORDANT MUSICAL SOUNDS with Mrs. Harris nodding approval. George Harris CHATS with other WORSHIPERS.

GEORGE HARRIS

We live close to the Wagoners down river. Mary and I are on a Donation Land Grant. The land is good.

SETTLER'S HUSBAND

You haven't been bothered by the Indians?

GEORGE HARRIS

They come begging. We've given them flour, and vegetables from our garden.

Mary Harris bends and helps the girl with the flute.

MARY HARRIS

Hold down this key.

Charles Bray and Benjamin Dirkson talk with other MEN.

DIRKSON

(provoked)

They are off the reservation. Palmer's over there acting like nothing's happened. He needs to get them back on the reservation.

MAN

The treaty allows them to go off the reservation.

BRAY

(incensed)

Did you hear me! They're not LIVING on the reservation? You men come to our next meeting.

ANOTHER MAN

What do you expect to accomplish? Palmer is doing the best he can. General Lane is East trying to help—

BRAY

You don't understand. Our job at these meetings is to get the volunteer militia to do what Palmer and Fort Lane can't or won't do.

DIRKSON

We are organizing politically to get the right judges, the right people in the legislature, the right governor...

Palmer ENTERS.

JOEL PALMER

... and the right Indian Agent.

BRAY

At least one who would spend more time down here keeping the Indians on the reservation.

JOEL PALMER

Easy there, Charles. There are some good treaty abiders and some not so good.

BRAY

(pointing across the street)

And then you have those heathens over there from that rascal Tipsu's band begging for food.

Palmer glances at the "heathens."

> JOEL PALMER
>
> Out of Christian charity I would like to invite them to eat with us.

The men fall silent. Meanwhile, CHATTER goes on around them.

> BRAY
>
> (arrogant)
>
> You were hired to teach the savages cultivation, not to feed them.

> DIRKSON
>
> You're likely to start a war in our churchyard. Go talk to Reverend Matson.

> PALMER
>
> (visibly upset)
>
> I will.

Palmer walks to the minister.

Mary Harris starts to play a SIMPLE MOZART MELODY. BOYS AND GIRLS run around the various groups playing tag.

Tecumtum WALKS - stands next to Kitty. Mary and Adam show Giles their purchases.

Worshipers line up and fill their plates. The minister standing next to Palmer looks at the bedraggled, hungry Indian families and then at Tecumtum et al. Bray APPROACHES.

MINISTER

We can't feed these people here or those over there.

JOEL PALMER

I just came in from the reservation a couple days ago. Many have died over the winter. Chief Apserkahar and his wife Sally...

BRAY

Oh! You know the savage's names? Which warlord was he? Sally did you say? One of his many squaws?

JOEL PALMER

(ignoring Bray)

Chief Tecumtum, over there, lost one of his children to dysentery. I would ask you to welcome all of them to eat with us; but I'm a visitor here.

Dirkson APPROACHES.

MINISTER

(hesitating)

Ah, Mr. Bray and Mr. Dirkson here are on the church board. I thought with your influence you could...

JOEL PALMER

They have just heard my opinion.

BRAY

I would oppose inviting any of the heathens.

(pointing across

the street)

Those beggars are from Tipsu's band. A few weeks ago renegades from his tribe killed a man and his dog - dumped the two of them in front of his cabin. His wife and children came home and found him in a lake of his own blood.

DIRKSON

(pointing)

Mr. Palmer, you go over there and talk to those men and women who gave up their homesteads on Bear Creek.

Some are without husbands and some without wives. If you can convince them to have the Indians eat with us, I may change my mind.

Mrs. Harris puts her flute away after APPLAUSE from those around her, including Kitty and Tecumtum.

Kitty courageously walks close to Mrs. Harris - pulls out her reed flute from her quiver - shows her flute to Mrs. Harris, who steps out of the line to look at it.

Kitty offers it to her. Mrs. Harris demurs and gestures that Kitty play it. Kitty looks at Tecumtum, who nods. She PLAYS the same simple tune that Mrs. Harris played a moment earlier. She plays the tune with no errors using a different scale.

All the attention from the worshipers including Bray, Palmer, et al focus on Kitty. Kitty finishes her tune and the men and women close by, APPLAUD. Mary Harris invites Kitty to eat with her family.

Kitty looks to Tecumtum, who in turn looks to Palmer. Giles runs over to take Kitty's hand. Palmer ignores Tecumtum. Giles drops Kitty's hand - runs to Palmer. Palmer looks at the minister, Bray, and Dirkson. He looks at Tecumtum - shakes his head.

> TECUMTUM
> (facing his family)
> Come.

Some in the line gesture for them to come and eat with them. Giles stands between the worshipers and Tecumtum and family. Giles looks at the Minister. Bray and Dirkson put their "not welcome" hands up.

Palmer angry, walks to the head of the food line. He grabs one of the chicken legs and raises it.

> JOEL PALMER
> I brought some of this chicken today. May I quote scripture, since your own minister does not have the courage to say what should be in his heart, and what I know is in some of your hearts, though you lack the courage to speak?

Some BOOs start as Palmer steps forward.

MR. HARRIS
(incensed)
Are we not civilized enough to hear Agent Palmer speak?

JOEL PALMER
When I was eleven years old, my mother compelled me to memorize these Bible verses when I chased a beggar off our porch:

Tecumtum and his family slowly WALK AWAY. Giles, torn, is left standing alone.

JOEL PALMER (O.S.)
"I was hungry, and you gave me not meat; I was thirsty, and you gave me not drink; I was a stranger, and you took me not in; naked and you clothed me not.

Tecumtum and family untether their horses - RIDE AWAY.

EXT. JACKSONVILLE HOME - CONTINUOUS

The impoverished Indian family begs at a pioneer's home. A PIONEER GIRL AND MOTHER give them a loaf of bread and garden vegetables. The family walks to the next house and are shooed away by a PIONEER MAN AND HIS WIFE. The man holds a gun in his hand.

JOEL PALMER (O.S.)
Then the so-called believers answered

(MORE)

JOEL PALMER (O.S. CONT'D)
Jesus, saying, "When did we see you hungry or thirsty or a stranger, or naked or sick, and did not give you what you needed." Then Jesus answered them, saying, "Verily I say unto you, inasmuch as you did it not to one of the least of these poor souls you saw today, you did it not to me."

EXT. NOISY BAR - CONTINUOUS

Cultus Jim's horse is still at the hitching post.

GUNSLINGERS and MINERS ENTER AND EXIT. Griffin EXITS - walks away.

INT. NOISY BAR - CONTINUOUS

Shorty, Charlie, a HUSTLER GAMBLER, AND THREE GUNSLINGER/MINER GAMBLERS (can use same gunslingers from earlier scenes) are playing poker. SOMEONE RAISES, SOMEONE CALLS, and SOMEONE FOLDS. They all glance frequently at Cultus Jim, who sits at a table by himself.

Ben Wright is at the bar with other GUNSLINGERS and MINERS. He wears a holster with a pistol. He walks over to Cultus Jim, who has a tobacco pouch, whiskey bottle and a drink in front of him. He sits down - silently stares at Cultus Jim. Cultus Jim stares back - SMILES - offers his tobacco pouch to Wright.

Wright takes the pouch - removes some tobacco - begins rolling a cigarette.

Near the bar is a rack with holsters and guns, and muskets lined up together. One newer rifle's stock has carvings and a colorful leather wrap. The gunslinger at the bar who ran down Walking Bear's father, Crooked Foot, eyeballs Cultus Jim.

GUNSLINGER

(glancing at the rack)

I thought those savages couldn't have guns.

BARTENDER

That's not how it is. Each tribe is allotted a certain number of guns for hunting.

GUNSLINGER

It don't look like a hunting gun to me. Makes no sense you selling him whiskey.

BARTENDER

What are you talking about? I don't have a grudge against the Indians like a lot of the folks around here, and the chief's son over there knows it.

GUNSLINGER

Well, I don't like it, and I wouldn't mind finding an excuse to plug his ass.

BARTENDER

You so much as put a hand on your pistol grip and you'll have a lead ball through the back of your head.

> GUNSLINGER
>
> You're the tough guy here, aren't you?

> BARTENDER
>
> That's why I stay in business. If you don't like it, there's the door.

The gunslinger STALKS OUT. Charlie has come up to the bar for another drink. Cultus Jim gets up - finishes his drink, takes his bottle and tobacco pouch and staggers to the back door of the bar - EXITS. Charlie comes back to the card table - sits down. Shorty's getting up.

> CHARLIE
>
> You in, Shorty?

> SHORTY
>
> Nah. I gotta take a piss.

Shorty GOES OUT the back door. Wright FOLLOWS.

Charlie folds his hand.

> CHARLIE
>
> Count me out on this one, BART.

Charlie walks to the back door - EXITS.

EXT. OUTHOUSE - CONTINUOUS

Shorty stands outside the outhouse door. Cultus Jim opens the door, COMES OUT.

> SHORTY
>
> Hey, chief, why ain't you on the reservation?

CULTUS JIM
You white chief?

SHORTY
Yeah! I'm white chief.

CULTUS JIM
You not chief. You smell like skunk. Come to chief's sweathouse. Get clean smell.

Cultus Jim LAUGHS.

Suddenly Shorty GUTS Cultus Jim with a Bowie knife. Cultus Jim tries to reach for his knife. WRIGHT comes from behind the outhouse. He grabs Cultus' hair - SLASHES his throat - SLASHES his throat again.

The gunslinger stands to the side as a lookout. He has an axe and a pail of lye in his hand. GRUNTS and GROANS are heard. Wright takes the axe - BEHEADS Cultus Jim.

In a quick one-two-three, Shorty and Charlie pull Cultus Jim's buckskin jacket over where his head used to be, then drag him into the outhouse. They lift the whole toilet seat. and DUMP HIM in the outhouse pit. The Gunslinger pours lye into the pit. He throws the bucket in, drops the seat down. He WALKS AWAY around the corner of the building. Charlie and Shorty ENTER the back door of the bar.

WRIGHT drops the bloody head of Cultus Jim in a leather mailbag. He PUMPS/WASHES his hands from an outside pump - takes the leather mailbag and DISAPPEARS AROUND THE SIDE of the building.

EXT. STREET BUILDINGS - OFFICE - CONTINUOUS

TOWNSPEOPLE PROMENADE, including the Harris family. Settlers window shop. Bar patrons go in and out of the bar. Wright RIDES BY with Cultus Jim's horse behind.

INT. OFFICE - CONTINUOUS

Bray and Dirkson, still in their Sunday clothes are plotting with Griffin and Lupton.

> GRIFFIN
>
> Major Lupton and I have twenty volunteers ready to go out to Little Butte Creek.
>
> DIRKSON
>
> We can't put them on the payroll.
>
> GRIFFIN
>
> They don't care. These boys are in it for the joy of killin'.
>
> BRAY
>
> You don't understand. We want to get us on the government payroll.
>
> You've got to go out and get the Jacksonville people in on the fighting.
>
> GRIFFIN
>
> Well, ain't we doing that by going out to Little Butte Creek?

DIRKSON

We're going to have a meeting tonight. Agent Palmer and Captain Smith from The Fort are going to be there. They been talkin' to the Chiefs.

GRIFFIN

What for? We already know they been robbin' and tradin' for guns and horses.

DIRKSON

Palmer knows it, too.

GRIFFIN

Yeah, but he wants to move em', not exterminate them. That won't get us any money.

There's a KNOCK on the door. Dirkson gets up - peeks through the window. He opens the door. Wright ENTERS. He walks to the table and drops the leather bag on it. Bray gets up.

BRAY

What's this? You finish the job already.

WRIGHT

Yeah.

Dirkson quickly goes to the safe and pulls out a packet - gives it to Wright. Wright glances in the packet. He pulls the roll of bills out and stuffs them in his pocket - leaves the envelope on the table next to the leather bag.

                    DIRKSON
          You have proof?

Wright nods at the bag. Bray quickly opens the leather bag with Dirkson standing next to him. They GASP and close it quickly. Griffin and Major Lupton BREAK UP WITH LAUGHTER.

                 MAJOR LUPTON
          How's that for proof?

                    DIRKSON
          Get it out of here.

Dirkson pulls out another envelope.

                    DIRKSON
          This is an advance on the old Chief.
          There's double that when you bring me
          his head.

He pulls the money out of the envelope and hands it to Wright. Wright stuffs the money in his pocket, takes the mailbag, DEPARTS.

EXT. STREET - CONTINUOUS

Wright walks down the street to the hitching post. He rolls a cigarette - lights it - attaches the bag to Cultus Jim's horse - mounts his Appaloosa and RIDES AWAY.

EXT. EDGE OF TOWN - CONTINUOUS

Shorty and Charlie wait on their horses. Wright RIDES UP. The reins of another horse carrying supplies is handed to Wright.

CHARLIE

Did Bray pay up?

WRIGHT

Yeah.

They RIDE AWAY into the woods.

EXT. WOODS - DAY (LATER)

Mary, in her same Native American wardrobe runs from tree to tree looking for Adam. A pine cone drops on the ground next to her. She looks at it. Another drops. And another. She looks up but can't see anything. Another drops and hits her on the head. She looks up again, walks around the tree. Sees Adam, points and LAUGHS.

Mary RUNS and HIDES. Adam SCURRIES down from the tree. Adam runs from tree to tree. He waits, turns around and comes back. He gets on his hands and knees and slowly crawls through a thick layer of leaves and crevasses. He sees her moccasins. They roll about affectionately wrestling. The game of love becomes erotic, intimate, sexual.

EXT. FOREST TRAIL - DAY (LATER STILL)

It clouds over. A light spring snow is falling. Adam and Mary ride through the woods.

Back in the trees, WRIGHT, SHORTY, and CHARLIE wait for them to pass. Wright picks up the trail and they follow.

EXT. JACKSONVILLE - METHODIST CHURCH - NIGHT

Spring snow falls. Horses, and horses with wagons and buggies are tethered outside the church.

INT. CHURCH MEETING

Captain Smith, Joel Palmer, Major Lupton, Bray, Dirkson, B. B. Griffin, the Methodist minister, and 20 OTHER SETTLERS AND A FEW MINERS are present. PRIMARY CONVERSATIONS ARE OVERLAPPED WITH OTHER CONVERSATIONS.

BILL LATHAM, A ROUGH-HEWN MINER, stands.

> LATHAM
> (shouting over the
> din)
> I ain't used to being in a church so I don't want to offend, but there ain't a miner on the Illinois or the Rogue or the Applegate who can't get a squaw for the price of a gun.
>
> Them miners will sell a can o' powder fer ten dollars, a box o' caps fer three dollars, and them lead musket balls fer a dollar apiece. 'Pending on how long them miners want to keep them squaws, and what they want 'em fer, them Indians are gettin' as much as they want. And that includes bran' spankin' new rifles and revolvers.

A LOT OF TALK BETWEEN people in response to Latham. Captain Smith looks at Palmer.

CAPTAIN SMITH
Did you know that?

JOEL PALMER
We can't stop it. Broken promises.

Dirkson rises to speak.

DIRKSON
I would like to address Captain Smith. Mr. Latham here has told me that Chief John has been stockpiling guns since he went off the reservation. He needs to be put in irons and brought back to the reservation.

JOEL PALMER
One in five Rogue Valley Indians died of white man's diseases last winter. Many more would have died of starvation if I'd kept them on the reservation. What few government subsidies given from the last treaty have been stolen by white people.

DIRKSON
Wasn't it your job to stop it? I believe I was addressing the Captain.

You, Captain, better be letting General Lane out East know we have a major crisis here. Chief John will lay you and your blue-eyed pups to waste unless you get more reinforcements.

CAPTAIN SMITH

Reinforcements are on their way.

JOEL PALMER

I know the citizens of Jacksonville and the majority of you here are determined to exterminate the Indians. It's not going to happen while I am their agent. I will move them before I let you go out and slaughter them.

BRAY

You can't stop us. We're marching in the morning to get the marauding savages out on Little Butte Creek.

CAPTAIN SMITH

You'll be dealing with the courts if you—

MAJOR LUPTON

Courts don't operate in southern Oregon, Captain. I heard you're also protecting runaway savages from California at the Fort. We have volunteers on their way to get them, too.

CAPTAIN SMITH

(twitching)

It's my job to protect them until justice is served, and by God I will.

Captain Smith STORMS OUT. Palmer faces Major Lupton.

JOEL PALMER

You're an arrogant son-of-a-bitch. You and the volunteers can stand outside the Fort's gates 'til Hell freezes over. You take one step through the gate and I'll order the Captain to shoot.

BRAY

You're not stopping us, Mr. Palmer.

JOEL PALMER

You are breaking the treaty. You will answer to—

Palmer is drowned out with BOOS. George Harris comes to the front.

MR. HARRIS

May I speak... May I speak? I know those Indians. They are peaceful. We saw them in town today.

GRIFFIN

I saw women and children out begging, while the bucks are out thievin' and killin'.

JOEL PALMER

You call them bucks, heathens, marauders, red devils, savages, rascals, renegades, redskins, killers.

(MORE)

JOEL PALMER (CONT'D)

In the time I've been in this valley, I have seen much more drunkenness and debauchery from our own people than—

BOOS again drown out Palmer.

GRIFFIN

(ignoring Palmer)

Let's get started, Major.

Palmer walks by the Major.

JOEL PALMER

What do you know about the military, Major? What military campaigns have you been in?

MAJOR LUPTON

(arrogant)

It's about extermination, Palmer. And I'm rich with experience.

Palmer EXITS. Dirkson, Griffin, Bray, and Major Lupton shake hands.

DIRKSON

Would the Reverend come forward and give his blessing?

The Methodist minister comes forward and raises his hand.

EXT. TECUMTUM'S VILLAGE - NIGHT (LATER)

Ridge Runner sits outside the plank house wearing the deer head - rifle sitting across his lap.

INT. TECUMTUM'S PLANK HOUSE - NIGHT

The Shaman has his hand raised. He is telling a story. The crowded cabin is warmed by a pot-bellied stove fed by the children. Walking Bear and one of the children PLAY STRING GAMES as they listen. Three other children, slightly younger, look transported with rapt attention to the unfolding story.

Kitty, River Maiden, Bear Woman, and Tecumtum recline next to the stove surrounded by blankets and deerskin coverings. Adam and Mary snuggle in a lovers' embrace.

The Shaman walks among the squatting and reclining family, using large sweeping gestures to make a point.

Tecumtum fiddles with his stone pipe, gets tobacco, stokes it - gives a stick to one of the boys to stick in the stove for lighting it. The boy returns the burning stick to Tecumtum.

Begin with an IMITATION OF THE LOST LANGUAGE.

> SHAMAN
> Before there were people on the earth, the Chief of the Sky Spirits grew tired of his home in the Above World.
>
> The air was always brittle with an icy cold. So he carved a hole in the sky with
>
> (MORE)

SHAMAN (CONT'D)

a stone and pushed all the snow and ice down below until he made a great mound that reached from the earth almost to the sky.

My grandfather's ancestors called the mound Shasta Mountain.

The Sky Spirit broke off the small end of his giant stick and threw the pieces into the rivers. The longer pieces turned into beaver and otter; the smaller pieces became fish.

Then he took the remaining pieces and threw them into air where they became birds.

TECUMTUM

No, no my friend. When leaves dropped from trees, Sky Spirit picked them up, and blew upon them.

Tecumtum EXHALES a puff of smoke.

TECUMTUM

... and so made the birds.

The Shaman walks over to the wood pile, picks up a stick, and waves it around casting shadows on the walls.

> SHAMAN
>
> Then he took the big end of his giant stick and made all the animals that walked on the earth, the biggest of which were the grizzly bears.

EXT. EDGE OF TECUMTUM'S VILLAGE - CONTINUOUS

Wright, Shorty, and Charlie creep slowly, carrying their guns in the ready position.

> SHAMAN (O.S.)
>
> Now when they were first made, bears were covered with hair and had sharp claws, just as they do today. But they walked on two feet and could talk like people.

INT. PLANK HOUSE - CONTINUOUS

Adam and Mary get up and stalk around the plank house with buckskin coverings over them, attempting to look like fierce bears.

> SHAMAN
>
> They looked so fierce that the Sky Spirit sent them away from him to live in the forest at the base of the mountain.

Pleased with themselves, Adam and Mary sit down. Mary hugs Adam.

> SHAMAN
>
> Pleased with what he'd done, the Chief of the Sky Spirits decided to bring his

> (MORE)

> SHAMAN (CONT'D)
> family down and live on the earth himself.

Kitty gets up, stokes the fire, then adds a log. She remains standing, prepared.

> SHAMAN
> Late one spring while the Sky Spirit and his family were sitting around the fire, the Wind Spirit sent a great storm that shook the top of the mountain. It blew and blew and roared and roared...

All in the plank house make WIND BLOWING SOUNDS.

> SHAMAN
> Smoke blown back into the lodge hurt their eyes, and finally the Sky Spirit said to his youngest daughter, "Climb up to the smoke hole and ask the Wind Spirit to blow more gently.
>
> Tell him I'm afraid he will blow the mountain over."

Kitty pantomimes climbing up a smoke hole.

> KITTY
> Wind Spirit, blow gently...blow gently.

> SHAMAN
> As his daughter started up, her father said—

                    TECUMTUM

"Be careful not to stick your head out at the top. If you do, the wind may catch you by the hair and blow you away."

                    SHAMAN

The girl hurried to the top of the mountain but stayed well inside the smoke hole as she spoke to the Wind Spirit.

As she was about to climb back down, she remembered that her father had once said you could see the great water from the top. She wondered what it looked like and her curiosity got the better of her.

Kitty crawls, then slowly moves to a walking position. She stands tall at the door, opens it, puts her head out.

EXT. OUTSIDE PLANK HOUSE - CONTINUOUS

The killers see Kitty and Ridge Runner with his deer head on. Kitty affectionately taps Ridge Runner on the shoulder. Kitty looks to the west.

Shorty and Charlie raise their guns.

INT. PLANK HOUSE - CONTINUOUS

Kitty is looking out from the door.

                    SHAMAN (O.S.)
She poked her head out of the hole and turned toward the west, but before she

                    (MORE)

SHAMAN (O.S. CONT'D)
could see anything, her father pulled her down the mountain and threw her into the ice and snow.

She—

Tecumtum quickly gets up.

TECUMTUM
No, no, my friend. Father didn't throw his daughter into the ice and snow. The Wind Spirit caught her long hair.

Kitty grabs her hair and pulls herself backwards back inside the house, closing the door behind her.

Tecumtum looks at Kitty and Mary, then at River Maiden - smiles - puffs on his stone pipe.

SHAMAN
The Wind Spirit caught her by her long hair, and pulled her out of the mountain, and blew her down over the ice and snow.

Shaman begins to COUGH - looks at Adam. Adam gets up and stands beside Shaman. He looks at the children.

ADAM
Maybe it's time to give the Chief of the Sky Spirit's youngest daughter a name.

BEN
Call her Raven.

ADAM

Raven? Why Raven?

BEN

Because of all that smoke that got in her hair going up the smoke hole.

All LAUGH. Adam looks at Shaman, who nods his head.

ADAM

Raven landed among the scrubby fir trees at the edge of the timber and snow line, her long black hair trailing over the snow. A grizzly bear found the little Raven when he was out hunting food for his family.

Shaman gets up - puts a bearskin over his head. He bends over, Kitty leans across his back. The two move slowly around the room to the LAUGHTER OF THE CHILDREN. River Maiden signals the children to sit at her feet. Shaman GRUNTING, deposits Kitty among them.

ADAM

He carried her home with him, and his wife brought her up with their family of cubs. The little raven-haired girl and the cubs ate together, played together, and grew up together.

Kitty and the children pantomime cubs eating and playing together.

ADAM

> When she became a young woman, she and the eldest son of the grizzly bears were married.

Kitty gets up - brings back her shoulders to accentuate the maturity of her breasts. She shows off her dentalia and earrings.

ADAM

> In the years that followed they had many children who were not as hairy as the grizzlies.

Kitty and River Maiden stroke the children's arms.

ADAM

> After many years had passed, the mother grizzly bear knew that she would soon die.

Bear Woman pantomimes a feeble gait as she walks around the room with a stick, using it as a cane.

Adam looks to Shaman to see if he's ready to take over the story telling. Shaman shakes his head and smiles.

ADAM

> Fearing that she should ask the Chief of the Sky Spirits to forgive her for keeping his daughter, she gathered all the grizzlies at the lodge they had built.

Kitty gestures to Mary to gather around the mother grizzly bear. Tecumtum passes his pipe to Bear

Woman. He slowly gets up. He walks to the door, opens it, and WALKS OUT, closing it after him.

EXT. PLANK HOUSE - CONTINUOUS

Wright points at Tecumtum. The chief takes a leak.

> ADAM (O.S.)
> Then she sent her oldest grandson in a cloud to the top of Shasta Mountain, to tell the Spirit Chief where he could find his long-lost daughter.
>
> When the father got this news, he was so glad that he came down the mountainside in giant strides, melting the snow and tearing up the land under his feet.
>
> Even today his tracks can be seen in the rocky path on the south side of the mountain.

At the right time, Tecumtum RAPS on the door.

INT. PLANK HOUSE - CONTINUOUS

> ADAM
> As he neared the lodge, he called out—

Bear Woman limps with stick over to the door and OPENS IT - sees Tecumtum.

> TECUMTUM
> "Is this where my little daughter lives?"

ADAM

He expected his child to look exactly as she had when he saw her last.

When he found a grown woman instead, and learned that the strange creatures she was taking care of were his grandchildren, he became very angry.

Tecumtum ENTERS and stalks around the room looking as menacing as he can. The children play out the pantomime. They run from Tecumtum.

ADAM

A new race had been created that was not of his making.

He frowned on the old grandmother so sternly that she promptly fell dead.

Bear Woman swoons into River Maiden's arms.

ADAM

Then he cursed all the grizzlies:

TECUMTUM

"Get down on your hands and knees. You have wronged me, and from this moment all of you will walk on four feet and never talk again."

All the children GIGGLE as they crawl around.

ADAM (O.S.)

He drove his grandchildren out of the lodge, put his daughter over his shoulder, and climbed back up the mountain.

Kitty leans over Tecumtum's bent body and they shuffle around the room. Then they sit down.

ADAM

Never again did he come to the forest.

Some say that he put out the fire in the center of his lodge and took his daughter back up to the sky to live.

Those strange creatures, his grand-children, scattered and wandered over the earth. They were the first Indians, the ancestors of us all.

All APPLAUD Adam's completion of the story.

EXT. PLANK HOUSE - CONTINUOUS

Wright, Shorty, and Charlie crawl closer.

CHARLIE

Do you think he can see us?

Wright and Shorty duck behind other trees with guns pointed at Ridge Runner.

CHARLIE

Look what he's wearing. Is he a witch doctor or something?

Charlie looks at Wright.

> SHORTY
>
> What do you think? I don't see a gun.

> WRIGHT
>
> Chief John's in there.

> CHARLIE
>
> If we could get a little closer, we could plug him.

Charlie puts his hat out on one side of the tree, peeks out the other side. He puts his hat on, steps out, aims his gun. In a flash, a gun raises from beneath Ridge Runner's deerskin coat. Ridge Runner FIRES, hitting Charlie squarely between the eyes.

> SHORTY
>
> Holy Jesus! Let's get out of here!

Ridge Runner is up, after them. Adam APPEARS at the door. He runs to Charlie's body, turns, RUNS BACK INTO the plank house. Warriors come out of other plank houses.

EXT. TREES - CONTINUOUS

Wright and Shorty race into the woods.

> WRIGHT
>
> We need to split up. I'll catch you back at the horses.

> SHORTY
>
> Why do we have to split up?

WRIGHT

They won't know which trail to follow. And they won't want to get caught in a cross fire. You go that way.

Shorty RUNS OFF to the right. Wright remains, sliding down into the brush.

INTERCUT SCENE

Shorty runs - Ridge Runner runs through the trees - gets ahead of Shorty. Shorty approaches the horses. On the other side of the horses, Ridge Runner is waiting, hidden. Shorty SEES HIM, goes for his revolver. Ridge Runner SHOOTS him at point blank range.

Ridge Runner bends - picks up Shorty's gun. He stands up. WRIGHT is there. Wright SHOOTS Ridge Runner, tears off his deer head, scalps him. Wright leaps on his horse, RACES AWAY.

EXT. INDIAN VILLAGE AT LITTLE BUTTE CREEK - DAY (EARLY MORNING)

Embers from a number of fires glow as the sun peeks over the horizon. Roosters CROW. Major Lupton and Griffin RIDE INTO the tribe's campsite followed by volunteers HOOTING AND HOLLERING AND CURSING.

Only WOMEN, CHILDREN, AND OLD MEN AND WOMEN are roused from the few makeshift shelters. They, along with livestock, inhabit the campsite. It's mayhem with SCREAMING AND PLEAS for lives. The Indians have no guns. A few old men raise bows and arrows in defense.

A Gunslinger draws a knife and slashes to death an Elderly Man who can hardly move. Another Gunslinger, with patience and skilled deliberation, systematically FIRES his revolver, killing Women, Children and Elders.

The beggars seen earlier in Jacksonville are among the slaughtered. Many gunslingers and miners PUSH women into the shelters and rape them, then SHOOT or stab them. They EXIT pulling up suspenders and wiping bloody knives.

A number of Indian scalps are taken. One miner starts to scalp a child he has just killed, thinks better of it, takes an elder instead. Others are less discriminating.

Griffin, pistol in hand, URGES the volunteers to mop up any who may be getting away. Some participating settlers hesitate, some pull back. Indians try to escape by going across the creek. Major Lupton and other volunteers pursue them, SHOOTING rifles or revolvers, or knifing them with large Bowie knives. A very few manage to ESCAPE into the woods.

Griffin and Major Lupton provide the *coup de grace* at point blank range to dying Indians.

Major Lupton approaches an elderly man who was unable to let fly his arrow before he was shot. Blood oozes from his chest and shoulder. Thinking him dead, Major Lupton holsters his pistol - looks down - draws his Bowie knife to start carving off his scalp. He leans forward.

Suddenly, with the bow at his feet, the elder lifts his leg, bends the bow with his feet, pulls the string taut with his left hand and lets fly an arrow into Lupton's chest, mortally wounding him. Major Lupton CRIES OUT, then falls, clutching at the arrow.

EXT. RESERVATION – DAY (LATER)

An ADOLESCENT BOY covered with sweat and dirt ENTERS the reservation. WORD of the tragedy at Little Butte Creek SPREADS QUICKLY throughout the reservation. WARRIORS as MESSENGERS RUN INTO the forest.

EXT. JACKSONVILLE - CONTINUOUS

Griffin and the volunteers ride into Jacksonville. Scalps dangle from horses. Some riders wave the Indian scalps. The corpse of Major Lupton and another wounded man are on litters.

TOWNSPEOPLE CROWD the street. A mixed combination of APPLAUSE to horror greet the volunteers. HOLMAN and GILES are there.

DIRKSON and BRAY COME RUNNING from their offices.

ONE OF JACKSONVILLE'S DOCTORS checks the wounded. He looks at Major Lupton, shakes his head. Griffin and volunteers ENTER/EXIT the bars with bottles of whiskey and come back to their horses to show off their trophies. Palmer ARRIVES - looks, HURRIES AWAY.

ONE SETTLER, on closer inspection, sees the scalp of a young child. Others, including Holman, recognize scalps of women with leather buckskin bands still attached to the hair. They EXPRESS THEIR HORROR to others. Giles covers his eyes - LEAVES.

The minister looks, pulls back, then goes around shaking hands with the volunteers.

EXT. FORT LANE - CONTINUOUS

Captain Smith and Lieutenant Crook lead forty dragoons from the fort.

EXT. RESERVATION - APSERKAHAR'S VILLAGE - DAY (FOLLOWING DAY)

Apserkahar's people are in a panic as they hurriedly gather all their belongings - load wagons, gather corralled horses. FOUR FRIGHTENED WHITE CARPENTERS carry tools - hurry to get their horses and wagons to depart.

Tecumtum, Adam, Mary, and 20 of his warriors RIDE INTO the reservation. The chief dismounts and mounts one of the white man's wagons. Apserkahar's people surround Tecumtum.

> TECUMTUM
> (shouting)
>
> My plea, to my brother's village and my village who, through many battles, marriages, births, and deaths between our people, do not go to the white man's Fort.

There is RUMBLING among the people of Apserkahar's village.

> TECUMTUM
>
> My son Cultus Jim is dead by the white man's hand. We must fight.

Mary separates from Adam - runs to WEEPING survivors ENTERING from Little Butte Creek. They hug and WEEP together. Many of her people separate from Tecumtum and gather around her. Tecumtum stops - looks at Mary.

Adam looks back and forth at his father and at Mary. He walks towards Mary - stops, then turns back and stands next to his father below the wagon.

SUDDENLY 20 WARRIORS RIDE IN. They see the white carpenters. Four warriors from Mary's village grab - drag the WHITE CARPENTERS to Mary. She turns from the weeping families. Mary looks at Tecumtum.

> MARY
> These white men belong to my village.
> They are under my protection.

> TECUMTUM
> Those men are thieves. Come look.

The LEAD WARRIOR from Mary's village looks at Tecumtum.

> LEAD WARRIOR
> You now the war headman. Lead us.

> MARY
> (interceding)
> No! No more war for my village.

The warriors ignore her. Tecumtum COMMANDS.

TECUMTUM

Wait for the big war. Come to my village. Old enemies will come and stand with us in this great war for our land.

LEAD WARRIOR

No. We kill now.

A number of warriors from Mary's village run to the corral and get their horses. Half the warriors from Tecumtum's village join the other warriors and warriors from Mary's village. Adam runs to them.

ADAM

Stay and fight with me. I will lead with my father in the great war.

A few warriors from Tecumtum's tribe pull away - gather around Adam. Warriors from Mary's village are divided. Some stay and some prepare to leave. Ten warriors go to their belongings and get their guns. They join the other warriors and RIDE away.

Tecumtum gets down from the wagon - walks to Mary - stands beside her. He pleads one more time to Mary's village.

TECUMTUM

Soon the white man will take all of us to a terrible land. Brother Leschi from the north warns that all red people will die forever unless we go to war. Come to my village.

One of the frightened Carpenters forces his way past the braves - walks to his wagon, unleashes the horse, climbs on the wagon to leave. He signals the other carpenters who are still surrounded to climb on his wagon of tools, lumber, blanket coverings.

Tecumtum steps in front - puts his hand up. Then climbs up on the wagon. The other warriors from Tecumtum's village restrain the other three carpenters.

Tecumtum lifts a blanket. Indian baskets are revealed. The chief looks inside a basket. He reaches in, lifts out strands of dentalia and other stolen items. Members of Mary's village come forward and reclaim stolen items.

Tecumtum picks up an ax from the tools. He looks at the carpenter, who tries to remain calm.

> TECUMTUM
> I do not want the white man's house
> you never built for my family.

Tecumtum raises the ax and SPLITS the carpenter's head. The other carpenters attempt to break away.

A warrior quickly raises his gun and SHOOTS one carpenter. The warrior takes his knife out for scalping. He falls upon the wounded carpenter.

Adam and Mary look on, horrified. Tecumtum raises his hand - comes down off the wagon.

> TECUMTUM
> Release him.

He turns to the other young carpenters.

                    TECUMTUM
        Take him. Go back... tell your people, we
        are at war.

The carpenters quickly pick up the wounded carpenter, climb on the wagon of the dead carpenter and LEAVE.

Mary RUNS INTO Apserkahar's plank house. Adam FOLLOWS.

INT. APSERKAHAR'S PLANKHOUSE - CONTINUOUS

Mary packs her belongings.

                    ADAM
        Hurry! Father's leaving.

Adam takes one of Mary's packs and starts to help. She reaches over and takes it back.

                    ADAM
        Come with me.

Mary continues to pack.

                    ADAM
        Come with me.

Mary begins to WEEP. Adam takes her in his arms.

                    ADAM
        Come with me.

SOBBING, Mary finally speaks.

MARY

I must stay with my village. We have dead to bury. Many of my people are already waiting for me at the fort.

(pleading)

Come with me. Agent Palmer will take my people out of this valley of death.

ADAM

I am my father's eyes. I smell blood in the air. I must go with Father.

Mary clings to Adam. Adam pushes her away - DARTS OUT the door. Mary buries her face in a blanket.

EXT. BURNING AND SMOLDERING SETTLER'S CABINS - DAY

A cabin smolders, surrounded by beheaded cattle. Chickens and ducks peck around the yard. A dirty doll lies on the ground outside. TWO CHARRED LITTLE GIRLS lie dead among ashes. Hogs grunt as they eat next to the cabin. A closer look reveals the hogs are chewing on the flesh of a NAKED DEAD MAN, charred by fire.

EXT. WARRIORS - CONTINUOUS

MONTAGE

WAR CRIES fill the air as the WARRIORS DIVIDE INTO SMALLER GROUPS. They burn cabins and attack fleeing families.

A couple WARRIORS place absconded guns on a travois with a variety of other stolen supplies. They RIDE OFF. BODIES of a MAN and a COUPLE WOMEN lie on the ground.

END MONTAGE

EXT. MEADOW - CONTINUOUS

George Harris splits cedar. FRANK REED, a hired man, works on a split rail fence nearby. Harris' son David, climbs on the fence near Reed. SEVEN WARRIORS RIDE SLOWLY toward them. They ATTACK. Mr. Harris YELLS.

> MR. HARRIS
> Come quickly! Frank, David, get to the cabin!

EXT. HARRIS CABIN - CONTINUOUS

Mrs. Harris and daughter Sophie hang clothes out to dry. They hear Mr. Harris's YELL over the RAUCOUS WHOOPS of the Indians. They drop the clothes - run to the cabin.

EXT. MEADOW - CONTINUOUS

> MR. HARRIS
> (yelling)
> Mary, Mary!

Harris runs to get his gun leaning against the fence nearby. He turns, runs for the house. The WHOOPING warriors race on their horses to cut off Reed's path. They reach young David first. One warrior scoops him up. Another warrior stops, FIRES his gun at Reed, bringing him down.

Other warriors close in on Harris, who runs through the vegetable garden. A few feet behind, they leap off their horses. Harris turns, SHOOTS an Indian at point blank range.

Mrs. Harris stands in the doorway with a shotgun in hand, Sophie hiding behind her. Mrs. Harris FIRES and wounds a warrior. Indians FIRE back at her and at Harris, who stumbles. As he gets up, he is SHOT. He crawls to the house leaving a bloody trail across dropped white sheets.

Mrs. Harris reloads, FIRES off another round, scattering the Indians. She drops the gun, drags her husband in. She SLAMS the door - bolts it. It SPLINTERS from bullets.

INT. HARRIS CABIN - CONTINUOUS

> HARRIS
> (groaning)
> Hurry! Take my gun. It's loaded.

A WARRIOR points a gun through the window, FIRES, hitting Sophie in the arm. She SCREAMS.

> SOPHIE
> Mommy! I got shot.

Mrs. Harris turns, FIRES, hits the Indian who falls over the window frame. She runs over and pushes him out, then pulls the curtains and peeks through. Sophie gives her a revolver. Mrs. Harris looks through the curtain. She FIRES the revolver.

The Indians keep up their YELLING AND HOWLING, as they continue to SHOOT at the cabin. Mrs. Harris checks Sophie's wound - throws a clean cotton blouse at Sophie.

> MRS. HARRIS
> Wrap that around your arm.

Sophie is CRYING.

> SOPHIE
> Is Daddy dead?

Mrs. Harris runs over to Harris. Bends over him.

> MRS. HARRIS
> I think so. He's not breathing. Did you see David?

Another SHOT rings out. A music stand holding sheet music falls over. A flute in an open case rests nearby.

Mrs. Harris fires another SHOT through a crack in the doorway. She glances through the doorway.

> SOPHIE
> I saw one of the Indians pick him up and ride off.

Mrs. Harris grabs her husband's Kentucky rifle, - runs from window to window peeking through. She FIRES another shot from her Allen revolver. A warrior YELLS in pain.

EXT. INDIANS - CONTINUOUS

The Indians draw back. Some light fires to the outbuildings. One approaches the door of the cabin, holding a torch. A SHOT rings out from inside the cabin. More SHOTS come from the warriors. Smoke and splinters come from the exterior wall of the cabin.

Other warriors drag their wounded behind trees and shrubs. A torch lands on the roof.

EXT. FOREST TRAIL – DAY (LATER)

Griffin and other volunteers including Giles ride fast on horseback. All the horses foam at the mouth and drip with sweat. They ride by the smoldering cabin seen earlier. They come across the hog-eaten remains of the naked man's body. A VOLUNTEER RETCHES. They RIDE AWAY at a full gallop.

EXT. FOREST TRAIL - DAY

INTERCUT SCENE

A detachment of dragoons, led by Lt. Crook, rides past a burning cabin. They see warriors in a clearing ahead and give chase. Lt. Crook and the dragoons RUN INTO THE VOLUNTEERS. A GUNFIGHT with the warriors ensues.

The Indians DISAPPEAR into the trees, dragging their wounded. Griffin and volunteers aggressively FOLLOW. Giles balks from fatigue. Giles stays back. He holds a pistol in his hand.

Lt. Crook holds his dragoons from going into the woods. Some of the volunteers COME BACK, exhausted. One of the volunteers approaches Lt. Crook.

ONE VOLUNTEER

We can't ride no fu'ther. We left Jacksonville last night. We don't have no food and our horses can't go no longer.

LT. CROOK

Where are the rest of the volunteers?

ONE VOLUNTEER

They're attacking the reservation, chasing down Chief John.

LT. CROOK

We'll reconnoiter from here. Sentries, to your posts. At least fifty yards all around the site. Water the horses at the creek, and then corral them.

I'm going to take a few soldiers with me to see what other damage they've done. You get some rest and food. Then get back to your homes. They're going to need protection.

Lt. Crook turns to Giles.

LT. CROOK

I was told you know the families down river.

GILES

Yeah, I do.

EXT. HARRIS CABIN – DAY (LATER)

Lt. Crook, Giles, and a half dozen dragoons RIDE UP. They dismount - cautiously walk around Harris's partially burned cabin. One soldier picks up a blood-covered sheet from the scattered laundry.

Lt. Crook goes to the front door, tries to open it. It is locked. He searches around the smoldering outbuildings. Giles YELLS through the door.

                GILES

    Mr. Harris? Mrs. Harris? Sophie? David?
    Are you in there?

There is no answer. Soldiers force the door in, revealing Harris's body. A brush pile outside the cabin moves. Two soldiers point their musketoons.

              MRS. HARRIS (O.S.)
            (faintly)
Giles.

Giles runs to the brush pile.

                GILES
    Mrs. Harris.

              MRS. HARRIS (O.S.)
    Help me. Help.

Lt. Crook and Giles tear the brush aside. Mrs. Harris and Sophie lie clinging to each other, very much alive. They are filthy with dirt and powder - too tangled in the brush to get up.

> MRS. HARRIS
>
> My husband is inside. They killed him! They took my son, David.

Lt. Crook reaches in, helps Mrs. Harris, while Giles helps Sophie out of the brush.

EXT. FORT LANE - CENTRAL QUAD - DAY

Captain Smith STEPS OUT OF his office carrying a sheet of paper. He walks among the HUNDREDS OF INDIANS. He walks up to Mary. Smith reads from a document without fanfare.

> CAPTAIN SMITH
>
> It has come to my attention that more Indians have arrived here at the Fort. All males twelve years and older shall be on the rolls. Anyone not enrolled or attempting to leave the Fort will be considered dangerous and will be shot.

Mary faces her people.

> MARY
>
> Come, sign the paper. No more war.

The Indians congregate, some RELATING THE DECREE to others. A NUMBER OF MALES come forward and begin to sign a register that two soldiers hold.

> MARY
>
> Where is agent Palmer?

                    CAPTAIN SMITH
> He's bringing in Chief John. Soon the chief will be hanging from the gallows in Jacksonville. You'll be right there with him if you don't keep your people with you.

Captain Smith walks back into his office. Mary walks among her people. Lt. Crook is parceling out clothing, including blankets and used shoes.

EXT. GENERAL LANE - CONTINUOUS

General Lane, Palmer, and 20 dragoons ENTER Fort Lane. A number of Indian families travel with them. The many Indians in the quad step aside as they pass. Lane and Palmer dismount. The dragoons corral their horses. Mary steps forward. Lane and Palmer ignore Mary. They ENTER Captain Smith's office.

INT. OFFICE - CONTINUOUS

General Lane and Palmer take off coats and accept coffee from a soldier. General Lane paces.

                    GENERAL LANE
> What do we do, Joel?

Palmer turns to Captain Smith.

                    JOEL PALMER
> Captain?

                    CAPTAIN SMITH
> You didn't see Chief John or any of his people?

JOEL PALMER
The chief has gone down river.

Captain Smith walks to the window - looks out.

CAPTAIN SMITH
It's probably better.

GENERAL LANE
If I know Chief John, he'll find his way back and attack the Fort.

CAPTAIN SMITH
He won't attack this Fort with our two howitzer cannons. If I have to, I'll put his own people in the crossfire.

Palmer paces.

PALMER
John's too smart. He wants us out on his terrain to fight his war.

CAPTAIN SMITH
(boasting)
I'll fight his war when we get the redskins out of here.

Palmer looks out the window - sighs - shakes his head.

CAPTAIN SMITH
Over three hundred of them out there and forty of us.

JOEL PALMER
Half of them have no shoes or blankets.

CAPTAIN SMITH
We can't feed them.

JOEL PALMER
We can't leave in this kind of weather.

General Lane is looking at a territorial map.

GENERAL LANE
We are at war. I want them moved.

JOEL PALMER
We need soldiers.

CAPTAIN SMITH
We can spare you, Lt. Crook - no more than a half dozen soldiers.

JOEL PALMER
Walking 300 people over 200 miles?....

Not to mention the Jacksonville militia waiting to attack the Indians while under my protection.

GENERAL LANE
I understand Mary is the headman now. Or should I say headwoman? She's got control over the warriors. They can back up the Lieutenant.

Palmer shakes his head.

GENERAL LANE

Do I have to tell you this is an order to get them out of here? NOW!

Palmer doesn't answer - walks over to the window.

INT/EXT. QUAD - CONTINUOUS

Palmer looks out at the hundreds gathered around small fires to keep warm.

CAPTAIN SMITH

I'll get Lt. Crook.

Captain Smith EXITS. Two dragoons escort Captain Smith as he walks through the Indians who huddle in groups. General Lane walks over - puts his hand on Palmer's shoulder. He also looks out at the huddling families around fires.

GENERAL LANE

Remember when we were back in Ohio standing outside our legislative office?

JOEL PALMER

I remember. It was spring. We talked about bringing our families west.

GENERAL LANE

We're here, Joel. About to present a new territory to the United States.

PALMER
(distressed)

I feel like a traitor.

INT. OFFICE - CONTINUOUS

Palmer walks away from the window - pours himself more coffee. Lane looks at Palmer - turns, looks out the window.

> GENERAL LANE
> Do you believe in Manifest Destiny?

> JOEL PALMER
> What are you talking about?

> GENERAL LANE
> The fact that the Indians cannot be Christianized or civilized; that it is the destiny of the Anglo-Saxon race to rise and ultimately prevail, as the Indians and their way of life fade out of existence.

A long pause. Palmer looks like a wounded animal.

> JOEL PALMER
> We are in different camps, Joe. You're either on a pro-slavery kick, or Indian extermination...

> GENERAL LANE
> ... I didn't say extermination...

> JOEL PALMER
> (visibly upset)
> I'm getting these human beings out of this wretched valley. Then you can

> (MORE)

> JOEL PALMER (CONT'D)
> freely play out your "Manifest Destiny."
>
> Go ahead, Joe. Wage war on Chief John and the red people out there.

Palmer gets his coat on - heads for the door.

> GENERAL LANE
> Joel, I think your attempt to save the Indians is doomed to failure.

Palmer doesn't turn back.

> JOEL PALMER
> You've lost sight of the human soul.

> GENERAL LANE
> What?

> JOEL PALMER
> I said, "you've lost sight of the human soul."

Palmer EXITS.

INT/EXT. QUAD

General Lane watches as Palmer walks up to Mary.

EXT. TRAIL OF TEARS - DAY

300 Indians are walking - a few elderly riding on wagons pulled by mules or horses. Soldier and warrior escorts vigilantly guard them, primarily for fear of attack. Warriors with guns are spaced between the dragoons.

A PARTIAL MILITIA of ARMED VOLUNTEERS a short distance away, ride on mules and horses - waiting for an opportunity to attack.

EXT. SLAUGHTER ON THE ROGUE RIVER - CONTINUOUS

Adam runs along above the river. GUNSHOTS - YELLING - WAILING. He looks over a cliff. Below, VARIOUS SMALL INDIAN VILLAGE PEOPLE move in canoes and rafts down river. Griffin and several hundred volunteers, Giles among them, shoot the Indians with DEADLY FIRE. Only a SPORADIC RETURN OF GUNFIRE comes from the Indians.

EXT. RIVER'S EDGE - GILES - CONTINUOUS

Giles reloads his musket, raises it, aims at a warrior, FIRES. The warrior buckles, falls into the river. The Indians attempt to flee but have no place to go in the rocky terrain. Canoes capsize and the elderly, children and women fall into the rapids, many drowning.

EXT. FOREST - ADAM - CONTINUOUS

Adam RUNS to his horse. Adam RIDES through the woods. He stops, gets off his horse, tethers it to a tree. He RUNS through the trees. He hears a PHEASANT CALL. He ANSWERS WITH A CALL. He turns in another direction. A WARRIOR LEAPS OUT of the woods. Adam and the warrior greet each other. The warrior points.

                    WARRIOR
  Tecumtum says you must travel at night.

                    ADAM
        I will.

Adam waves. They separate and run in different directions. Adam lowers himself - CREEPS through the trees. He stops. Hears sounds of HORSES AND VOICES. He peeks through trees. He sees the ARMED VOLUNTEER MILITIA.

He sees the tail end of the Indians, who have slowed to a crawl on Oregon's Trail of Tears. Adam, exhausted, reaches into his leather bag - pulls out jerky - eats. He watches through the trees.

EXT. TRAIL OF TEARS - EVENING

INTERCUT SCENE

The Trail of Tears march has stopped. Indians gather wood and light fires. Soldiers ration out food. The Militia between Adam and the Indians maintain a wary eye.

Adam WORKS HIS WAY to the front where Lt. Crook and Palmer are located. He sees an opening - runs. Volunteers spot him - give chase. A couple volunteers get a COUPLE SHOTS off.

The volunteers abruptly stop when Adam gets to Palmer and Lt. Crook. Lt. Crook points his musketoon at the volunteers.

                JOEL PALMER
                 (shouting)
        He's now under the care of the United
        States Army. Keep your distance.

> VOLUNTEER
> (shouting back)
> Anybody leavin' or laggin' gets shot.

Adam stands by Palmer.

> JOEL PALMER
> You have a message.

> ADAM
> Father wants a powwow with you.

> JOEL PALMER
> I will find your father as soon as the people here are in a safe place.

> ADAM
> Where is Mary?

> JOEL PALMER
> She's leading Chief Joe's village. Lieutenant, take Adam back to Mary.

Palmer turns to Adam.

> JOEL PALMER
> If you try to leave, you will surely get shot.

Lt. Crook and Adam go back through the many who are suffering, shivering. Rags cover frosted feet.

EXT. MARY - CONTINUOUS

Mary aids an ELDERLY WOMAN who is feverish. Mary brings a cup of hot broth to her mouth. CHILDREN huddle with ANOTHER WOMAN sitting near Mary. The woman's hands shake as she drinks the broth.

Lt. Crook and Adam approach Mary. Lt. Crook gives his coat to Mary, who wraps it around the woman. Mary sees Adam. She gestures to another woman to help. Lt. Crook assists ANOTHER FAMILY.

Mary throws her arms around Adam. They walk off to the side.

> MARY
> Why did you come?

> ADAM
> To see you.

Mary looks closely at Adam.

> MARY
> You are not telling me everything.

> ADAM
> To see agent Palmer. My father wants a powwow.

Mary glances over to THREE WOMEN from Tecumtum's village

> MARY
> The women and children over there belong to your village. They want to go back to their husbands.

ADAM

Only the women can come with me.

MARY

Let someone else take them. Stay.

ADAM

Father's gathering warriors from other tribes by the great water. I feel a deep fear inside.

MARY

Your father will not surrender his people?

ADAM

Father is angry. He has many guns and many warriors ready to fight.

MARY

Do not take those women.

ADAM

I have given my promise to their husbands. I will speak with Palmer first.

Mary walks away. Adam follows.

MARY

(heartbroken)

I have new life inside me. The baby will die when you go...

(MORE)

MARY (CONT'D)

I want to die but cannot. I am responsible for my people... Our baby's death will tell the story of my grief.

Mary WEEPS. Mary clings to Adam.

ADAM

Both our hearts are broken. Mine cannot mend if I stay here. Yours cannot mend if you leave your people. Only the Great Spirit knows our destiny.

Adam and Mary return to the groups of people who huddle around fires. Adam walks to the THREE WOMEN. They greet each other with hugs. The women quickly gather their belongings. They leave some articles of clothing to those in need.

Palmer and Lt. Crook WALK OVER to Adam and Mary.

JOEL PALMER

Those women are from your people?

ADAM

Yes.

JOEL PALMER

You are taking a great risk by taking them with you.

ADAM

You will let me go?

JOEL PALMER

You would not leave your father unless you had a purpose. I am going to help you. The three women will show him he can trust me to protect your people. I will meet with your father when I am done here.

ADAM

My father is at war with the white people.

JOEL PALMER

Your father respects me. A scout and I will travel to find you. Tell your father many soldiers from the ocean are coming to join Captain Smith.

ADAM

My father has an army of warriors.

JOEL PALMER

Only the people here will be safe from the soldiers. The headmen and the villages will be protected by the United States Army if they surrender.

Adam is defiant.

ADAM

My father will never surrender his land or his people.

> JOEL PALMER
>
> Your people will die out if he stays in this valley.

> ADAM
>
> My father says that is better than dying on a reservation under the white man's laws.

Palmer paces. He looks over at the militia. He looks at Mary.

> JOEL PALMER
>
> Your village and all the people here are safe with me.
>
> To save Tecumtum, you must go with Adam and plead with him to surrender to Captain Smith before hundreds of volunteers get to his people.

Mary looks around at all the suffering people.

> JOEL PALMER
>
> Very few, if any, will die here. Many more people will die each day by not going to Fort Lane. I want you to go with Adam. Tell Tecumtum that I have kept my word.

Mary quickly grabs her belongings. Palmer walks over to Mary.

> JOEL PALMER
>
> Take a gun... Adam, you need a gun.

> ADAM
>
> I have a gun with my horse.

> JOEL PALMER
>
> We are going back to the front of the camp. Go when Lt. Crook and I shoot our guns.

Palmer takes Adam's hand - shakes it. Palmer looks at Mary.

> MARY
>
> I will go with Adam.

Palmer walks back to Lt. Crook. The two walk to the front of the caravan.

The GUNS GO OFF. SOLDIER ESCORTS and VOLUNTEERS run/ride to the front.

Mary makes sure the women's WEEPING CHILDREN get support from relatives or other village members.

An OLD INDIAN WOMAN comes to Mary and Mary buries her head in the woman's bosom - then kisses her many times.

Adam, Mary, and the three women CRAWL AWAY into the night.

EXT. RIVER - TECUMTUM - DAY

At the river's edge, Tecumtum and a dozen warriors wait for two canoes and a towed flat raft. THREE INDIANS in each canoe paddle the canoes to the shore, where warriors wade out and pull the raft in.

Wooden boxes from the raft are carried and loaded on horse and mule drawn wagons. Tecumtum opens one of the boxes - pulls out a rifle. Warriors quickly open boxes and gather guns and ammunition.

Tecumtum gives one of the Indians a leather pouch. One Indian from the raft opens the bag - pulls out large gold nuggets. He looks in the bag, nods his head. They clasp arms - get back in their canoes and PADDLE BACK DOWN RIVER. Tecumtum, warriors and wagons LEAVE.

EXT. FOREST - CONTINUOUS

One woman rides on Adam's horse. Adam, Mary, and the other two women walk. A PHEASANT CALL. Adam RETURNS THE CALL. They tether the horse to a tree - walk down to the river - drink water from the river.

The PHEASANT CALL REPEATS. Adam, looks up and a horse and cart with a horse tied behind, stands next to Adam's horse. The INDIAN seen earlier on the trail, WAVES.

Adam, Mary, and the women quickly walk back to the horses and wagon. All hug each other. The three women climb on the horse drawn wagon and DEPART with the Indian. Adam and Mary ride away on the two horses.

EXT. FOREST - MOMENTS LATER

Adam and Mary guide their horses.

> MARY
> What if Agent Palmer puts all villages together on the same land?

                    ADAM

Father wants his own land.

                    MARY

What will you do?

                    ADAM

When there is no war, I will live with our children in your village.

Mary smiles.

Suddenly Wright and a half dozen gunslingers EMERGE from the trees. Adam and Mary are trapped.

                    WRIGHT

You come with us.

Adam looks at Mary. He SLAPS his horse. Adam and Mary ride for their lives - Wright and gunslingers close behind.

Two draw pistols and SHOOT. Mary is swept off her horse by a branch. She is taken prisoner. Adam DISAPPEARS in the trees. Wright briefly follows - turns around - signals the gunslingers to holster their guns. Wright puts a lasso around Mary's neck.

EXT. FOREST - ADAM - CONTINUOUS

Adam stops his horse - listens. He makes a PHEASANT call. He REPEATS IT again. A DIFFERENT BRAVE COMES out of the forest.

ADAM
Go to my father. Ben Wright and other bad men have Mary. Go along the river near Big Bend.

The brave RUNS off. Adam turns, RIDES INTO the trees.

EXT. CAMPSITE - NIGHT

The gunslingers are sprawled around a campfire.

EXT. WRIGHT AND MARY - CONTINUOUS

In the shadows Mary sits against a tree with a rope around her neck, the other end wrapped around the tree. Wright approaches - puts a knife to Mary's throat. He forces her down.

EXT. GUNSLINGER AND HORSES - CONTINUOUS

A knife slices a sleeping gunslinger's throat. The INDIAN WARRIOR untethers the horses.

EXT. WRIGHT AND MARY - CONTINUOUS

In the fire's shadows, Tecumtum and Adam, in war paint, pounce on Wright with knives. At the same time, GUNFIRE ERUPTS.

Adam cuts the rope around Mary's neck as Wright struggles with Tecumtum, who repeatedly stabs him.

Tecumtum drags Wright over next to the campfire.

Two gunslingers lie dead. Three stand with their hands up, surrounded by Kitty and a half dozen Indians pointing rifles and pistols at them.

WRIGHT is still alive. He GURGLES blood. Kitty stands next to Tecumtum. The chief gestures to the gunslingers to sit down. Mary takes a pistol and strikes Wright. Wright spits blood at her. Adam lifts Wright - holds him from behind. Tecumtum hands his knife to Mary.

Mary puts her face close to Wright's. He spits at her again. Kitty comes over - pulls open Wright's bloody shirt. Mary plunges the knife deep into Wright's chest. Wright falls. Mary straddles Wright. Mary carves out Wright's heart - raises it skyward - takes a bite of it, and spits it out. She hands the heart to Kitty. Kitty takes a bite, spits it in Wright's face. She throws the heart to a warrior, who tosses it into a pan and places the pan over the campfire.

Tecumtum nods to the warriors. The warriors slice the throats of the gunslingers. The warriors quickly gather guns - start a NOISY WAR DANCE around the fire. One brave takes the heart out of the pan - takes a bite - passes it on.

Tecumtum and Adam look at each other. Tecumtum smiles. He bends over Wright's mutilated body, slowly pulls the gold and other money from his pockets.

ADAM
Father, I seldom see you smile.

TECUMTUM
My revenge for Ridge Runner and Cultus Jim. Now they live free with our ancestors.

Tecumtum gestures to his warriors to remove everything from the dead. They try on shirts and pants, inspect pockets.

Wright's and the Gunslinger's horses are brought in by a warrior. Tecumtum, the horses, and the rest DISAPPEAR in the trees.

MONTAGE OF MELTING SNOW AND THE CHANGE OF SEASONS.

EXT. BIG BEND - EARLY SUMMER - DAY

80 SOLDIERS from Captain Smith's detachment surround a large open tent, which serves as Smith's quarters. Hundreds of Indians are huddled around small fires to keep warm.

Chief John, Mary, and Adam ENTER ON HORSES. FOUR DRAGOONS accompany them. The huddled Indians rise with immediate recognition and CACOPHONY of WELCOMING SOUNDS.

> JOEL PALMER (O.S.)
> You have a sickness, Captain. You have fallen in love with war. Go back to the fort. Protect the people who have surrendered.

> CAPTAIN SMITH (O.S.)
> I will not let that savage choose his own time and place to fight this war.

A JUNIOR OFFICER runs toward the tent.

INT. TENT - CONTINUOUS

                JOEL PALMER

In my letter to General Lane, I have asked why more troops have not come.

I do not believe you're up to the task of defeating Chief John without more soldiers.

The junior officer ENTERS.

                JUNIOR OFFICER

Chief John is here with a woman and subchief.

Palmer leaps up. Tecumtum, Mary, and Adam ENTER with TWO OTHER JUNIOR OFFICERS. Palmer warmly reaches out his hand. Tecumtum and the rest of the family do not take his hand. Puzzled, he looks at Mary. Mary looks away. After a long silence, Palmer speaks.

                JOEL PALMER

Chief Toquahear from Sam's valley has gathered all his people and brought them to Fort Lane.

All Chiefs on the coast, the Chiefs from Cow Creek and the Umpqua have surrendered. Chiefs Chocultah and Lympe, warriors who fought bravely along the river, have surrendered.

Their people are here. I ask the great Chief Tecumtum to surrender your guns and remain here for protection.

There is a long silence.

> JOEL PALMER
> What will Chief Tecumtum do today?

> TECUMTUM
> I will not surrender my people or my guns. I want all the volunteers by the river to go back to Jacksonville.

Adam goes to his father and WHISPERS. Tecumtum puts up his hand to Adam.

> TECUMTUM
> (turning to Palmer)
> Where will the headmen and families go after they surrender their guns?

> PALMER
> The Chiefs and families will go on the reservation to the north by the great water. There you will be protected from white men.

Tecumtum signals Mary and Adam to come close. They draw to the side of the tent and WHISPER among themselves.

> CAPTAIN SMITH
> What's going on?

> JOEL PALMER
> Somehow I think the idea of going away from the valley has not sunk in. I don't

> (MORE)

JOEL PALMER (CONT'D)
think Tecumtum really heard us.

Tecumtum, Mary, and Adam turn and head for the tent door.

CAPTAIN SMITH
If you leave, more soldiers will come. The war will go on. Mr. Palmer promised in the treaty that you will have peace.

Tecumtum ignores Captain Smith - turns, comes back, takes Palmer's arm. He looks into Palmer's eyes, ignoring Captain Smith.

TECUMTUM
It is not your war that kills our people.
It is your peace that kills our people.

Palmer is speechless as Tecumtum continues to grasp his arm, looking deep into Palmer's eyes. Palmer finally looks down. Tecumtum slowly releases his grip and returns to Mary and Adam.

He turns and looks at Smith, then walks over and grasps Smith's arm.

TECUMTUM
You are a great Chief.

He stands side by side with Smith facing the others in the tent.

TECUMTUM
I am a great Chief. This is my country.

Tecumtum turns and looks outside.

> **TECUMTUM**
> I lived here when those trees were small... no higher than my head. My heart is sick from fighting, but I will not leave this land. I will not lay down our guns and go to a reservation. I will fight.

Tecumtum turns and WALKS OUT of the tent. Adam and Mary look at Palmer. They EXIT. Captain Smith YELLS at Tecumtum.

> **CAPTAIN SMITH**
> Chief John! Chief John!

EXT. TENT - CONTINUOUS

INTERCUT

Captain Smith STEPS OUT of the tent - Palmer close behind. Tecumtum stops - walks back to Captain Smith.

> **CAPTAIN SMITH**
> We will catch you and hang you. But if you go to the reservation, you can live in peace.

Palmer attempts to intercede. Smith pulls away. Smith points to wagons and horses under the trees.

> **CAPTAIN SMITH**
> See those wagons, blankets, clothes? You will have everything good, plenty of food... If you do not come with your village, you see that rope?

Tecumtum, Mary, and Adam get on waiting horses.

> CAPTAIN SMITH
> (shouting)
> We will hang you.

Palmer pushes Captain Smith towards the tent.

> JOEL PALMER
> No, you won't. The Chief and I had an agreement.

Tecumtum, Mary, and Adam start riding away. Captain Smith tries to step by Palmer. Captain Smith YELLS.

> CAPTAIN SMITH
> I'm going to stop him.

Palmer grabs Captain Smith. Tecumtum HEARS Captain Smith - stops. He looks at Adam. Adam nods his head - gets off his horse. Adam walks up to Captain Smith.

> ADAM
> My father, the Great Tecumtum, gives Captain Smith one more day. He asks you to surrender by the time the sun sets tomorrow or he will hang you and kill all your soldiers.

Captain Smith comes undone. Bewildered, he looks at Palmer. Palmer smiles without humor.

> JOEL PALMER
> He has challenged you to a duel.

CAPTAIN SMITH
That insolent savage!

He turns to a couple junior officers.

CAPTAIN SMITH
We're breaking and moving to higher ground. Get the howitzers loaded and ready for relocation.

Palmer is determined. He waves to Mary to come. Mary gets off her horse and walks to Adam and Palmer.

JOEL PALMER
(in Captain Smith's face)
Captain, go back in the tent... away from me... NOW!

Reluctantly Captain Smith LEAVES.

JOEL PALMER
(looking at Mary)
Tell Chief John, Captain Smith will not surrender. Tell him Agent Palmer will take his people to the great water. Tell the great Chief if he fights, I will come back with more soldiers.

It is the will of the Great White Father that all Indians in Oregon territory live on a reservation to stop all wars.

MARY

You came over the mountains to our land. We welcomed you to live with us side by side. Your Great White Father has betrayed our people. I will stay and join the great Chief Tecumtum in the war against the white people.

EXT. BIG BEND - FINAL BATTLE PREPARATION - DAY

MONTAGE

Captain Smith prepares infantry with muskets and dragoons with musketoons. With horses, soldiers pull howitzer cannons to the top of a knoll. The captain is in his element and excitement is in the air. Day turns to sunset.

Captain Smith inspects the boundaries of the knoll. The soldiers eat, smoke, clean the muzzles of their guns and write letters.

Birds SING their night songs, the CRICKETS and OTHER NIGHT SOUNDS leave a sense that all is well.

EXT. TECUMTUM'S CAMP - FINAL BATTLE PREPARATION - NIGHT

Tecumtum and Adam, painted with the same markings of the warriors from Tecumtum's village, pass the pipe to OTHER HEADMEN AND SUBCHIEFS painted with different markings. Mary is painted with the markings of her village. As the Chief of her village, she shares the pipe.

Some subchiefs and warriors wear white men's hats, shirts, and pants. Adam inspects their muskets - returns them. Adam takes rifles from a travois and gives one to each subchief. He shows each how to use the gun.

Mary, Kitty, and other women furnish ammunition and supplies to the subchiefs. Subchiefs raise the rifles in gratitude and return to WARRIORS from their villages.

WOMEN from their villages provide food and water to the warriors.

END MONTAGE

EXT. BIG BEND BATTLE SCENE – DAY (MORNING)

INTERCUT BATTLE SCENE

EXT. CAPTAIN SMITH - CONTINUOUS

Captain Smith, accompanied by junior officers, watch forty warriors slowly walk up the slope, guns raised over their heads. Adam leads the warriors.

EXT. TECUMTUM AND MARY - CONTINUOUS

Tecumtum and Mary stand at the edge of the forest on a small hill. They watch the different groups of warriors spread out.

EXT. ADAM AND WARRIORS - CONTINUOUS

Adam and forty warriors face a howitzer cannon.

                ADAM
Captain Smith, Captain Smith!

Captain Smith raises his hand.

> CAPTAIN SMITH
> Be in the ready position to fire.

Captain Smith exposes himself - walks toward the warriors. He stops about thirty yards away.

> CAPTAIN SMITH
> Where is Chief John? I will speak only with Chief John.

Adam and the warriors slowly, cautiously continue to approach.

> ADAM
> We come to surrender. Sit down with the Captain. After the powwow, we surrender guns.

> CAPTAIN SMITH
> Put your guns against the rock over there. Then come sit and have a powwow with me.

Adam points up past the stationed howitzers.

> ADAM
> No. We will sit in the shade with the Captain. Talk of peace.

> CAPTAIN SMITH
> Stop!

Smith retreats back up the hill. He raises his hand. The soldiers stand ready to fire.

> CAPTAIN SMITH
> (shouting)
> Put down your guns.

The warriors suddenly spread out, run up the hill toward Captain Smith, SHOOTING. Smith gives the COMMAND TO FIRE. The soldiers FIRE and the war is on.

(NOTE: The Director and Expert Choreographers will obviously direct the battle scenes. The following battle scenes offers a combination of actual historical battle events colored by a bit of fiction).

The HOWITZERS BLOW huge pieces of earth and boulders in the air. An Indian is thrown into the air by the BLAST. Adam and his warriors RETREAT down the hill.

Warriors attack from all sides, up and down the hill.

HOWITZER CANNONS FIRE but are mostly not helpful due the attack from all sides of the hill. The soldiers' counterattacks manage to force warriors back down the hill. The battle rages on.

Each charge of the Indians is choreographed by Tecumtum. Some warriors, hot from running up and down the hills remove their shirts. Their bodies show the markings of their village.

Tecumtum's SHOUT is stentorian; so loud that during lulls in SHOOTING, his voice ECHOES. Soldiers as well as the Indians hear his commands.

> TECUMTUM
> WEST!

After an attack by Indians up the west side, Captain Smith hears the word "RETREAT." He TALKS to his junior officers and soldiers WHO PROVIDE NEWS from all fronts over the small battleground.

Tecumtum's voice, against the backdrop of RAUCOUS INDIAN YELLS, gets to the emotions of the soldiers, whose muskets and musketoons are no match for the warrior's rifles.

The WORDS from Tecumtum and the many warriors seem to come from only a few feet away. The sudden attacks and retreats while the soldiers reload are choreographed to psychologically wear down the soldiers.

The SUDDEN APPEARANCE and DISAPPEARANCE of WARRIORS, from only a few feet away, destroys any semblance of a counterattack. The soldiers are trapped on the edges of the battlefield—immobilized—fighting for their lives.

The warriors SHOUT personal statements at single soldiers such as "BAD SHOT", "BOSTON HIT TREE (ROCK, CLOUD)," "BOSTON BLIND IN ONE EYE," "I HAVE LASSO TO HANG YOU," "ME CUT OFF GOLDEN HAIR ON HEAD," "YOU DIE TODAY," "WE HAVE HORSES. SOON WE HAVE SCALPS."

Tecumtum's VOICE RINGS through the CACOPHONY OF INDIVIDUAL VOICES AND GUNFIRE. "SOUTH," "RETREAT," "NORTH," "SOLDIER GUN NO FIRE," "SOLDIER TIRED," "SOLDIER HUNGRY," "SOLDIER HAVE NO TIME TO EAT," "SOLDIER NO PLACE TO GO," "SOLDIER NO PLACE TO HIDE," "SOLDIER DIE TODAY."

The wounded soldiers are dragged to the center of the battlefield where Captain Smith is continuously informed about the battle.

Indians CARRY THEIR WOUNDED down the hill into the brush.

EXT. CAPTAIN SMITH - CONTINUOUS

           JUNIOR OFFICER

They're coming through the rocks on the south end.

           CAPTAIN SMITH

We can't move the cannons in time. Take six men from Sweitzer's command to protect the south rim. We must maintain access to the river.

           JUNIOR OFFICER

Sir, we no longer have access to any water. We're sealed in, Sir.

           CAPTAIN SMITH

Under no conditions shall you give any more ground to those savages! And under no condition will you counterattack. Right now that would be suicide.

Get a tally of the dead and wounded. Save what ammunition you have left for the final attack.

The MOANS of the wounded and the numbers of dead keep mounting. Many of the wounded CRY FOR WATER.

All becomes quiet as the SUN SETS.

EXT. BATTLEFIELD - NIGHT

CONTINUE INTERCUTTING

The soldiers build little fortifications of trenches, branches, and blankets using any tool at hand including musket heels, sticks, and their hands. Each soldier's face shows desperation. They prepare for the next attack.

The SHOTS from warrior guns are now more to terrorize than to attack. The TAUNTS of the Indians never stop.

Soldiers are so closed in they have to view dead comrades and hear the WOUNDED CRY FOR WATER AND FOR DEATH.

As soldiers wait for another attack, rocks are thrown into the fortifications. "PLAY GAME WITH ME, FRIEND. YOU CATCH ROCK, THROW IT BACK, I CATCH ROCK, WE PLAY GAME, FRIEND."

A soldier throws a rock back. He begins WEEPING. Silence again amidst the GROANING and WOUNDED.

EXT. BATTLEFIELD - TECUMTUM - CONTINUOUS

Tecumtum, Adam, and Mary creep close to the soldiers. A soldier begins to slumber on his blanket. Suddenly, Adam pulls the blanket away. The soldier, too fearful to go after the blanket, only SHOOTS his musket into the night. Adam, Mary, and Tecumtum TAKE TURNS SPEAKING. Mary creeps close to another soldier who is WEEPING. She throws a rock at him. He jumps up.

SOLDIER

Where are you?

MARY

Hello, Boston. My name is Mary. You put down gun, I give you water.

ADAM

You shoot gun again, I have lasso for you.

A beat.

MARY

Soldier now cold. No blanket. You want to go home to family?

Tecumtum slides up even closer. Mary tries to pull Tecumtum back.

TECUMTUM

(shouting)

Captain Smith! Captain Smith! See the tree. I hang you. Take out blue eyes.

Adam, Mary, and Tecumtum slide behind a boulder. SHOTS ring out from the soldiers - a few hit the boulder. A return FUSILLADE comes from the warriors.

CAPTAIN SMITH

(SHOUTING)

Hold your fire! Save your ammunition until you see them.

Tecumtum stands - tosses a loose lasso over the rocks.

                    TECUMTUM
            Captain Smith! Captain Smith! Tomor-
            row you hang.

The battleground becomes silent except for the MOANS and CRIES for water from wounded soldiers.

EXT. BATTLEFIELD - DAY – (MORNING)

It has been a sleepless night for all the soldiers. The food and water have been gone for hours. The barricaded soldiers use dead horses, branches, saddles, trenches, and blankets as their means of protection.

EXT. TECUMTUM - CONTINUOUS

Tecumtum stands on a mound, Adam, and Mary beside him. All three hold lassos. They are distanced from any attack by Captain Smith and soldiers.

                    TECUMTUM
                    (yelling)
            Hello, Captain Smith. Good sleep last
            night? You ready to go to reservation? I
            give you wagons and horses. I give you
            water and plenty to eat. You get many
            things on reservation.

            You not go on reservation? Tecumtum
            hang Captain Smith with this rope. You
            see this rope?

Many warriors have ropes. They wave them around. Some throw them over branches on trees as they do a war dance.

                    TECUMTUM
> Captain Smith. We have rope for all soldiers. Put down guns. We have pow-wow.

Captain Smith is defiant. His face twitches. His pressed uniform is filthy, as are his soldiers' uniforms.

EXT. CAPTAIN SMITH'S CAMP - CONTINUOUS

Captain Smith faces his junior officers.

                    CAPTAIN SMITH
> I will not surrender to that bastard. For God's sake, someone shoot in the air to let him know we aren't surrendering.

From a protected position, a couple frightened soldiers SHOOT in the air.

                    CAPTAIN SMITH
> Stay ready for the next attack.

Captain turns to a JUNIOR OFFICER next to him.

                    CAPTAIN SMITH
> My God, we're not going to last out the day.

Another determined braver junior officer SHOOTS in the air.

Silence.

Suddenly there is a full scale attack up the slopes. BLOOD CURDLING CRIES and WAR WHOOPS fill the air. The first warriors jump the barricades. They are met with muskets as the first hand-to-hand combat unfolds. The soldiers fight furiously for their lives.

Just as it looks like the Indians are going to overwhelm the soldiers, the soldiers start CHEERING.

EXT. ATTACK OF THE REINFORCEMENTS - CONTINUOUS

Soldiers led by Lt. Crook and Joel Palmer, launch an attack from both sides and the Indians are caught in a CROSS FIRE. The warriors fighting hand-to-hand stop, turn, and race down the hill in full retreat, reinforcement soldiers running after them. Warriors quickly DISAPPEAR in the trees.

The last of the Indians battle Lt. Crook's men, who try to cut them off from retreat. Palmer SHOOTS at retreating warriors with a revolver. A soldier next to him falls, wounded. Palmer grabs his musket and SHOOTS, bringing down a retreating warrior.

Soon all the soldiers are in full pursuit as the Indians DISAPPEAR into a precipitous ravine. Palmer YELLS to Lt. Crook.

> JOEL PALMER
> Lieutenant, don't go in there. Take care of your wounded and set up camp.
>
> I'm going back to headquarters to hurry the rest of the Indians down river.
>
> LT. CROOK
> What if the Chief comes in to surrender?

> JOEL PALMER
>
> He's not going to. He still has a few warriors from other tribes under his command.
>
> I'm going to send messengers out to Chief John to try to negotiate a surrender before the Jacksonville militia volunteers get here.

EXT. TECUMTUM'S CAMPSITE - DAY

Hundreds of warriors are gathered around Tecumtum.

> ADAM
>
> Palmer was there. I saw him shoot a Klamath. He will speak with us.
>
> TECUMTUM
>
> Palmer is no longer a peacemaker. He makes war like the volunteers.
>
> ADAM
>
> If Palmer wanted war, he would march with the volunteers, not the soldiers.
>
> Speak to him, Father.
>
> TECUMTUM
>
> No. I will speak with subchiefs.
>
> ADAM
>
> The warriors from other tribes who
>
> (MORE)

              ADAM (CONT'D)
    have not left want to surrender.

    Their families are down by the river
    waiting. You're the only one who still
    wants to fight.

              MARY
    My uncle. You have won every battle.
    But now there are too many soldiers.

Tecumtum walks to a private place among the trees. Warriors follow. He waves them away. He sits down, takes out his pipe, looks over the landscape.

EXT. SOLDIERS' HEADQUARTERS - CONTINUOUS

The camp is filled with more surrendered Indians. Lt. Crook assists soldiers in passing out bread. Indian women share provisions. Some warriors play shinny as they wait. Healthier children fraternize with some of the soldiers.

Lt. Crook walks to the tent - ENTERS.

INT. TENT - CONTINUOUS

Palmer is in the tent with junior officers. He is at the table writing. Lt. Crook walks up to Palmer.

              JOEL PALMER
    Ah, here you are. Now that Smith and
    the reinforcements are leading the
    other tribes to the ocean, you are in
    command.

> LT. CROOK
> Where are you going?

> PALMER
> I'm waiting for Chief John.

> LT. CROOK
> How are we going to do this?

> JOEL PALMER
> The rest of the Indians here need to be on their way to the coast. Ships are waiting.

> LT. CROOK
> Who's going with you?

> JOEL PALMER
> Nobody. The warriors out there will protect their village people and me.

A junior officer ENTERS.

> JUNIOR OFFICER
> Sir, the volunteers from Jacksonville are approaching camp.

Lt. Crook and Palmer quickly rise and EXIT.

EXT. TENT - CONTINUOUS

Griffin RIDES IN with twenty volunteers, including Giles, and a group of HUNGRY, WOUNDED INDIANS. Griffin approaches Palmer.

GRIFFIN

These are my prisoners. I gave orders to take no prisoners. It's only by the grace of God and the kindness of some of my men that these aborigines are here today.

Palmer ignores Griffin - SIGHS - turns to Lt. Crook.

JOEL PALMER

We can't move these poor wretches until they get medical attention, some food and rest.

Griffin wants immediate attention from Palmer. He stands toe to toe with Palmer.

GRIFFIN

People in Jacksonville want you to resign. I will keep these prisoners until there is someone other than the Lieutenant here to release them to.

Griffin signals the volunteer militia to dismount. They circle the soldiers and the congregated Indians. There's tension everywhere.

Lt. Crook and Palmer ignore Griffin and the militia as he, Lt. Crook, and soldiers attend to the new group of suffering Indians.

GRIFFIN

(yelling)

You're a goddamned Indian lover.

                    JOEL PALMER
                   (shouting back)
And you're an insolent, money-grubbing pig. You helped start this war.

                    GRIFFIN
And we're here to finish it.

Palmer goes back to helping unload food from a wagon. Griffin points his gun at Palmer.

                    GRIFFIN
Go ahead and feed the savages. Like I said, we're staying.

Three dragoons on horses RIDE INTO camp. Lt. Crook leaves Palmer - approaches the dragoons.

                　LEAD DRAGOON
More Indians are coming into camp.

                    LT. CROOK
With families?

                　LEAD DRAGOON
Looks like a whole village. I counted seventy-three, including the children.

Palmer stops doing what he is doing.

                    GRIFFIN
It might be a trick.

He signals a dozen men to mount up. Palmer comes running.

JOEL PALMER
Mr. Griffin, let them come.

Lt. Crook walks up to Griffin.

LT. CROOK
You have my order to be in the ready position.

GRIFFIN
You and your officers are all the same. I am not under your command and I don't need your orders. I'm not going to massacre them unless the savages start something first.

There's a RUSTLING and SOFT TALKING among the Indians.

Lt. Crook and Palmer look to the top of a hill. Only Tecumtum COMES OVER the crest. Then COME Adam and Mary. Next Shaman, River Maiden, Bear Woman, Kitty. Tecumtum's Children, and Walking Bear, the Warriors, and the REST of Tecumtum's village slowly follow.

Palmer faces the soldiers and volunteers. Giles forces his way to the front of the volunteers.

JOEL PALMER
You are watching a great Chief and his people. Call your men to attention.

LT. CROOK
Attention!!

The soldiers come to attention. The volunteers do not. Instead they place their guns in the ready position.

Giles lowers his gun down. Ashamed, he slowly withdraws back behind other volunteers.

Tecumtum turns to his warriors. They line up and come forward to Palmer. Palmer points to a rock. The warriors deposit their guns one by one against the rock.

Adam comes forward next and deposits his gun.

Mary follows - deposits her gun.

Slowly Tecumtum walks towards the rock, looking much like an Ohio farmer in his short-sleeved shirt and pants. Suddenly he turns, points his gun at Griffin. Fifty volunteers raise their guns. Lt. Crook leaps between. Tecumtum smiles and puts his gun against the rock. Palmer offers his hand. Tecumtum rejects the hand.

Tecumtum turns, looks around, looks to the sky. He gives a LONG WAIL. The Shaman comes to one side of him. Adam and Mary come and stand next to him. They lock arms around shoulders.

They begin a RHYTHMIC WAIL as they start a slow traditional dance.

Mary, Kitty, River Maiden, and Bear Woman, and all the rest who are able, join them. Those who can't, keep time, using BASKETS, BONE RATTLES, and HANDS as Tecumtum's village dances the dance of their ancestors.

The soldiers and volunteers encircling a proud people.

CAPTION: SEVEN YEARS LATER

EXT. FOREST - APPLEGATE RIVER - DAY

Adam, Mary, and Kitty ride by a pioneer's farm. A BOY AND GIRL play on the fence. When they see the Indians, they run to their PARENTS who are gardening nearby. Adam, Mary, and Kitty ride on.

EXT. TECUMTUM'S VILLAGE - CONTINUOUS

Adam, Mary, and Kitty tether their horses - walk slowly over the grounds they lived on at Deer Creek. Weeds and brush cover the charred and rotting wood resting in the pits where the plank houses once stood. Moss and lichen cover indentations in boulders where for centuries women ground acorns and seeds into flour with pestles.

Adam picks up a small pole by the river that once served as an aid to netting salmon. He carries the pole to the burial ground of his ancestors.

Kitty empties Tecumtum's quiver of his stone pipe, woodpecker feathers, dentalia, arrowheads, and ashes. They finish the burial. The pole marks the place. Mary attaches feathers to the pole. Adam covers the earth.

Kitty takes her reed flute from her quiver. She carefully unwraps the flute from the calico wrapped around it. She PLAYS. Adam and Mary keep RHYTHM WITH A BONE RATTLE and DENTALIA.

THE SOUND OF A WHIRLWIND AND SURREAL IMAGES of ANCESTORS AND ANIMALS INDIGENOUS TO SOUTHERN OREGON DANCE/MOVE AND DISSOLVE

ACROSS THE SCREEN - ENDING WITH A COYOTE RUNNING - LOOKING OVER ONE SHOULDER - LOOKING OVER THE OTHER SHOULDER.

Adam's VOICE OVER matches the action.

> ADAM (V.O.)
>
> We lived on this land as long as Father and Mother can remember. No one knows when we came.
>
> In the forest, there are no more moccasin tracks of my brothers. Only the tracks of coyotes. In the meadows, the tracks of wheels, oxen, horses, and cattle and earth turned over.
>
> No more women and children gathering berries, Camus bulbs, and acorns with their laughter and play, singing songs to the wild flowers, coming home to see smoke curling up from the lodge, hearing yells of my brothers as they dive into the river after the sweat lodges.
>
> Our way of life is gone forever. Now I see only the shadows of my life.
>
> In the night, when darkness creeps, the ghosts of my ancestors and my past steal my consciousness, I feel as though I will suffocate from the pain of my loneliness.

FADE OUT.

BLACK

Mary and 300 of her people left Fort Lane on February 22, 1856. They walked under military escort for thirty-three days, covering the 263 miles to the Grand Ronde and Siletz reservation in northwestern Oregon. Beginning July 11, 1856, Tecumtum and his people walked under military escort, 200 miles north along the Oregon coast to the reservation.

Disease and racism took their toll on the Native Americans. By the early 1900s, only a handful of Rogue River Indians could be identified on the Siletz and Grand Ronde reservations. The reservation land had been reduced to one-fifth its original size.

Tecumtum remained defiant until his death on June 6, 1864. He often took some of his family off the reservation to hunt. After Tecumtum's death, Adam disappeared. Some say he went back to the land of his ancestors at the foot of Mt. Shasta. Kitty, Mary, and other family members remained on the reservation.

Joseph Lane, Joel Palmer, and the citizens of Jacksonville and southern Oregon continued to play a significant role in Oregon's fight for statehood. Most of the soldiers from Fort Lane and Big Bend went on to fight in the Civil War.

Mary Harris re-married and settled in southern Oregon.

In September, 2000, the head of the federal Bureau of Indian Affairs apologized for the agency's "legacy of racism and inhumanity." Specifically, the agency acknowledged its participation in "the ethnic cleansing that befell the Western tribes" as well as the deliberate spread of disease, forced relocations of tribes, attempts to wipe out Indian languages and cultures, and the cowardly killing of women and children.

THE END

AFTERTHOUGHTS ON PEACE THAT KILLS

Our foster child, D——, moved back to live with her grandmother after eighth grade. Time and changing relationships left our family with seven years of many happy memories with D——.

In my real-life private clinical practice, I soon realized that I became immersed in a world of psychological crises and critical incidents, beyond the run-of-the-mill neurotic ailments so often seen in clinical settings. I could not leave hard-core, seemingly impossible cases alone.

Soon, lawyers, judges, and other mental health professionals, including the administration at SOU were contacting me as a consultant and problem-solver when critical issues/incidents arose. And then, television news channels contacted me for my take on the latest newsworthy mental health issues and events. Intriguing cases came to my office every week where I was called upon to evaluate, report, recommend, do psychotherapy, testify in court - anything to fix the problem.

What was wrong with me? Why did I let illusion and my fantasy life take over again?

I had FOUR CASES that became composites and the spine of my next screenplay, *Raspberry Heaven*.

Case One: A shy male college student who masturbated while rubbing flannel shirts. I choreographed a series of experiences that broadened his outlook on his sexuality. Enough said. This was one of a number of interesting cases that I had when I went through my phase of doing sex therapy.

Case Two: I completed many Child Abuse Evaluations. One case involved two sexually and physically abused children living in a remote area with an ex-military, abusive stepfather. Intervention included removal of the children and courtroom expert testimony to give the stepfather jail time.

Case Three: More abuse issues. The case involved an alcoholic/drug-addicted mother who gave her children barbiturates to cope.

Case Four: I saw many Vietnam veterans coming back to SOU after seeing frontline action during President Johnson's troop buildup to win the war of attrition in Nam. I was anti-war while I watched the war expand to over 500,000 "boots on the ground." On national television, we watched napalm dropping from planes destroying Vietnam villages. We kept getting news on body counts. Some of my ex-Navy friends who were in pilot training with me were flying those planes. Some of the ex-students from my classes were the "boots on the ground" who became a number in General Westmoreland's philosophy of counting bodies. It was all about ratios. Ten of them, one of us.

Because I had some background in the military (the vets never got my full story), I saw veterans with PTSD after Vietnam. Some vets shared their horror stories and confessions. Some had the need to resolve domestic relationship problems; others I saw over time as they made attempts to heal and make sense of their incomprehensible actions during the war. I suffered with them as they struggled with marital conflict, depression, alcohol and drug abuse, and feelings of rejection and alienation by those around them. Finally, I saw veterans after their years of isolation (living in the backwoods in southern Oregon) with the need to arm themselves to keep the enemy away.

All of the above were modified into composites and became scenes and parts of scenes in the feature film *Raspberry Heaven,* and in other completed screenplays.

Take a break and watch Raspberry Heaven on Amazon Instant Video.

Back to *Blurred Realities.* But wait. Is this first book long enough? I think I'll let the book publisher decide.

In my life, I'm running out of time. So, I better get on with putting more of my blurred fantasies life on paper. Second book title written in screenplay format. *Prodigal Son.*

Catch you later after you read *Prodigal Son,* another screenplay that has been gathering dust in my closet of secrets.

THE ORIGINS OF PRODIGAL SON

I feel compelled again to give you a little history.

I was a Preacher's son, with a warm loving Mother who told Bible and other self-created stories about good and evil. As she told her stories, they were illustrated and dramatized on flannel graph. At bedtime, Mom also recited portions of the Psalms, the Books of Revelation, and some of the New Testament by heart. She orated the allegorical classic, John Bunyan's *Pilgrim's Progress* to the parishioners of Dad's churches, all by memory. I got the desire to tell my stories from Mom. I also got some memory skills from her.

www.screeningformemoryloss.com.

Dad was the stern taskmaster who preached of sin and salvation. He brought evangelists to town to pitch their tents on Sunday. I was short on receiving the "Glory of God," so was saved a few times when he brought evangelists to town. Tents were put up, crowds gathered, and salvation came to me through tears and self-recriminations and self–contempt as a first-class sinner.

I "backslid" on Mondays when I peeked under the carnival tent (same tent), watching ladies drop grapefruit from vaginal vaults.

The problem for me is that I kept coming up with one less God than the contemporary monotheistic religions of the world. By nineteen years of age, I was carrying the Rubaiyat of Omar Khayyam in my pocket. The

Yin and Yang of religion plays out in all my screenplays and in much of the history of my life.

My latest revision of the screenplay *Prodigal Son* transformed the leading psychologist's character profile from atheist to evangelical Christian. Why? I wanted to seek out a different set of producers who want to make money on low budget, independent films. What a hypocrite I am to bow to the evangelical Christian population just to sell a screenplay.

Welcome to the political *zeitgeist* 2018, the year of tweeting fake news by Donald Trump.

The following screenplay is not autobiographical other than to reveal how child, adolescent, and adult experiences play out in the stories one tells.

We had the normal amount of small town mischief growing up with five brothers and one sister. Gardens were raided, outhouses were tipped, empty houses were broken into, tree houses were built and slept in, naked ladies were viewed, and mouths were soaped for cussing.

When I was sixteen, Dad died. To put a stamp on his life, he died in the pulpit in prayer before giving his sermon on New Year's Day, 1953. Parishioners claim his hands never unfolded. Now that should give me pause as to what I believe about eternity. At least he didn't fall on me on one of those Sundays when I was called up from the front row of the congregation to sit on the steps behind him for doing mischief.

Prodigal Son borrows a lot from life experience. Many scenes have a semblance of truth, starting with the phone call from a blind, distraught, suicidal adolescent.

PRODIGAL SON

(RETRO VERSION - TIME PERIOD: 2008-2010)

FADE IN:

MUSIC "WISH ME A RAINBOW" ACAPPELLA WOMAN'S VOICE (RENEE TRULSON'S VOICE).

EXT. SOUTHERN OREGON ROGUE RIVER - DAY

THREE HAPPY CHILDREN. KATY TRULSON, 14 and blind; HER BROTHER, MARK TRULSON, 9; FRIEND CAMILA ALBERS, 9; AND 2-YEAR-OLD BORIS, THE FAMILY DOG.

MUFFLED UNINTELLIGIBLE CHATTER.

EXT. RIVER'S EDGE (1) - DAY

In swimming suits, they sit below a cliff next to the Rogue River's whirling rapids. Their shorts, tops, and an aged lunch box lay nearby.

They are looking at, sorting, adding to the collection of colored stones, shells, and small dead animal skulls. Katy feels each cherished find. She HUMS the melody: Wish Me A Rainbow.

>   KATY
> Give me the squirrel's head.

Camila hands Katy the squirrel's head. Katy feels every inch of it. Katy breaks into verse.

                                KATY
                              (singing)
          "I want all these treasures the most that
          you can give, so wish me a rainbow as
          long as I live."

Katy goes back to HUMMING.

                                KATY
          Wow! I'm feeling the eye sockets.

Mark gets up - makes his way up to the cliff top above large boulders. From twenty feet up, he YELLS and JUMPS into the river's pool away from the strong currents. He swims to the edge.

                            YOUNG MARK
          C'mon.

Camila gets up, taps Katy on the shoulder.

                            YOUNG CAMILA
          C'mon on, before anybody sees us.

Excited, Katy hands the skull and sunglasses to Camila, who deposits the collected artifacts and glasses in the lunch box. Camila takes Katy's hand. They navigate to the top.

EXT. CLIFF TOP BOULDERS (1) - DAY

Camila directs Katy to the cliff edge. Katy JUMPS into the river.

EXT. UNDERWATER (1) - DAY

Bubbles and Katy swims to the top.

EXT. RIVER'S EDGE (1) - DAY

Katy BURSTS out of the river, SPEWING water.

> YOUNG MARK
> Over here.

Katy DOG PADDLES to Mark, who reaches in to help her out. Camila JUMPS from the cliff into the river - swims to the edge.

CAPTION: 5 YEARS LATER

EXT. UNDERWATER (2) - DAY

DREAM SEQUENCE: SUBTLE UNDERWATER SOUNDS.

Submerged underwater, a barely visible YOUNG FE-MALE BODY floats by rocks, fish, moss, leaves and branches. Slowly, the body gets harder and harder to see. The body DISAPPEARS.

INT. MARK'S BEDROOM - NIGHT

A DISTANT CRY. 14-year-old MARK TRULSON bolts up in bed. He is sweating profusely. He has a vacuous stare - BREATHES HEAVILY - turns his pillow and lies back down, staring at the ceiling.

EXT. ASHLAND, OREGON - DAY

Copter shot showing Ashland and slow ZOOM in to the Middle School and soccer field.

EXT. SCHOOL SOCCER FIELD - DAY

A flag-football game with the SOUNDS, GRUNTS, AND THE USUAL LANGUAGE OF COMPETING MIDDLE

SCHOOL PLAYERS. Some players play more aggressively than others.

A SPASTIC, OBNOXIOUS, MYOPIC KID with thick glasses, who came out of the chute different, disrupts play by not following the rules of the game.

Mark, a slight boy with long blond hair (resembling Katy's hair in earlier scene), wearing post-punk/grunge shorts and standard P.E. white t-shirt, also stands out on the field, basically because he's stepping aside rather than blocking defensive players.

Mark gets looks from backfield players who gesture in frustration at his lack of investment in the game. The myopic kid KICKS the football away - then runs after it before the football can be put in play. Once the football's in play, the myopic kid takes the flag from his own team member who carries the ball.

BIG BOY, the most aggressive defensive player, moves in. He pushes the myopic kid. His glasses fall off. Big Boy picks up his glasses and throws them to the sideline.

                    BIG BOY
        Go fetch!

The myopic kid staggers around looking for his glasses to the LAUGHTER of the rest of the players. The game moves forward without him.

Mark walks to the sideline and picks up the glasses - gives them to the myopic kid, who stares at Mark - then comes back again to disrupt the game. The ball is hiked. While in the air, the myopic kid INTER-CEPTS/KICKS/PUSHES the football Mark's way. The loose football rolls towards Mark.

Mark hesitates - suddenly picks up the football, runs with intense, reckless abandon. He jukes a number of the big guys on defense, then gets BLIND-SIDED by Big Boy, who, rather than grab at the flag, bowls him over.

Mark, hurt, slowly gets up. Big Boy walks up to him - pulls the flag from his waist.

> BIG BOY
> Welcome to Ashland.

BIG BOY reaches out his hand to help. Mark refuses to be helped. DIEGO, a Hispanic male standing next to Big Boy, smiles.

> DIEGO
> Great moves. What's your name?

> MARK
> Mark.

The SCHOOL BELL RINGS. P.E. is over. Mark lags behind as the rest of the boys trot to the locker room. The myopic kid wanders off, oblivious to anyone else. He picks something up from the path - inspects it.

Diego and a COUPLE OTHER BOYS hang back to introduce themselves to the new boy on the block.

Mark intentionally averts his eyes and separates himself from them. The boys shrug their shoulders and MOVE ON ahead. Mark slowly ENTERS the school building.

INT. SCHOOL LOCKER ROOM – DAY

Some of the boys CHATTER, change shirts and DEPART. Mark ENTERS. Big Boy walks over to Mark.

> BIG BOY
> Did I hurt you, Fag?

Mark turns his back as he changes shirts, ignoring Big Boy.

> BIG BOY
> What's with you, Queer!

Big Boy SNAPS Mark with his shirt. Mark whirls around and WHACKS Big boy with his backpack. Big Boy dives into Mark - punches him. Mark swings back. They go at it. The COMMOTION brings the P.E. TEACHER IN, who separates the boys.

> P.E. TEACHER
> You guys have a problem?
>
> (beat)
> You can work it out with the school counselor, and a little after school detention.

Both boys have BLOOD on their faces. Big Boy wipes the blood off his face with a paper towel.

> BIG BOY
> Freak!

Big Boy LEAVES with his friends. The P.E. instructor stays - looks at Mark. Mark avoids eye contact. The instructor shrugs - LEAVES. Mark is alone - checks himself out at the mirror and sink. He scratches hard on his bloody lip - making it bleed more.

He stares vacantly at himself - finally takes a paper towel, wets it, and cleans himself off. He has a couple of nasty bruises on his cheek. He checks his knuckles - shows no emotion. Mark WHACKS an open locker with the palm of his hand - picks up his backpack and DEPARTS.

INT. SCHOOL CORRIDOR - DAY

It's lunch. STUDENTS deposit backpacks, books, and stuff in their lockers. Mark ENTERS - goes to his locker - deposits some materials from his backpack - takes out a cassette player and headphones - puts them on - grabs his lunch sack from his backpack. He walks by a number of students who ignore him.

EXT. SCHOOL QUAD - DAY

STUDENTS mill around in cliques during lunch break. Many have their own lunches. OTHERS COME from finishing lunch inside.

Mark ENTERS - picks a spot seeking as much separation as he can from the other students.

A GROUP OF GIRLS from across the quad TALK excitedly. It's typical teenage middle school flirtation time, with the furtive glances and the personal dramas. 14-YEAR-OLD-CAMILA from the group of girls, looks Mark's way.

Mark, self-absorbed, eats his lunch. Camila watches Mark, looks back - chats with the girls. Some glance his way. Camila leaves them - walks to Mark. Mark doesn't notice. Camila walks up - pulls Mark's headphones off.

CAMILA
Why didn't you call me?

MARK
I didn't feel like it.

Mark looks down and away - unties/reties his one tennis shoe. He periodically glances at her, but avoids meeting her direct gaze.

CAMILA
You know cassette players aren't allowed. They'll take 'em.

MARK
What the hell is it with this school?

Mark puts the cassette player and ear phones in his backpack. Camila looks at Mark's bruise on his face.

CAMILA
I heard about the fight. They're calling you weird.

Mark remains silent.

CAMILA
So why didn't you come over with your parents and Lindy on Sunday?

Mark shrugs - glances at Camila's group of friends.

MARK

Your friends are looking over here.

CAMILA

So?

MARK

What do they know about me?

CAMILA

I just told them our parents are friends and that I've known you forever.

Mark is untying/retying his second tennis shoe.

MARK

Your friends are waiting.

CAMILA

Why are you such a pain in the ass, Mark?

Camila walks off. Stops - turns.

CAMILA

Call me tonight, or I'm calling you.

Mark pulls out his cassette player. Goes back to listening to MUSIC.

EXT. TRULSON HOME - DAY

INT. HALLWAY - DAY

BORIS, the boxer lies at Mark's bedroom door. He MOANS and SCRATCHES on the door.

INT. MARK'S BEDROOM - DAY

MUSIC

Mark wears sunglasses. A half-gallon of orange juice and a whiskey bottle sit on his dresser. Mark takes a drink from a cup. He calls on his phone. An open phone book lies on the bed.

Mark stands - poses in front of the dresser mirror. In the low lit room, Mark is dressed in a girl's t-shirt with perceptible breasts protruding, and a pair of girl's jeans.

Mark sits on the bed.

> RECEPTIONIST (O.S.)
> Dr. Steinberg's office.

> MARK
> My name is Katy. I want to talk to Dr. Steinberg.

> RECEPTIONIST (O.S.)
> Dr. Steinberg sees patients by office appointments. What was your name again?

> MARK
> Katy.

> RECEPTIONIST (O.S.)
> Katy, he's not taking any new patients. If you want to get on a list, I can take your—

Mark ends the call - checks the phone book - calls the next number. He gets up - looks at himself in the mirror.

                    SECOND RECEPTIONIST (O.S.)
          Family Psychiatric Services.

                              MARK
          Can I talk to one of your counselors?

                    SECOND RECEPTIONIST (O.S.)
          We do not make appointments by telephone. Are you a patient of—

Mark BANGS his fist on the dresser. Boris BARKS – SCRATCHES.

                              MARK
          Shut up, Boris.

Boris keeps MOANING and SCRATCHING. Mark agitated, makes another call - gets the MESSAGE.

                    THIRD RECEPTIONIST (O.S.)
          Dr. Rowland will not be back in her office until Tuesday, September seventeenth. If you would like to...

Mark takes another drink - hurriedly consults the phone book. The bedroom is sparse with unpacked cardboard boxes lining one wall. A few posters aligned with those alienated from Pop Culture are on the walls. Mark's backpack sits next to the dresser.

                    FOURTH RECEPTIONIST (O.S.)
          Dr. Vitali's and Dr. Howard's office.

MARK

Is Dr. Vitali or Dr. Howard in?

FOURTH RECEPTIONIST (O.S.)

They're both in session. Do you wish to make an appointment?

MARK (O.S.)

(breathing hard)

There's no one to talk to me?

FOURTH RECEPTIONIST (O.S.)

Are you a patient of—

MARK (O.S.)

I'm not a patient.

(voice raised, intense)

Can't I decide if I want to be a patient by talking to one of them?

FOURTH RECEPTIONIST (O.S.)

Of course. Dr. Howard has a waiting list and both Dr. Vitali and Dr. Howard have initial reduced consultation fees if you wish to make an appointment. Would you like—

Mark lets out a SCREAM of frustration, HEAVY BREATHING AND WHIMPERING. He throws the phone book.

The CAMERA focuses on a poster.

DISSOLVE TO

INT. YMCA - POSTER - DAY

The camera pulls back from an old-fashioned poster of an earlier and more innocent time with TEACHER, PARENTS, AND CHILDREN.

INT. YMCA - BUSY PRESCHOOL ROOM - DAY

IMPROVISED BANTER. RENEE TRULSON, late thirties, talks animatedly with ANOTHER PARENT as children play. She glances often over at 4-YEAR-OLD GIRL, LINDY TRULSON, who plays with ANOTHER BOY AND GIRL, CHELSEY.

          ANOTHER PARENT
Thursday works for me.

          RENEE TRULSON
          (laughing)
You know, I can't get her in the car unless I promise a play date with Chelsey.

          (glances at the pre
          school teacher)
I'll leave a note with Bonnie.

Both walk to the children.

          RENEE TRULSON
C'mon Lindy.

          LINDY
          (emphatically)
We're not done playing.

                    RENEE TRULSON
            We have to go. You're going to Chelsey's
            on Thursday.

Chelsey SHOUTS with glee, followed by Lindy's SQUEAL of delight. The boy wanders off to another toy and other kids.

                         LINDY
            When's Thursday?

                    ANOTHER PARENT
            The day after tomorrow.

                         LINDY
            Can I go now, Mom, pleeeeease?

The girls drag on their mother's arms and chant:

                  LINDY AND CHELSEY
            NOW! NOW! NOW!

Both parents get "stuff", drag their children to the door. They wave back to the PRESCHOOL TEACHER, other parents and kids.

EXT. GROCERY STORE - DAY

Renee and Lindy EXIT grocery store pushing a grocery cart. Lindy hangs onto the side of the cart. Renee unloads the groceries as Lindy crawls into the car seat.

INT. MARK'S BEDROOM - DAY

                         MARK
            What if it's an emergency?

Mark is STILL INTENSE - EMOTIONAL.

> **FIFTH RECEPTIONIST (O.S.)**
> I can give you a number for Help Line.

> **MARK**
> I don't want Help Line. I've tried that before.
>
> (he sobs)
> They're not going to keep me from killing myself.

> **FIFTH RECEPTIONIST (O.S.)**
> I can provide you with other emergency services—

> **MARK**
> I have a handicap.

> **FIFTH RECEPTIONIST (O.S.)**
> What kind of handicap?
>
> (pauses)
> What kind of handicap?

Silence. Mark hangs up. More agitated, Mark rocks his body, BREATHING HARD. He dials again.

> **SIXTH RECEPTIONIST (O.S.)**
> Christian Counseling. Dr. Beck's office.

MARK
(sobbing)
Can I please speak with Doctor Beck?

SIXTH RECEPTIONIST (O.S.)
Are you a patient, then?

MARK
No, but I want to be...if she will only talk with me.

SIXTH RECEPTIONIST (O.S.)
It's a he. Doctor will talk with you if you will leave your number.

I didn't get your name.

MARK
I'm Katy.

(sobbing)
I want to die.

EXT. PSYCHOLOGIST'S BUILDING/OFFICE - DAY

INT. RECEPTION OFFICE - DAY

FREIDA NELSON
You want emergency numbers, then.

CHOKING sounds.

MARK (O.S.)
Please! Don't hang up! I'm so—

More CHOKING and COUGHING sounds. FREIDA NELSON, in her late fifties, remains businesslike on the phone. She speaks with a Norwegian accent.

> FREIDA NELSON
> I'm listening. But I don't know for how long.
>
> You're just going to have to calm yourself down now. Doctor won't be out for another half hour.

The SOBBING SLOWLY SUBSIDES.

> MARK (O.S.)
> Do you know what it's like to be blind?

> FREIDA NELSON
> You blind then?

> MARK (O.S.)
> Right after I was born.

> FREIDA NELSON
> Now isn't that something? It's been a hardship for you. I'm sure God has blessed you in other ways. How old are you, then?

There is silence. Freida glances at the door to the Doctor's office.

> FREIDA NELSON
> Are you still there?

The SOBBING BEGINS AGAIN.

> MARK (O.S.)
> (confused)
> Eighteen. No! Fourteen.

> FREIDA NELSON
> Eighteen? Fourteen? Now which is it?

INT. DR. BECK'S OFFICE - DAY

DR. BECK mid-forties, Christian psychologist, is upset with his client ANGIE LAMSON - early thirties, disheveled and agitated.

> DR. BECK
> I don't do well with clients who come to their appointments hung over.

Dr. Beck gets up. The client, Angie Lamson gets up.

Dr. Beck opens the door.

> ANGIE LAMSON
> (exasperated)
> You hate me. You're kicking me out.

> DR. BECK
> Yes, I am. Let's go out and make another appointment.

> ANGIE LAMSON
> Dr. Andrews wouldn't have done this to me.

DR. BECK

Angie, Dr. Andrews isn't here anymore. He would have—

ANGIE LAMSON

—listened.

Angie pauses as Dr. Beck opens the door.

ANGIE LAMSON

But I killed him.

DR. BECK

Don't do this today, Angie. We've gone over this and—

ANGIE LAMSON

(tearful)

I don't care what you say! He loved me. I felt safe with him.

Then he died for me. I'm Evil! And I'm rotting inside.

Dr. Beck closes the door.

DR. BECK

Alcohol isn't helping.

(pauses)

You know, I'm not going to buy into your hung over histrionics today.

Dr. Beck opens the door again. Angie won't leave. She sits down - puts her head in her hands - lets out a LOUD, FRUSTRATED, SELF-LOATHING YELL.

> ANGIE LAMSON
>
> I can't get out of where I am.

> DR. BECK
>
> Tell me why you go to the bars the night before you see me?

Angie gets up - goes to the door - opens it - hesitates.

Dr. Beck gets up, closes the door again. He takes her wrist - Angie pulls back.

> DR. BECK
>
> Let me see.

She looks at him - gets TEARY. Dr. Beck pulls up the sleeve of her sweatshirt revealing numerous RAZOR CUTS on her arm.

> ANGIE LAMSON
> (surprised)
> How did you know?
>
> (looking down at her arm)
> Why do I do this?

Dr. Beck SIGHS.

> DR. BECK
>
> The other day when you talked about being disconnected from feelings, did the cutting help you?
>
> > ANGIE LAMSON
> >
> > (plaintively)
>
> I don't know.
>
> > (pauses)
>
> I don't know what I feel except that I hate me.

Angie pulls down the sleeve of her sweatshirt. The two look at each other. Dr. Beck reaches out - takes Angie's hand.

> DR. BECK
>
> What do you want me to do?

Angie pulls her hand back - opens the door.

> > ANGIE LAMSON
> >
> > (with a sudden emo-
> >
> > tional shift)
>
> You sure didn't help me today.

Both EXIT to the reception room.

EXT. RECEPTION OFFICE - DAY

Freida SPEAKS INTO the phone.

> > FREIDA NELSON
>
> Katy, hold on a minute.

Freida covers the phone.

> DR. BECK
> Angie wants another appointment.

Freida looks at Angie.

> FREIDA NELSON
> You look awful!

> ANGIE LAMSON
> You and your Doctor here are something else.... Is next Thursday open?

Dr. Beck points to the phone. Freida nods her head.

> FREIDA NELSON
> Someone new. Another story.

Dr. Beck gives Angie a pat. Angie turns and hugs him. Dr. Beck smiles - RETURNS to his office. Freida SIGHS and looks at Angie.

> FREIDA NELSON
> He does like you, you know.

> ANGIE LAMSON
> (grabbing a tissue
> from the box)
> I know.

Freida puts the phone down - writes down Angie's name on the schedule. She picks up the phone - listens.

> DR. BECK (O.S.)
> This is Dr. Beck.

Freida hangs up, gets up, comes around the desk and gives Angie a hug. Angie buries her head into Freida's shoulder.

INT. DR. BECK'S OFFICE - DAY

> MARK (O.S.)
> What kind of shrink are you?

> DR. BECK
> A clinical psychologist.

> MARK (O.S.)
> (a voice of emotion
> and frustration)
>
> I've been to psychiatrists, psychologists, counselors—about a hundred others who were supposed to help me. I never got better. I got worse.

> DR. BECK
> So why are you calling now?

Around Dr. Beck's office, a family picture stands out showing Dr. Beck, a mountain bike enthusiast with his family, wife and two college age daughters - all on mountain bikes. Some Christian books and icons are part of the decor.

> MARK (O.S.)
> My name is Katy. I'm blind. Can you just talk to me for a minute?

Dr. Beck checks his watch.

EXT. STREET - TRULSON HOME - DAY

Renee Trulson slowly turns into the driveway of the Trulson home. The phone conversation continues.

> MARK (O.S.)
> I've heard about psychologists counseling over the phone. Do you do that?

> DR. BECK (O.S.)
> I don't. How old are you?

A beat.

> MARK (O.S.)
> Eee...I'm fourteen.
> (sobbing and choking)
> Can't you just talk to me now? I'll pay you.

> DR. BECK (O.S.)
> (hesitating)
> I'm listening, Katy.

EXT. GARAGE - DAY

Renee and Lindy unload the groceries from the car.

> MARK (O.S.)
> I've been blind since right after I was born. I just moved to Ashland.

I hate it here... I wish I was dead.

EXT. TRULSON HOME - CONTINUOUS

Renee and Lindy ENTER through the door to the kitchen.

> MARK (O.S.)
> I don't want people to look at me. I hated all those therapists looking at me in their offices. I couldn't see them. I didn't want them to see me.

> DR. BECK (O.S.)
> Why is it so important that they don't see you?

There is silence.

Boris BARKS with excitement. NOISE COMES FROM RENEE AND LINDY FROM THE KITCHEN.

INT. MARK'S BEDROOM - CONTINUOUS

Mark glances at the bedroom door - runs over to make sure it's locked.

> MARK
> Are you there?

> DR. BECK (O.S.)
> I am. Was that your dog barking?

> (beat)

> DR. BECK (O.S.)
> Are you there?... Let's make a deal. I'll give you an hour of time on the phone, after you give me an hour in my office.

Mark's hands shake.

> DR. BECK (O.S.)
> I will need your parents or responsible adult to come by with—

Mark takes another quick drink from the glass of orange juice on the dresser. He swallows wrong. Severe COUGHING, CHOKING and what can be interpreted by sound as SOBBING.

> MARK
> I can't breathe.

> DR. BECK (O.S.)
> Katy, talk to me... Do you have asthma?

INT. KITCHEN - CONTINUOUS

RENEE DEPOSITS THE GROCERIES AS BORIS BOUNDS INTO THE KITCHEN JUMPING ON RENEE AND LINDY. LINDY DROPS HER SWEATER AND RUNS TO MARK'S BEDROOM, BORIS FOLLOWS.

INT. HALLWAY - CONTINUOUS

Lindy gets to Mark's bedroom door, tries to open it - then BANGS on it.

> LINDY
> Mark! Open the door! Right now! Mark! Let me in!

INT. MARK'S BEDROOM - CONTINUOUS

Mark has his hand over the phone. He listens.

> DR. BECK (O.S.)
> I know you're there. Katy?... Katy?

With his hand covering the phone, Mark brings the phone to his ear. He waits as Lindy insistently BANGS on the door.

> LINDY (O.S.)
> I know you're in there. Mark? Mommy, Mark won't open the door.

Mark hears the phone go dead - puts the phone on the dresser. He hastily takes off his t-shirt, exposing a bra. He unfastens the bra - changes the pair of slacks - throws them and the whiskey bottle in a canvas bag - delivers everything to the back of a cluttered closet. He quickly pulls on his shorts as his mother RAPS on the door.

> RENEE TRULSON (O.S.)
> Mark, let your sister in.

EXT. NEW HOUSE CONSTRUCTION - DAY

A building project (house) is in progress. Off to one side, BEN TRULSON, early forties, one of two SUPERVISING CONTRACTOR/BUILDERS are teaching/assisting MALE AND FEMALE HIGH SCHOOL STUDENTS in a Habitat for Humanity project.

One MALE STUDENT is inactive, goofing off by himself. Ben gestures to the student to get on board with the other students, who are moving lumber. The un-invested male student resists.

BEN TRULSON

So what are you going to do? You want to bag the program?

The student shuffles uncomfortably. He glances at the other students. Ben gets close - gestures to the student to move away from the others.

BEN TRULSON

Hey! I'm not trying to embarrass you. They know you've been goofing off. I'm not going to ask if you're using, but you've been dragging your ass around all week and I'm—

UNINVESTED STUDENT

I'm not using.

(KICKING the gravel)

My parents are separated again.

Ben walks around to face the student.

BEN TRULSON

Why didn't you talk to me?

The student shyly looks up at Ben.

UNINVESTED STUDENT

You're new. I don't know you.

BEN TRULSON

So are you talking to anybody?

                        UNINVESTED STUDENT
Sometimes my mom, until she starts bad-mouthing Dad.

                        BEN TRULSON
How about Sam over there? You've known him since you started the project.

                        UNINVESTED STUDENT
He said, "Don't bring your problems to work. It's a great way for someone to get hurt."

                        BEN TRULSON
I think you may have misunderstood Sam. That's why Sam and I are doing this. Not just for the people who will move into this house, but for you guys as well.

The student sees the VAN ARRIVING and looks away.

                        BEN TRULSON
Don't walk away from this moment.

                        UNINVESTED STUDENT
I'm thinking I don't want to come back.
I'm dropping out of school.

The student grabs a backpack and walks toward the bus. Ben catches up to him - walks beside him - puts his arm around his shoulders.

                    BEN TRULSON
I'm going to save a spot for you the rest of this week.

The student walks on to the van and ENTERS.

The rest of the high school kids helping on the work project play HACKY SACK. They look over to Ben.

                    BEN TRULSON
Who's coming tomorrow?

Three of the five students raise their hands.

                    BEN TRULSON
How about the rest of you?

                    ONE STUDENT
We got baseball tomorrow. We're coming Friday.

                    BEN TRULSON
You guys did a great job today. We start framing tomorrow. So bring your muscles and strong backs and your sign off sheets.

                    FEMALE STUDENT
Yes, boss. Hey! Who gets the house, anyway?

Ben joins the circle and the sack is kicked to him. He misses. He picks it up and makes a BUMBLING KICK, then throws it to the student who kicked the sack to him, who in turn starts the rotation again.

>   BEN TRULSON
>   A mom with three kids. She's going
>   back to school.

A CHORUS OF "COOL!" The students grab backpacks and get in the van. The Uninvested Student glances out at Ben as the van DRIVES AWAY.

EXT. TRULSON HOME - DRIVEWAY - DAY

Ben drives his pickup truck into the driveway - exits with a leather case. A tricycle sits next to the garage door. He takes the tricycle to the back and ENTERS the house.

INT. KITCHEN - DAY

Renee meets Ben at the door. Gives him a hug.

He puts leather case by the wall and walks to the kitchen sink to get a drink of water.

>   RENEE TRULSON
>   We've got to talk.

Ben pats his stomach.

>   BEN TRULSON
>   No dinner? No Lindy run and kiss
>   Daddy?... Where's Lindy?

>   RENEE TRULSON
>   I'm bad. I'm not coping. I put Lindy on
>   video games. Pizza's coming.
>
>   I'm hoping that will get Mark out of the
>   bedroom.

Ben walks to Lindy. Renee follows.

INT. PLAYROOM - DAY

Lindy's bare feet dangle on Boris' back, moving back and forth as she plays a game. Ben bends down - gives Lindy a hug.

> LINDY
> Watch me, daddy!

> BEN TRULSON
> In a minute, honey. Mommy and Daddy are going to talk in the kitchen.

Renee and Ben return to the kitchen.

INT. KITCHEN - DAY

Ben Trulson glances through the kitchen window out into the yard.

> BEN TRULSON
> Where's John?

Renee comes over to Ben - wraps her arms around him as they look out into the back yard.

INT/EXT. KITCHEN - DAY

> RENEE TRULSON (O.S.)
> John had to take Emily back to the Doctor. He put the plants in the garage.
>
> By the way, you have to sign the papers
>
> (MORE)

> RENEE TRULSON (O.S. CONT'D)
> on the nursery. We are now the proud owners of forty years of Mom and Dad's heart and soul.

INT. KITCHEN - CONTINUOUS

> BEN TRULSON
> How does that make you feel?

> RENEE TRULSON
> I'm sad that my parents won't see me carry on what they made.
>
> I want to show you some plants I brought home earlier.

Renee moves away from Ben.

> RENEE TRULSON
> Something more important is happening with Mark. You're going to need to sit down for this.

Ben goes to the fridge - grabs a beer - looks to Renee who gives the signal for two.

> RENEE TRULSON
> First I get a call from Miranda. Then I get a call from Camila. I tried to call Mark this afternoon and he was on the phone for at least a half hour. Then I get a call from the school. He's not turning in assignments.

BEN TRULSON

So what else is new? Maybe he's made a friend?

RENEE TRULSON

Don't think so... That's not all. He was in a fight at school.

BEN TRULSON

Well, that's good news. At least he's connected to something.

RENEE TRULSON

It's not good news. We have an appointment with the counselor with Mark. Monday at 11:00.

The PIZZA DELIVERY GIRL arrives. Renee takes money off the counter and completes the transaction at the door. Renee gets plates while Ben gets napkins as they talk.

BEN TRULSON

Does he know this?

RENEE TRULSON

Yeah. Probably.

BEN TRULSON

I'll go get him.

RENEE TRULSON

Hold your horses, Ben. Let's do this as a team.

BEN TRULSON
So what do you have in mind?

RENEE TRULSON
Confront him. The whole damn thing.
(yells)
Lindy, Pizza!

LINDY (O.S.)
Just a sec. mommy, I got to level three.

Ben is up pondering - pacing.

BEN TRULSON
Let her stay. Things may heat up.

Renee calls to Lindy.

RENEE TRULSON
Okay, I'll keep the pizza warm.

Ben stops, turns to Renee.

BEN TRULSON
Take a deep breath.

RENEE TRULSON
You, too.

INT. MARK'S BEDROOM - DAY

Mark has his head phones on. Ben RAPS on the door.

BEN TRULSON (O.S.)
Dinner... Pizza.

Ben waits. Mark takes off his head phones unlocks the door and ENTERS the hallway.

INT. HALLWAY - CONTINUOUS

              BEN TRULSON

You locking us out again?

              MARK

Locking Lindy out.

They walk to the kitchen.

INT. KITCHEN - CONTINUOUS

              BEN TRULSON

Did you take Lindy out and play with her?

              MARK
              (mumbles)

Yeah.

              BEN TRULSON

Did you get her to put the tricycle in the garage?

Mark thinks.

              MARK

Nooo!

All dish up pizza for themselves. MARK checks the fridge. He grabs a container of milk - gets a glass.

> RENEE TRULSON
> I didn't see the orange juice in there.

> MARK
> It's in my bedroom.

Mark heads for the bedroom with a full plate of pizza.

> BEN TRULSON
> Where' you going?

> MARK
> Back to my room.

> BEN TRULSON
> Sit down. Let's talk.

Mark reluctantly comes back, SIGHS, slouches down on the kitchen chair - chomps on his pizza.

> MARK
> I don't wanna' talk.

> RENEE TRULSON
> You had problems at school today.

> MARK
> Yeah. I was called a faggot.

> RENEE TRULSON
> Is that how you got the bruise on your face?

> MARK
> Yeah.

> RENEE TRULSON
> Tell us about it.

> MARK
> There's nothing to tell.

Mark gets up and heads to the bedroom. Renee and Ben get up.

> BEN TRULSON
> Come back here. We're not done.

> MARK
> I'm done.

MARK comes back - takes a last big bite of his pizza and deposits the rest on the table.

> RENEE TRULSON
> Who were you on the phone with this afternoon?

Mark walks away. Renee steps in front of him.

> MARK
> Camila.

> RENEE TRULSON
> No, you weren't.

Renee and Mark stand toe to toe.

> RENEE TRULSON
> You're lying, Mark. Talk to us.

MARK

I'll talk to you later.

Renee and Mark play shifting offense and defense with their bodies. The conversation LEAPS IN EMOTIONAL INTENSITY to an explosion of anguish and angry feelings.

RENEE TRULSON

You've been saying that for five years. We moved here to give you another chance.

MARK

No, you moved here because Grandma died, and you always wanted to live here and run the nursery.

Mark ELBOWS Renee aside. Ben suddenly PUSHES HIS WAY between Renee and Mark.

BEN TRULSON

(grabbing Mark by

the shoulders)

And you can get on with your life rather than be frozen forever because of an accident.

RENEE TRULSON

(Forcing herself be-

tween Ben and Mark)

Ben! Stop!

                    BEN TRULSON
We're in this now and I'm not going to stop.

                    (grabbing Mark's shirt
                    as MARK pulls away)
We're not a family anymore because of you.

Mark breaks free as Renee firmly pushes Ben back. Mark is in tears.

                    MARK
                    (shouting)
I'm really a big problem for you. Right!... Right!

                    BEN TRULSON
Yes!

Renee puts her hand over Ben's mouth.

                    MARK
                    (exploding)
You never asked me if I wanted to move here. I'm not going to that appointment with some retarded counselor and I don't care if I am suspended from school. And I'm not going to a school with a bunch of asshole rednecks.

Mark heads for the bedroom - Renee follows.

INT. HALLWAY - CONTINUOUS

> RENEE TRULSON
> (shouting)
> Ashland? Rednecks? Come on! Miranda and I went to that school... Who were you talking to on the phone?

Mark doesn't answer. ENTERS the bedroom - SLAMS the door.

> RENEE TRULSON
> When you can calm down, we're going to talk later.

> MARK (O.S.)
> Yeah... Later.

Ben catches up to Renee - checks the bedroom door.

> RENEE TRULSON
> Wait. He's up to something. We'll hit him again later.

INT. KITCHEN - CONTINUOUS

Ben and Renee come back to the kitchen - sit down. Ben is pacing - finally sits down. Lindy WALKS IN, Boris slinking, FOLLOWS.

> LINDY
> Are you all done yelling at each other?

She goes over and climbs in her father's lap. Ben is shaking from the tension. Lindy looks up at him. Cuddles him. Renee serves pizza.

INT. MARK'S BEDROOM - DAY (LATER)

Mark paces back and forth. He stops. Puts his headphones on - tears them off. He grabs his phone - sits on the bed. Gets up, looks in the closet - glances at his bedroom door - checks the lock on the door - comes back to his bed. The phone RINGS.

> MARK
> (whispering, irritated)
> Camila, go away.

The phone keeps ringing.

EXT. DR. BECK'S UPSCALE URBAN RESIDENCE - DAY

INT. WORK OUT ROOM - DAY

Dr. Beck runs on the treadmill. He's listening to CHRISTIAN ROCK MUSIC. Sweat pours down his face. HIS WIFE, LYN WALKS IN with the phone. She walks over, turns the MUSIC OFF.

> LYN
> It's the exchange. I have a number for a girl named Katy. What do you want to do?

Dr. Beck slows the treadmill down to a walk - grabs a towel and wipes his face.

> DR. BECK
> She's not a client, yet. But you know me, curiosity's going to kill me someday.

                    LYN

Call it for what it is, Robert.

                  DR. BECK

Yeah, yeah.

                    LYN

Daughter number two just popped in
for a free meal so make up your mind.

Lyn turns to leave.

                    LYN
                 (mumbles)
Messiah complex.

                  DR. BECK

What'd you say?

Lyn EXITS.

Dr. Beck hops off the treadmill - takes the phone and slip of paper. Dr. Beck takes a drink - sits down on the seat of the Bowflex. He relaxes for a moment.

A HYMN IS HEARD on the piano from another room. Dr. Beck's daughter's VOICE COMES THROUGH WITH "LIVING HE LOVED ME, DYING HE SAVED ME," from the Original Trinity Hymnal, #689. Lyn joins in on the singing. He HUMS, then calls.

INT. MARK'S BEDROOM - DAY

Mark is listening to music. The phone RINGS. Mark TURNS DOWN the MUSIC.

MARK

Hi.

INTERCUT PHONE CONVERSATION

INT. WORK OUT ROOM - DAY

Dr. Beck gets up, closes the door.

DR. BECK

Have you calmed down?

INT. MARK'S BEDROOM - DAY

MARK

No.

DR. BECK

(pauses)

I've made a decision to not do an appointment over the phone.

MARK

Why?

DR. BECK

Something doesn't ring true about what's happening here.

MARK

You don't believe I'm blind?

DR. BECK

I need an identity. A street address, the names of your parents. Your parent's permission to talk to you. Then I'll keep the bargain.

An hour on your terms for an hour on mine.

Mark paces.

MARK
(emotional)
I don't think you really care about what's happening to me.

INT. WORK OUT ROOM - DAY

MOLLY, Dr. Beck's college-age daughter, ENTERS.

DR. BECK

Oh I do. I get sucked into other people's pain. It's the Christian thing to do.

Molly strongly nods her head as she gives her father a kiss on the cheek. She points to her watch. Dr. Beck nods - signals he's getting off the phone.

MARK (O.S.)

I thought all psychologists were agnostics.

DR. BECK

I am a Christian. Didn't you see that in the yellow pages? Oops, I'm sorry.

Molly gives the sign of the cross to tease dad.

> MARK (O.S.)
> I'm not coming to your office.

> DR. BECK
> Call Help Line. I'm hanging up now.

Mark starts CHOKING AND CRYING.

> MARK (O.S.)
> My dad... He's been doing things to me.

A beat.

> DR. BECK
> Do you have a friend?

> MARK (O.S.)
> Why?

> DR. BECK
> Have your friend bring you to my office.

> MARK (O.S.)
> I'd rather meet you someplace else.

> DR. BECK
> Where do you want to meet? It will have to be in a public place - like a park or restaurant.

A beat.

MARK (O.S.)
When?

DR. BECK
Tomorrow. I'm done at the office at five o'clock. On my way home.

MARK (O.S.)
How about a park?

DR. BECK
(thoughtful)
No, I don't trust you that you'll be there. How about a restaurant?

MARK (O.S.)
I... I guess.

DR. BECK
How will you get there?

Molly WHISPERS.

MOLLY
Larks.

MARK (O.S.)
I can have someone with me.

DR. BECK
How about Larks. 5:15. It's on Main Street. Easy to walk to. I can meet you in the hotel lobby. You know Larks?

> MARK

Yeah, my parents used to take me there.

> DR. BECK

Tell your friend I'll have a San Francisco Giants baseball cap on.

Hello?... Hello?

There's silence. The phone is dead. Molly shakes her head.

> MOLLY

Oh dear, dear papa. What kind of idiotic thing are you doing now?

> DR. BECK

You want to meet me at Larks at 5:30?

> MOLLY

What about the person you're talking to on the phone?

> DR. BECK

A probable no show.

EXT. TRULSON BACKYARD - NIGHT

CRICKETS and OTHER NIGHT SOUNDS.

> BEN TRULSON (O.S.)

Wynken and Blynken are two little eyes and Nod is a head...

INT. TRULSON HOME - LINDY'S BEDROOM - NIGHT

Ben lies on the bed, Lindy next to him. He READS a children's poem to Lindy, who is almost asleep. Boris sleeps on the floor.

> BEN TRULSON
> "...and the wooden shoe that sailed the skies is the wee one's trundle-bed. So shut your eyes while father sings of wonderful sights that be.
>
> "And you shall see the beautiful things as you rock in the misty sea. Where the old shoe rocked the fisherman three. Wynken, Blynken, and Nod."

Lindy tries to keep her eyes open. Halfway through the verse she's in the land of Nod. Ben waits - watches Lindy. He finally gets up - turns off the lights and EXITS.

INT. KITCHEN - Continuous

Ben walks to the kitchen.

Renee sits at the table looking at a catalogue of native Oregon plants. Tears drop on the catalogue. She wipes them off.

> RENEE TRULSON
> Here's what the new plantings will look like next September - and December - now February. Take a look at April and all summer.

Renee reaches back and grabs Ben's hand. He puts his other hand on Renee's neck. Boris ENTERS - lies down next to Renee's feet.

> BEN TRULSON
> What's going on?

The sound of RIVER RAPIDS and Renee's SHOUTING VOICE (OFF SCREEN) - Boris BARKS (OFF SCREEN)

> RENEE TRULSON
> I'm screaming inside. I'm back there again.

FLASHBACK (5 YEARS EARLIER) - RENEE'S POV

EXT. ROGUE RIVER - DAY

ROARING RIVER RAPIDS

> RENEE TRULSON (O.S.)
> Mark... Over here! Mark!

Mark's VOICE PIERCES through the ROARING RAPIDS.

> YOUNG MARK (O.S.)
> I can't see... I can't find her.

Ben runs in and out of the rapids down river. Boris BARKS as he JUMPS in and out of the river. Young Mark's head bobs up and down out in the middle of the river.

> RENEE TRULSON (O.S.)
> This way! Over here. Now!

Mark goes under, comes up again - SCREAMING.

> YOUNG MARK
>
> No!

Mark goes under again. He comes up. Renee enters the raging river - loses her balance.

> MARK
>
> She was there and then she wasn't...
>
> I can't see!
>> (seeing Renee go under)
>
> No, Momma, no!!

Mark swims - wades towards his mother. Ben runs toward Renee.

> RENEE TRULSON (O.S.)
>
> I'm hearing Mark: "No, Momma, no."

END RENEE'S POV - CONTINUE FLASHBACK - BEN'S POV

> BEN TRULSON (O.S.)
>
> I came running... I couldn't hear what Mark was yelling. I thought he found Katy.

Renee keeps slipping in the river rapids. She gets her feet under her as Mark gets next to her. She grabs him - pulls him out of the rapids. He fights her to go back in.

> RENEE TRULSON
>
> No!

She jerks him firmly as he falls to the water. She drags him to shore as he rages and fights to get away. As

Renee gets to shore, she turns - looks back, upriver. The other woman, (Camila's mother, MIRANDA), RUNS UP with a HYSTERICAL CRYING CAMILA.

                  BEN TRULSON (O.S.)
You got Mark out while I ran downstream.

That's when I found her.

Mark sits, head between his knees at the river's edge. Afraid to look, he pulls his head down further between his knees.

END FLASHBACK

INT. MARK'S BEDROOM – NIGHT

Mark, shirtless, sits on the floor with his head between his knees, rocking back and forth.

The whiskey bottle, orange juice container, and glass sit on the dresser. His cassette player PLAYS the same vocalist's theme song.

He slowly gets up - puts on the bra, Katy's t-shirt, slacks. He looks at a poster of family pictures of earlier times (five and more years before) with Katy dressed similarly with sunglasses. Mark puts on the sunglasses - reaches for the phone.

INT. DR. BECK'S BEDROOM - NIGHT

Dr. Beck and Lyn are kneeling beside the bed. An open Bible lies on the comforter. He is deep in prayer.

DR. BECK

I thank you Lord for giving me health and strength that I may be a witness for you. I ask you to continue to Bless Lyn, Alicia, and Molly with your love.

The phone RINGS

DR. BECK

Forgive me Lord for the times that I forget by running ahead and thinking I can manage my life without you. In Jesus' name, Amen.

LYN

Do you want me to...?

Dr. Beck lovingly touches Lyn's back then hops up as Lyn continues her own prayers in silence. He walks to the living room.

INT. DR. BECK'S LIVING ROOM - NIGHT

DR. BECK calls the exchange.

EXCHANGE (O.S.)

Sorry, Dr. Beck. She stated it was an emergency. It's Katy again.

DR. BECK

I have the number.

Dr. Beck grabs a notebook and pen - walks to a chair in the dim light and sits down. He calls.

MARK (O.S.)
                (choking and sobbing)
I want to die.
                    (a beat)
I want to die.

Another long silence as Dr. Beck closes his eyes. The SOBBING and CHOKING continues.

                    MARK (O.S.)
Are... are you there?

                    DR. BECK
                    (softly)
I'm here.

                    MARK (O.S.)
Why wasn't it me? I couldn't see.

Dr. Beck slowly opens his eyes and looks at a family picture of his two daughters on the lamp table next to him.

                    MARK (O.S.)
At night... at night it never goes away. Never goes away... the dream. The dream.

EXT. UNDERWATER (2,3) - DAY

FLASHBACK OPENING DREAM SEQUENCE

The UNDERWATER opening dream sequence DISSOLVES into a UNDERWATER MURKY ATMOSPHERE with weeds, a stump, and ANOTHER YOUNG FEMALE FIGURE. This time the figure is visually apparent.

Another long silence.

END FLASHBACK

INT. DR. BECK'S LIVING ROOM - NIGHT

> DR. BECK
> I've been waiting for you.

Another silence. The SOBBING and CHOKING subsides.

> MARK (O.S.)
> Waiting? It's all real to you?

> DR. BECK
> Oh, yes.

EXT. COUNTRY NURSERY - DAY

A country nursery with BUYERS PERUSING PLANTS outdoors.

INT. NURSERY - DAY

Lindy, HUMMING, is sneaking around the nursery - peeking out periodically to get her mother's attention. NPR is on in the background. Mom smiles and waves when she spots Lindy. A MAN WALKS away from the cash register pulling a cart with plants.

> RENEE TRULSON
> You need help?

MAN

Thanks, I can handle it.

Renee turns to Camila's mother, MIRANDA, chubby, late thirties.

MIRANDA

So he told her he wanted to see her after school.

RENEE TRULSON

And?

MIRANDA

Camila told me she wouldn't be home before 6:00. So what's that all about?

Renee works around the plants.

RENEE TRULSON

I never know what's going on with Mark. Camila didn't tell you?

MIRANDA

She doesn't know.

RENEE TRULSON

Ben and I had a terrible night. I couldn't stop crying after a fight with Mark. Then about two o'clock in the morning, Ben scares me half to death.

He wakes up screaming my name,

(MORE)

RENEE TRULSON (CONT'D)
RENEE! RENEE! Like that day on the river.

Then Mark is up wandering around in the middle of the night. We think he may be getting into the liquor cabinet, but we can't prove it. This morning we had to fight to get him to school.

LINDY
Momma, look at me.

Renee waves - Miranda is in tears.

RENEE TRULSON
Now I've got you crying.

MIRANDA
I was crying before you told me about Mark. Can I change the subject for one minute?

RENEE TRULSON
Go for it.

MIRANDA
About Saturday night.

RENEE TRULSON
(excited)
You had a date?

MIRANDA

It was terrible. I couldn't enjoy my food, not because I'm fat, but because the little mousy guy only ordered a salad for himself. Then, I couldn't really drink because I'm on anti-depressants... And the guy was a pervert who couldn't stop talking about his sex life.

RENEE TRULSON

Well, are you going to see him again?

MIRANDA

I wanted to like him... I'm so tired of being single.

Renee hugs Miranda. Miranda SIGHS.

MIRANDA

Sorry about that... How can I forget that day at your parent's cabin? It started so perfect.

FLASHBACK (5 YEARS EARLIER) - MIRANDA'S POV

EXT. ROGUE RIVER - CABIN - DAY

NOISY children are heard inside the house. Young Camila runs out, followed by Young Mark and KATY, with sunglasses. All are in t-shirts, shorts, swimming suits underneath. Boris runs out after the children run to a table - get drinks, then start running. Katy hangs on to Mark's shorts from behind.

                    MIRANDA (O.S.)
Camila came running out of the house after hearing us yell, "Ben's got a fish on the line." Then Mark comes running out with Katy hanging on to that pair of soccer shorts of his.

How they would chase each other. Every day was an adventure.

Camila looks back. Katy LAUGHING, clings confidently to Mark as he tries to KEEP up with Camila.

                    RENEE TRULSON (O.S.)
I yelled to Mark, "Tie your shoelaces, Mark, tie your shoelaces."

The children run down a path.

END FLASHBACK

INT. NURSERY - DAY

                    MIRANDA
Have you ever been back?

                    RENEE TRULSON
Never. And now with my parents gone, we inherited the cabin.

EXT. QUAD - STUDENTS - DAY

Mark and Camila are in an intense conversation off to one side.

CAMILA

You piss me off. You don't wanna see me or even talk to me, then you tell me you have a big favor to ask.

Then you don't wanna tell me what it's about.

MARK

Will you do it?

CAMILA

Do what?

MARK

Meet me at my house after school.

CAMILA

Why?

MARK

Dress in shorts and tennis shoes. You need to be on your bike.

CAMILA

Where' we going?

MARK

I'll tell you later.

Big Boy and ANOTHER BOY WALK UP.

BIG BOY

Is this idiot here your friend?

CAMILA

Yeah.

BIG BOY

Why is he such a freak?

Mark ignores Big Boy and Another Boy.

CAMILA

He's adjusting.

Another Boy looks at Mark - then Camila.

ANOTHER BOY

I want him on my team. He's got skills.

Mark quickly glances up - then looks away.

ANOTHER BOY

Dude. I'll block for you.

Big Boy and Another Boy WALK AWAY.

EXT. ASHLAND STREET - DAY

Mark and Camila ride bicycles through neighborhoods. Mark carries a backpack. They walk their bicycles on an Ashland street - Mark turns up an alleyway.

CAMILA

Is this follow the leader or do you have to go to the bathroom?

MARK

Padlock our bikes.

CAMILA

Yes, Sir.

Mark ENTERS the rest room. Camila waits and waits. Finally Mark PEEKS through the door.

MARK

Don't laugh.

CAMILA

At what?

Mark comes out dressed as Katy. He puts on the sunglasses. Camila is in shock.

CAMILA

Oh my God. You have gone crazy? I'm gettin' outta here.

Camila starts unlocking her bicycle.

MARK

How do I look?

CAMILA

You look like your sister. Why are you doing this?

MARK

Walk with me. We have to practice.

CAMILA

Why?

> MARK
> Let me take your arm. I'll tell you on the way.

Mark reaches out into thin air. Camila won't cooperate. The pantomime becomes comical. MARK is determined to be blind. Finally, he gets her arm and they start walking. Mark TRIPS on the concrete.

> CAMILA
> Serves you right.

Camila leads Mark right up to a lamp pole. Stops. She walks slowly - he HITS the pole.

> CAMILA
> You still want to do this?

Mark is serious.

> MARK
> Yes.

He HUMS the hit tune from the film's beginning credits: WISH ME A RAINBOW.

> CAMILA
> Don't do this.

Mark keeps HUMMING.

> MARK
> We're going to Larks.

They slowly walk along. Soon both are HUMMING "Wish me a Rainbow."

EXT. STREET - TRULSON HOME - DAY

Ben drives up - exits and ENTERS the residence.

INT. KITCHEN - DAY

Ben ENTERS the kitchen - Boris greets him. He glances at the newspaper on the table.

> BEN TRULSON
> I'm home.

Lindy COMES RUNNING IN - gives him a hug.

> LINDY
> I was at Chelsey's. We made brownies.

> BEN TRULSON
> I don't see any.

Lindy points to the counter.

> LINDY
> There.

> BEN TRULSON
> Where's Mommy?

> LINDY
> Mark's room.

> RENEE TRULSON (O.S.)
> Ben. You want to come in here.

Lindy RUNS BACK to her playroom. Ben walks to Mark's bedroom.

INT. MARK'S BEDROOM - DAY

On the bed is the poster of family photos, empty whiskey bottle, an empty container of orange juice on the dresser. Renee sits on the bed viewing the pictures. Ben ENTERS.

RENEE TRULSON
How stupid are we?

Ben notices the whiskey bottle - opens it - smells.

BEN TRULSON
Must be vodka.

RENEE TRULSON
That's not all. I packed this poster away three years ago. He dug it out when we moved here.

BEN TRULSON
How do you know?

RENEE TRULSON
I know, because I was sneaking it out now and then when I got really pissed at Mark, or when I needed a good cry.

BEN TRULSON
Pissed?

RENEE TRULSON
Yeah. Remember, Mark used to be such a shit one day and a sweet boy the next. Look around Ben.

BEN TRULSON
I'm looking... Well?

RENEE TRULSON
Sometimes you can be so dense.

BEN TRULSON
About what? Hey! Katy's tennis shoes.

RENEE TRULSON
One of her many pairs. In the canvas bag with the whiskey bottle - back of the closet.

BEN TRULSON
Now what?

Lindy WALKS IN. She notices the poster with pictures - climbs on Mom's lap and looks.

LINDY
How come I'm not in those pictures?

RENEE TRULSON
You weren't born yet.

Lindy continues to look at the pictures. Renee hands Ben a scrap of paper.

RENEE TRULSON
I called this number.

BEN TRULSON
And?

LINDY

Will I look like Katy when I get that big?

RENEE TRULSON

It's a Christian counseling center. A Dr. Beck is the psychologist.

BEN TRULSON

Mark's been seeing him?

RENEE TRULSON

"Katy" has been calling Dr. Beck on his bedroom phone.

LINDY

How can Katy be calling somebody? She's supposed to be in heaven.

BEN TRULSON

Lindy, go play with Boris.

LINDY

Come on Boris. Katy's come back from heaven.

Lindy EXITS.

LINDY (O.S.)

She'll play with me more than Mark does.

INT. OFFICE RECEPTION - DAY

Freida is up cleaning her desk, putting files away. Angie is reading a magazine. Dr. Beck ENTERS.

FREIDA NELSON
You leaving?

DR. BECK
The deal is on.

ANGIE LAMSON
What deal?

FREIDA NELSON
Sweetie, it's our little secret.

Dr. Beck looks at Angie.

DR. BECK
You look better today.

ANGIE LAMSON
I found an old - ah - really a new friend.

DR. BECK
Who may that be?

ANGIE LAMSON
I went back to AA. Mrs. Andrews was there.

> DR. BECK
>
> I'm glad for you and Mrs. Andrews. Where are you two going?
>
> FREIDA NELSON
>
> Larks.
>
> DR. BECK
>
> You ought to try Omar's. Fresh Seafood.

Freida sees Dr. Beck's look - turns back to Angie.

> FREIDA NELSON
>
> You'll want to do Omar's.

Angie nods her head.

Dr. Beck walks over, leans down and gives Angie a hug - EXITS.

EXT. ASHLAND MAIN STREET (1) - DAY

Mark and Camila are on Ashland's Main Street. Mark is a step behind. They walk by a shoe store. Camila stops. Mark hangs on to Camila's shirt.

> CAMILA
>
> Now that's an ugly pair of shoes.

Mark doesn't look.

> CAMILA
>
> Say something.

Mark stands there, head frozen - only listening. PASSERSBY seem aware they are passing a blind person.

                    CAMILA
             You wanna to go in?

                     MARK
             No.

They walk on. TWO OLDER WOMEN walk by - remark to each other.

                ONE OLDER WOMAN
             Are they beautiful or what?

               OTHER OLDER WOMAN
                  (takes a second look
                    at Mark)
             God's angels.

Camila looks at the two women - looks at Mark - puts her hand on Mark's hand. He flinches at first - lets her hand remain.

                    CAMILA
             We're crossing the street.

They wait for the light. Dr. Beck DRIVES UP to the light.

DR. BECK'S POV

Dr. Beck watches them cross. Arm in arm Camila and Mark get to the other side - walk down another street. Camila's hand remains on Mark's hand. The light turns green.

END POV

EXT. ASHLAND MAIN STREET (2) - CONTINUOUS

Dr. Beck still sits there in his car. A HORN startles him back to reality. The car lunges forward.

EXT. SIDEWALK STORES - DAY

Camila stops and looks in a clothing store window. Camila describes what she sees.

> CAMILA
> I wish you could see those shoes.

> MARK
> I like shoes that feel soft... like Mom gets me...

> CAMILA
> I know, I know. You're out of touch.

Camila looks at Mark/Katy

> CAMILA
> You gotta get a different top.

The dance is on. Camila is with Katy. They walk on - as if this was yesterday with only time, different music and clothing styles changing.

> CAMILA
> Same with those shoes.

EXT. ASHLAND MAIN STREET (3) - CONTINUOUS

As they approach the Varsity Theater, a STATION WAGON DRIVES UP to the curb. OUT JUMPS Big Boy,

Another Boy, Diego, and A COUPLE OTHER ADOLESCENTS. They line up to purchase tickets.

Camila stops abruptly.

> MARK
>
> What?

> CAMILA
>
> I think we may wanna walk the other way - some of my friends from school.

Big Boy and Another Boy spot Camila and Mark.

> BIG BOY
> (shouting)
>
> Camila. Where' you going? Hey, that's the faggot dressed up as a girl. C'mon.

Camila points the other way. She walks fast; Mark tries hard to keep up. Big Boy, Another Boy, and the other adolescents give chase.

> CAMILA
>
> They're coming.

Mark drops her arm and starts running full speed, Camila close behind. They cut into an alley, Big Boy and friends in full pursuit. Big Boy and friends surround Mark and Camila.

EXT. ALLEY NEAR VARSITY THEATER - CONTINUOUS

> CAMILA
>
> Go away, Matt.

Big Boy walks up to Mark - pulls his glasses off.

> MARK
> Gimme them back!

Mark reaches for the glasses.

> BIG BOY
> What's under the t-shirt?

Mark dives into Big Boy. Big Boy, forty pounds heavier, wrestles Mark to the asphalt. Another Boy pulls Big Boy back.

> DIEGO
> Let him go, Matt

> BIG BOY
> He's a faggot fake.

Big Boy pulls up Mark's t-shirt - pulls up the bra. Stuffed socks fall out.

Dr. Beck ENTERS.

> DR. BECK
> Hey guys. Get lost.

Dr. Beck faces Big Boy and the other adolescents.

> BIG BOY
> Who are you?

> DR. BECK
> Never mind. Go away.

Big Boy stares down Dr. Beck. Diego steps forward - grabs Big Boy's arm.

ANOTHER BOY
C'mon, we're missing the movie.

Big Boy and friends LEAVE as Diego gestures.

DIEGO
So he wants to be a girl.

Mark is still on the ground. His elbow is bleeding. Camila is in silent shock. Dr. Beck reaches down to help Mark up. Mark jerks away.

DR. BECK
You okay, Katy?

CAMILA
Who are you?... You know Mark?

Mark gets up - RUNS AWAY. Camila starts to follow.

CAMILA
Mark!!

She looks back at Dr. Beck - appearing frozen.

DR. BECK
I'm Doctor Beck. A psychologist.

CAMILA
(stammering)
Aaaah. Has Mark been talking to you?

> DR. BECK
>
> I can't answer that. How do you know Katy?

Camila looks at Dr. Beck with a puzzled look.

EXT. CAMILA'S HOME - DAY

INT. CAMILA'S BEDROOM - DAY

Camila's on the phone.

> CAMILA
>
> You're killing me. I was there. You don't care about what I feel...
>
> Mark listen to me. Mark! Stop! Wait!

Camila is shaking - HYSTERICAL. SHE SLAMS THE PHONE ON THE BED. She whirls around - hands over ears.

FLASHBACK (5 YEARS EARLIER) - CAMILA'S POV

EXT. CLIFF BOULDERS (1) - DAY

Boris is BARKING, next to Katy. Katy is staggering, hands out - she is approaching the edge of the rocky cliff.

Katy is ANGRY/SCREAMING.

> KATY
>
> Mark, I hate you! Where are you? Camila! Camila!

> YOUNG CAMILA (O.S.)
>
> Where—
>
> (SCREAMING)
>
> STOP! NOT THERE!

Katy FALLS - DISAPPEARS. Boris BARKING, comes running down through the boulders. Young Mark APPEARS FROM BETWEEN BOULDERS on the cliff - looks over the cliff - pulls off his unlaced tennis shoes.

> YOUNG CAMILA (O.S.)
>
> Mark! Stop! Wait!

Mark jumps - DISAPPEARS.

> YOUNG CAMILA (O.S.)
>
> MARK! MARK!

END FLASHBACK

EXT. TRULSON HOME - BACKYARD - DAY

Ben, Renee, and JOHN, gardener and yard helper, are setting plants on a plot of land in the back yard. In GARDEN TALK they discuss the pros and cons of the design of the plant placements.

Mark rides up with his backpack on his back. Mark hurries to the back door of the house.

> BEN TRULSON
>
> Mark, wait. How's Camila?
>
> MARK
>
> Okay.

BEN TRULSON
So what'd you do?

MARK
Stuff.

BEN TRULSON
Stuff? You've got a scratch on your arm.

MARK
My bike tipped.

Mark starts to leave.

MARK
I'm gonna go get a drink.

BEN TRULSON
Come back out. Tell us what you've been up to.

A HIGH PITCHED CRY for help comes from inside.

LINDY (O.S.)
Mom! Mom! Wipe me.

Ben and Renee's hands have dirt on them. Mark is about to enter the house.

RENEE TRULSON
Mark. Go take care of Lindy.

MARK
No way!

Mark EXITS into house. Renee looks at Ben. Ben shows his dirty hands. Renee gets up and HEADS IN.

> RENEE TRULSON
> Go figure. Soap works just as well on your hands as mine.

> LINDY (O.S.)
> Mama!

INT. KITCHEN - CONTINUOUS

Mark drinks a glass of water. Renee ENTERS. She comes over and washes her hands in the sink. Boris tries to get Mark's attention.

> LINDY (O.S.)
> Mom. Where are you? Wipe me.

> RENEE TRULSON
> Why don't you say hello to Boris?

> MARK
> Hello, Boris.

Mark GOES to his bedroom.

> RENEE TRULSON
> We'll be talking later.

Renee quickly takes a drink of water - puts the glass down.

EXT. ASHLAND SPRINGS HOTEL - LARKS'S RESTAURANT - DAY

Dr. Beck stands outside the hotel as Molly WALKS UP.

                    MOLLY
Stood up?

                    DR. BECK
Stood up. The blind girl almost made it.

                    MOLLY
What?

                    DR. BECK
I saw her and her friend. I think she got scared.

                    MOLLY
You sure you got it straight now, Dad? Not a figment of your imagination?

I'm famished.

Dr. Beck gestures to enter the restaurant.

                    DR. BECK
How was your day?

EXT. ASHLAND SCENES - NIGHT

MONTAGE

EXT. ASHLAND MAIN STREET - NIGHT

Dr. Beck and Molly walk arm in arm down Main Street.

EXT. CAMILA'S BACKYARD - NIGHT

Camila, with her mother, embrace in a hammock.

NIGHT SOUNDS, COYOTES YIPPING

EXT. TRULSON HOME - BACKYARD - NIGHT

Most of the plants are in place at the Trulsons'. A tent is up in the backyard.

MONTAGE ENDS.

The shadow of Renee and Lindy come through the tent canvas. Renee TELLS a bedtime story. COYOTES CONTINUE TO YIP.

           RENEE TRULSON (O.S.)

Mr. Coyote was getting very old and had to be more careful for his own safety. He had been walking for hours and hours through a beautiful valley when he came upon a large tree. Do you hear the coyotes?

           LINDY (O.S.)

Yeah. There are lots of them out there.

           RENEE TRULSON (O.S.)

And they are all very busy having fun out in the moonlight... But this Coyote was very tired and wanted to rest, but he also needed to be safe...

He kindly asked the tree, "Please open up so I can rest safely in your care." The tree opened up and Mr. Coyote went inside to rest, then it closed to keep him safe. Mr. Coyote slept for hours.

           LINDY (O.S.)

Mommy, I think I want to sleep inside.

                    RENEE TRULSON (O.S.)
You sure?

                         LINDY (O.S.)
Those coyotes out there aren't sleeping. The trees not big enough for them. They're gonna eat us.

The SOUNDS OF NIGHT and the YIPS of the coyotes.

                    RENEE TRULSON (O.S.)
Maybe Daddy can come out and check on us so no coyotes will come in the yard.

                         LINDY (O.S.)
Okay.

                    RENEE TRULSON (O.S.)
Well when Coyote woke up, he said, "Let me out, Mr. Tree," but nothing happened. He said, "Please let me out now!" And again nothing happened.

INT. MARK'S BEDROOM - CONTINUOUS

Mark peruses a map. He has clothing, a hunting knife, and snack packs on his bed next to his backpack. His window is open. He walks to the window - listens.

                    RENEE TRULSON (O.S.)
         Getting angry, Mr. Coyote knocked hard

                          (MORE)

> RENEE TRULSON (O.S. CONT'D)
> on the tree, but Mr. Tree would not open up.
>
> Mr. Tree said, "I'm upset with you Mr. Coyote for not having said "please" the first time you spoke to me." So Mr. Tree didn't let Mr. Coyote out.

INT/EXT. TENT - CONTINUOUS

Renee and Lindy come out of the tent - WALK to the house.

> RENEE TRULSON (O.S.)
> "Ah, come on you old ugly tree," Coyote cried. "Just let me out!"
>
> But that ugly old tree didn't answer. So Mr. Coyote decided to take off his arms one at a time and put them through a small hole that a woodpecker made.

Mark closes the window - goes back to the bed.

INT. LINDY'S BEDROOM – NIGHT (a few minutes later)

Lindy lies in bed wide awake. Renee sits at the end of the bed. She pantomimes the removal of all body parts - starting with pulling on Lindy's legs. Lindy GIGGLES. It becomes a cooperative play in bed.

> RENEE TRULSON
> Then Coyote put his legs through the hole one at a time by taking them off.
>
> (MORE)

                    RENEE TRULSON (O.S. CONT'D)
Then he put his whole body through by taking it off. "I'll show you Mr. Tree, you can't keep me in here."

Next Mr. Coyote tried to put his head through the hole, but it was too big. His ears were in the way. So he took off his ears and put them through the hole.

He tried to get his head through again, but his eyes were too big. So Mr. Coyote took his eyes off and put them through the hole.

                                LINDY
Mommy, did somebody take Katy's eyes out and hide them?

                          RENEE TRULSON
No, now it's time to close your eyes.

Renee puts the covers over Lindy.

Lindy closes her eyes. Renee puts her hands over Lindy's eyes.

                          RENEE TRULSON
That's all that Katy could see...

It's sleepy time now. We'll finish the story another night.

                                LINDY
Did Mr. Coyote get his eyes back?

                    RENEE TRULSON

> Not for a while. He had to get out of the hole and put his body back together first.

A kiss good night - and LIGHTS OUT. Renee EXITS.

INT. BEN'S AND RENEE'S BEDROOM/BATHROOM - NIGHT

Ben is out of the shower toweling himself off. He checks his face - combs his hair - brushes his teeth. Renee's mirror image ENTERS. She watches him. They look at each other to read the internal dialogue.

                    RENEE TRULSON

> I was thinking about that silly old coyote story I was telling Lindy. The one I would tell Katy and Mark.

                    BEN TRULSON

> And?

                    RENEE TRULSON

> Mark's in that hole in the tree and it's too small for him to get out.

                    BEN TRULSON

> That's because Katy's in there with him.

RENEE TRULSON

> I guess... Are we doing okay?

They ENTER the bedroom. Ben puts on a pajamas shirt.

BEN TRULSON

No.

RENEE TRULSON

You going to bed?

BEN TRULSON

Not necessarily. You want a glass of wine?

RENEE TRULSON

Yeah, I do. You coming back?

BEN TRULSON

Yeah. We're not done with this Dr. Beck.

Renee changes out of her clothes.

RENEE TRULSON

Bring me my book from the kitchen table.

Ben EXITS. Renee sits on the bed - lost in thought.

Ambivalent, she can't decide to take her socks off or leave them on - to shower or to wait.

RENEE TRULSON

You coming?

Ben ENTERS with the book, newspaper, and two glasses of wine. He's agitated.

BEN TRULSON

You taking a bath?

Renee is still lost in thought. She takes the book and glass of wine - takes a drink. Ben throws the paper on the bed - deposits the wine next to his bedside lamp.

> RENEE TRULSON

Are we calling a moratorium on confronting Mark tonight?

> BEN TRULSON

No! Not me. We live with a son who is not a brother to Lindy. I can't touch him. He's doing lousy in school. You're afraid of his anger. I'm afraid of your fricking feelings. Are we doing okay? What kind of a moronic statement is that?

> RENEE TRULSON

What are we going to do?

> BEN TRULSON

First, I want to talk some more with Camila.

> RENEE TRULSON

Why? Remember the history, Ben. She's not going to snitch on Mark.

That gets us back to Dr. Beck.

> BEN TRULSON

I want to talk to Mark tonight.

> RENEE TRULSON

Tomorrow.

BEN TRULSON
You gotta stop this bullshit.

Renee in underpants and bra, decides to put on a robe, sits at the end of the bed.

RENEE TRULSON
Let me finish the story.

Ben waits - watches Renee.

RENEE TRULSON
I found out from Miranda that Mark wanted Camila to go with him to Lark's to meet with this psychologist.

BEN TRULSON
What's this psychologist doing meeting with our son at Lark's?

RENEE TRULSON
I'm going to find out tomorrow. Anyway, Mark was dressed up as Katy.

BEN TRULSON
YOU'VE GOT TO BE KIDDING!

RENEE TRULSON
Some kids from school apparently saw Mark and confronted him.

BEN TRULSON
Why wouldn't they?

RENEE TRULSON

Dr. Beck saw the confrontation. Camila told Miranda that Dr. Beck called Mark "Katy."

BEN TRULSON

Katy?

RENEE TRULSON

I'm going to his office. Obviously Mark has been putting Dr. Beck on in phone conversations that he's Katy.

BEN TRULSON

I don't get it. I'm coming with you. So what if he has appointments all day?

RENEE TRULSON

He's going to see us. I know a little about ethics, you know.

BEN TRULSON

This madness is making me crazy. Mark dressing up again as Katy?

INT. MARKS'S BEDROOM - NIGHT

Mark is counting money. He has earphones on.

The phone rings. He takes off his earphones - answers the call.

MARK

Hello.

> DR. BECK (O.S.)
> I missed you at the restaurant.

Mark stammers.

> MARK
> I got scared.

INTERCUT BIZARRE PHONE CONVERSATION

INT. DR. BECK'S LIVING ROOM - NIGHT

> DR. BECK
> I'm willing to talk with you if you meet me at my office with your parents.

INT. MARK'S BEDROOM - NIGHT

> MARK
> My parents? I've changed my mind. I won't call any more.

> DR. BECK
> What are you afraid of? What's making you hurt so much, Katy?

> MARK
> Why do you say Katy when you know I'm not her?

A beat.

> DR. BECK
> Do you have any brothers and sisters?

Mark stammers.

MARK

Yeah... yeah. I have a brother and sister.

DR. BECK

Tell me about how you being blind affects your brother and sister.

MARK

What do you mean?

DR. BECK

Who gets most of the attention from your parents?

MARK

Katy.

DR. BECK

Are you talking about you or someone else?

MARK

You're confusing me.

DR. BECK

Tell me the names of your brother and sister.

MARK

My sister is Lindy.

DR. BECK

How old is she?

MARK

Five.

DR. BECK

What's it like for her to know she has a sister who is blind? Does she even understand at five years of age what it means to be blind? And how about your brother?

MARK

I don't want to talk anymore.

(pauses)

Did you hear? I don't want to talk any more.

DR. BECK

Are you sure now, Katy? I can tell you now this isn't something you can do yourself. It's too much for you to think about how your little sister and...

MARK

(sputtering)

My sister was born because my parents know deep down that I'm going to die, so they wanted to replace me without even talking to me and my brother. Everything is my fault because I'm blind.

DR. BECK

What about your brother? Who's going to take care of your brother if you die?

                    MARK

My brother doesn't need anybody. We don't get along.

                    DR. BECK

Why is that?

                    MARK

You'll have to ask him. I hate talking about him. I'm going now. I won't call you anymore.

                    DR. BECK

Let me talk to your brother...Let me talk to your brother.

Mark doesn't answer.

                    DR. BECK

Mark... Mark.

Mark gets off the phone. MARK is a boy on a mission. He fills his backpack. Dr. Beck slowly puts the phone down - sits still in the dim light.

EXT. PSYCHOLOGIST'S BUILDING/OFFICE - DAY

INT. OFFICE RECEPTION - DAY

Freida is nervous. She checks her watch. A PATIENT sits waiting.

                    FREIDA NELSON

I'm sorry. We have emergencies, you know.

The patient reads a magazine, checks his watch.

INT. DR BECK'S OFFICE - DAY

Dr. Beck looks at the poster of family pictures with Ben and Renee.

>   DR. BECK
> I can't get over the resemblance with whom I saw downtown.

>   RENEE TRULSON
> When Katy and Mark were little, they would play dress up. Mark would wear clothes that Katy outgrew. Then he would put on the sunglasses and walk around the house. I never saw a boy so determined to mimic Katy.

>   DR. BECK
> How do you mean?

FLASHBACK (10 YEARS EARLIER) - RENEE'S POV

INT. ROGUE RIVER - CABIN - KITCHEN - DAY

4-YEAR-OLD MARK is dressed in Katy's hand-me-downs with sunglasses on.

RENEE TRULSON (O.S)

> Eventually I would say it's time to stop. He would push it.

>   DR. BECK (O.S.)
> Jealousy?

                    RENEE TRULSON (O.S.)
    I suppose.

                    BEN TRULSON (O.S.)
    He'd get aggressive with her.

YOUNG 9-YEAR-OLD Katy ENTERS the kitchen. Mark tries to push her out. Katy strikes her brother. Mark pushes Katy back.

END FLASHBACK

INT. DR. BECKS OFFICE - DAY

                    RENEE TRULSON
    Then I would shame him.

                    DR. BECK
    Shame him?

                    RENEE TRULSON
    At that time, I thought it was better than burning his rear. I don't understand it? Sometimes they would live in their own fantasy world.

ANOTHER FLASHBACK (FIVE YEARS EARLIER) - RENEE'S POV

EXT. ROGUE RIVER CABIN - YARD - DAY

The three of them, Mark and Camila age 9, and Katy age 14, come up the path, Katy hanging on to Mark's soccer shorts. MARK dumps the shells, rocks, and bones and whatever kids collect. They cooperatively play - passing objects to Katy to feel. Mark gets bored - sees the soccer ball lying on the lawn - starts kicking the ball back and forth with Camila.

                RENEE TRULSON (O.S.)

Mark and Camila would take Katy on little adventure/collecting walks, which Katy loved. Then Camila and Mark would start playing their own physical games. Katy would get livid.

                DR. BECK (O.S.)

Angry at Mark?

BEN TRULSON (O.S.)

At Mark and Camila. She'd start screaming. "They're not letting me play." So Mark and Camila would start teasing her. They'd hide from her. It sometimes was fun and sometimes hostile and we'd have to get in there and stop it.

Katy, listening, tries to intercept the ball. They play keep away from her by throwing and catching the soccer ball. They finally let Katy get it. Then Mark and Camila run and hide.

Katy carries the soccer ball and throws it in Mark and Camila's direction. Katy throws a temper tantrum - begins to stamp the ground. Then scratches herself. Mark and Camila LAUGH.

END FLASHBACK

INT. DR. BECK'S OFFICE - DAY

RENEE TRULSON

Katy had a temper. She'd yell, "I'm going to tell Mom about all our secrets." That would bring them back.

DR. BECK

You let them keep their secrets?

BEN TRULSON

We did.

RENEE TRULSON

Was that wrong?

A beat.

DR. BECK

What are you going to do?

BEN TRULSON

You're the doctor.

RENEE TRULSON

We've been through this with professionals like you the last...
    (looks at Ben)
I don't know how many years. But now there's a new twist. He's acting out what he did when he was little, before Katy died.

> DR. BECK
> (rhetorically)
> Dressing up again. Just at an age when a lot of kids have an identity crisis.

> BEN TRULSON
> He's still all boy.

Ben gets up to leave.

> RENEE TRULSON
> Where you going?

> BEN TRULSON
> It's our problem to solve.

Renee doesn't budge. Ben stands at the door. Ben and Renee stare at each other.

> DR. BECK
> Obviously, you have heard of post-traumatic stress disorder.

> BEN TRULSON
> We've done the books and all the consultations. The point is Mark has stonewalled all efforts to get him to tell his side of the accident. Camila says she doesn't know how Katy got on the cliff.
>
> Are you coming, Renee?

Renee won't budge.

Renee starts CRYING. Ben SIGHS - comes back - sits down.

>DR. BECK
>
>Sometimes they can't tell their story. Was he angry at Katy the day of the drowning?
>
>BEN TRULSON
>
>Very.
>
>RENEE TRULSON
>(tearful)
>
>But Ben, we intervened, and they were over it.

Renee looks in her purse for a tissue. Dr. Beck hands her a box.

>DR. BECK
>
>Memories become cloudy. Especially for kids. You never know how they fill in the blanks.
>
>BEN TRULSON
>
>Have you had experience with PTSD?
>
>DR. BECK
>
>Sorry. I'm just thinking out loud. Yes, to PTSD. With trauma, it all gets shuffled around and his reality doesn't conform to what you may remember.
>
>BEN TRULSON
>
>His unreality.

>   DR. BECK
>
>   Apparently it's all real to Mark. And
>   now it's being acted out.
>
>   BEN TRULSON
>   Why?
>
>   DR. BECK
>   It's called readiness.

RENEE TRULSON

>   Readiness? It makes sense if I know
>   what you mean...
>
>   Our move to the valley... We vacationed
>   on the river every summer with my parents until Katy drowned.
>
>   Ben, I want to bring Mark in.

Ben looks at Dr. Beck. He's skeptical.

>   DR. BECK
>   I think we ought to pray about it.

Ben and Renee are startled. They look at each other.

>   BEN TRULSON
>   We're not Christians.
>
>   DR. BECK
>   What does that have to do with this? Do
>   you want to bring your son in?

Ambivalent, Ben, and Renee look at each other. There is a long silence. Dr. Beck BEGINS TO PRAY.

Slowly, after looking at each other, Ben and Renee bow their heads.

> DR. BECK
>
> Father in Heaven, I pray for divine direction. I ask for your compassion and wisdom with Ben and Renee as they pray with me. Help us to put our hearts and minds together to do our part. With your help, I ask you to bring forth a healing for their son, Mark... In Jesus' name, Amen.

His head remains bowed, eyes closed. Ben and Renee look at each other. Renee wipes tears away with the tissue. Finally, Renee begins to pray.

> RENEE TRULSON
>
> Creator of Heaven and Earth... You are me... I am you... May the winds of heaven blow softly on Mark–and the Great Spirit bless all who enter in his life.

INT. GARAGE - DAY

Mark pumps up his bicycle tires. When he's done, he fastens the air pump to his bicycle. His backpack sits on the concrete floor next to him.

> BEN TRULSON (O.S.)
> Thou conqueror of afflictions, help us to
>
> (MORE)

                    BEN TRULSON (O.S. CONT'D)
          be more mindful that our sorrows and
          suffering overwhelm our need to love
          and understand our son, Mark.

          Bring a balm of clear water to pour on
          the roots of our afflictions... Today, let
          us begin anew.

Mark RINGS the bell on the handlebars of the bicycle. Then Mark puts a hunting knife in his backpack. He HEARS A BICYCLE coming into the driveway. Mark panics. He hides his backpack and RUNS FROM THE GARAGE THROUGH THE:

INT. KITCHEN/HALL

To his:

INT. MARK'S BEDROOM

He locks the door.

Mark scrambles to hide anything in his bedroom that may reveal that he is going to run. The DOORBELL RINGS. A KNOCK on the outside door.

EXT. TRULSON HOME - DAY

Camila stands at the door - looks around. She walks to the garage - peeks in. She turns to leave as Mark opens the door. Mark COMES OUT.

                    MARK
          What are you doing here?

CAMILA
Your parents asked me to come over after school. I thought you were sick.

MARK
I'm not gonna go to that school.

CAMILA
I wouldn't either after the hole you put yourself in. So you really skipped today?

MARK
Yeah. It was a super long day.

EXT. TRULSON BACKYARD - CONTINUOUS

Mark walks away - stares into the new plant arrangement.

MARK
Time sure crawls when life sucks.

CAMILA
What?

MARK
I said, time sure crawls when life sucks.

CAMILA
That's the truth.

Camila walks around Mark.

CAMILA

I already told the kids at school we were playing a prank on some friends.

MARK

That's a bunch of shit. They know I don't have any friends.

CAMILA

Okay, I lied. I told them you were a transvestite. And you were going to get a sex change.

Camila goes over and sits on a backyard-covered swing.

MARK

Liar.

CAMILA

I got the pictures to prove it. You used to dress up in Katy's clothes.

MARK

So?

Mark sits down next to Camila.

CAMILA

So why can't you let Katy be dead?

Mark jumps up - walks away.

MARK

I want to live somewhere else.

CAMILA

Mark, get real.

A beat.

MARK

So what did my parents want?

CAMILA

Like I'm gonna tell you? You haven't done me any favors.

There is a combination of tension and attraction between Mark and Camila.

MARK

Have you and your mom ever been back to the house on the river?

CAMILA

No. I told Mom I wanna to go back. Why?

MARK

Just wondering. You want to go with me?

CAMILA
(surprised)
You're going? Yeah. Let's get outta here.

Camila gets up - goes to an area with flowers. She looks at them - looks at Mark.

CAMILA

You look so sad.

She picks a flower and puts it in her hair. Then she picks another and walks over to put it in Mark's hair. She stands close.

CAMILA

(teasing)

I've never given a boyfriend—

Mark pushes on her shoulders. Camila pushes her way back in.

CAMILA

I've always had the hots for you.

He accepts the flower in his hair but won't make eye contact.

CAMILA

Remember when we used to kiss?

Camila moves close.

MARK

(embarrassed)

Get away.

Camila slowly walks among the garden plants and flowers. Mark drags along behind.

CAMILA

I want it to be like it used to be.

She looks back at him. Mark stops.

CAMILA

Don't you?

MARK

It can't ever be like that again.

The Trulson car is HEARD driving into the driveway.

MARK

I'm outta here.

Mark throws off the flower and RUNS INSIDE the house.

CAMILA

Where' you going?

Camila walks around the side of the garage. She walks up to the station wagon as Renee and Ben EXIT. Renee has her purse and carries the poster. Lindy is in the car seat.

CAMILA

Want me to get Lindy out?

Renee nods.

RENEE TRULSON

Where's Mark?

CAMILA

He just went in.

BEN TRULSON

I'm surprised he came out to see you.

> LINDY

You going to play with me?

> CAMILA

I get to baby sit you.

Camila and Lindy walk hand in hand ahead of Ben and Renee. Ben stops Renee.

> BEN TRULSON

You ready for this?

> RENEE TRULSON

I'm too emotionally exhausted to think about it. Why not?

INT. MARK'S BEDROOM - CONTINUOUS

Mark looks frozen as he fiddles with his Swiss Army Knife - opening and closing the blades. A KNOCK on the door. He stuffs the knife in his pocket.

> RENEE TRULSON (O.S.)

Are you up?

> MARK

Yeah.

> RENEE TRULSON (O.S.)

Open up.

> MARK

I'm still sick.

RENEE TRULSON (O.S.)
Open up.

Mark opens the door and Renee and Ben WALK IN.

MARK
I thought you both had to work?

RENEE TRULSON
Come into the kitchen.

MARK
What's going on?

They walk to the kitchen.

INT. KITCHEN - CONTINUOUS

On the kitchen table lies the poster. Camila is looking at it.

BEN TRULSON
We're going to see Dr. Beck.

MARK
(sputtering)
Who?

RENEE TRULSON
Camila is taking care of Lindy.

Mark turns to go to the bedroom.

RENEE TRULSON
You can't run from this, Mark. We know everything.

Mark is aghast.

> RENEE TRULSON
> And we're going now.

> MARK
> But I'm sick.

> BEN TRULSON
> Go get in the car.

Mark takes a long look at his dad as Ben walks towards him. He looks at Camila as if she has betrayed him.

> MARK
> You're all mad at me.

> BEN TRULSON
> Madder than you can ever imagine.

Mark looks at his mother. She nods her head. Mark wants to cut and run. He walks to the door. Ben moves in the same direction ahead of him.

INT. OFFICE RECEPTION – DAY (LATER)

Ben and Renee WALK IN with Mark behind them. Freida gives Mark the once over.

> FREIDA NELSON
> So then, you're the person I was talking to. Doctor is waiting for you.

All walk to the office. Ben signals for Mark to go ahead.

Mark stops.

                    MARK
          I wanna go in alone.

Ben looks at Renee.

                RENEE TRULSON
          If that's what you want.

INT. DR. BECK'S OFFICE - DAY

Dr. Beck stands by his desk. Mark ENTERS. They look at each other. Dr. Beck breaks into a smile.

                  DR. BECK
          Before I saw you yesterday, I had a dream.

Dr. Beck gestures to Mark to sit down. Mark sits down.

                  DR. BECK
          I woke up soaked from sweat... We had a cabin at Diamond Lake. Our daughters were out playing in a canoe and it capsized. I laughed. They were good swimmers.

          Then my one daughter, Molly, didn't come up. It was late summer and the water had turned murky with green algae.

          My other daughter dove under. She kept coming up yelling, "I can't see under there. I can't see Molly."

                    (MORE)

DR. BECK (CONT'D)

I knew when you said, "I couldn't see," something important had happened to you. You said, "At night, at night it never goes away.... The dream, the dream."

MARK

It doesn't go away.

DR. BECK

Can you tell me about it?

MARK

My parents told you everything.

DR. BECK

That's their story and their struggle with Katy's death. But that's not your story.

Mark remains cautious - tries to change the subject.

MARK

You wanted to tell me about your dream.

DR. BECK

That's not why you're here.

MARK

Well, what happened to your daughter? Was it just a dream?

Dr. Beck sees that Mark is not ready to talk. He stands up - paces.

> DR. BECK
>
> So, I had this dream of being underwater looking for Molly. Every time I thought I was getting closer to her, she would disappear. Then I woke up. My wife said I was talking in my sleep. This dream is not new, except my wife said I cried Katy, not Molly. "Katy," she said. "Katy."

Dr. Beck sits down again in a rocking chair next to the couch that Mark is sitting in. Mark scans Dr. Beck's office. Dr. Beck looks at Mark - waits.

> DR. BECK
>
> When I saw you in the street, my heart leaped. "Katy's alive."

Dr. Beck waits.

> MARK
>
> And then you saw me in the alley.

> DR. BECK
>
> I did.

> MARK
>
> What happened in the lake?

> DR. BECK
>
> Oh, I found her. She had hit her head on a stump underwater.

MARK
Wait. Was, was she...?

DR. BECK
Dead? Oh no! Molly is my miracle daughter. It was touch and go after we found her and brought her to shore.

Mark gets up - begins to pace.

MARK
Well, I didn't find Katy.

Dr. Beck doesn't speak. He waits. Mark abruptly turns - faces Dr. Beck.

MARK
The dream. Why do I keep having the dream?

DR. BECK
Tell me the whole story.

MARK
(begins to hyperventilate)
I can't... I can't.

Mark walks towards the door - faces away.

DR. BECK
How did you get in the water?

MARK
I jumped from the cliff.

DR. BECK
Before that?

MARK
We were running from the cabin.

DR. BECK
Who was running?

MARK
Camila, Katy, and me. I fell.

DR. BECK
Everyone knows this?

MARK
Yes.

DR. BECK
Then what happened?

MARK
I jumped off the cliff.

Dr. Beck has recognized something.

DR. BECK
I found it.

Mark turns - faces Dr. Beck.

MARK
Found what?

DR. BECK

The empty space.

MARK

What're you talking about? There isn't any space. She fell off the cliff. I jumped in after her.

DR. BECK

I can take you there.

MARK
(puzzled)

Drive me there?

DR. BECK

We could do that, but we can do it here. I can tell you're ready.

MARK
(getting anxious and
frustrated)

Ready for what? You don't make any sense. I wanna get out of here.

Mark turns to the door, then turns back to look at Dr. Beck. Dr. Beck waits.

MARK

What do I have to do?

Dr. Beck gestures to Mark to sit down. Mark comes back - sits down.

DR. BECK

Watch my hands.

Dr. Beck moves two fingers in different directions in front of Mark.

DR. BECK

Please don't move your head. You left the house with Katy and your friend...

MARK

Camila.

DR. BECK

Then what do you see?

MARK

Camila.

DR. BECK

Who's behind you?

MARK

Katy. I was trying to catch up when I fell and then I—

DR. BECK

Don't close your eyes. Watch my hands. Time is slowing down. You see yourself falling forward... Back up... Back up.

Mark makes a sudden lunge forward.

FLASHBACK (FIVE YEARS EARLIER)

EXT. PATH - DAY

Young Mark makes a sudden lunge forward. Katy flies over Mark - rolls to the edge of the path. Camila runs ahead on the path, Boris following.

> DR. BECK (O.S.)
> Back up! Back up!

THE ACTION BACKS UP IN SURREAL SLOW MOTION.

Katy CRIES - angrily turns - FLAILS at MARK with her fists.

> KATY
> I HATE YOU! YOU HURT ME!

Mark still on the ground, HITS Katy back. Katy's sunglasses fall. Katy is out of control. She PULLS Mark's hair - SCRATCHES him - KICKS at him. She gets up - staggers/crawls ahead.

MARK'S POV

The POV PANS BACK to Mark's legs. The laces of one of his tennis shoes are caught in blackberry branches. He tries to free the lace. It's stuck. He rips the shoe off - angrily tries to pull his shoe free.

Katy staggers ahead.

> YOUNG MARK (O.S.)
> Katy! STOP!

                    KATY
                  (shouting)
            Camila, I'm coming!

Katy DISAPPEARS.

The POV goes back to the tennis shoe. MARK SCREAMS - tugs on the shoe to free it from the blackberry branches.

END FLASHBACK

INT. DR. BECK'S OFFICE - DAY

Mark is sitting on the floor sweating, crying, and rocking back and forth with the same motion as on the beach seen in an earlier flashback.

                  DR. BECK
            Mark... Mark. Can you talk?

Mark looks at Dr. Beck with glazed tearful eyes.

                   MARK
            Why am I sitting on the floor?

Mark leaps up and RUNS from the office. Dr. Beck FOLLOWS.

INT. OFFICE RECEPTION - CONTINUOUS

Mark RUNS THROUGH the office and OUT THE DOOR. Both Ben and Renee are standing. Ben RUNS AFTER Mark.

                RENEE TRULSON
            What happened?

DR. BECK

Come in, please.

Renee follows Dr. Beck. Freida walks to the door to check on Ben and Mark.

INT. DR. BECK'S OFFICE - CONTINUOUS

Dr. Beck gestures to Renee to sit down. Renee has a worried look - stays standing.

DR. BECK

Your son had an abreaction.

RENEE TRULSON

Abreaction?

DR. BECK

He recalled some aspect of the drowning of Katy that he, for one reason or another, hadn't remembered.

RENEE TRULSON

That's the reason for his scream? What was it?

DR. BECK

He didn't say. It was on the way to the river. Before Katy fell to the water.

RENEE TRULSON

Camila said she never saw what happened.

DR. BECK
There's more. Keep a close eye on him... Call me.

RENEE TRULSON
Should we make another appointment?

DR. BECK
Absolutely. He needs to find words for what he experienced today.

Renee turns to leave.

EXT. TRULSON'S DRIVEWAY - DAY

The station wagon rolls into the driveway. Mark leaps out - RUNS INSIDE.

INT. KITCHEN - CONTINUOUS

Camila and Lindy are at the table cutting and pasting.

Mark ENTERS - EXITS to his bedroom. Camila stands up to follow. Lindy jumps off her chair.

LINDY
Mark is mad.

IN WALKS Ben and Renee. Camila looks at them to get a reading on what's going on.

LINDY
Mark's mad again, Mommy.

RENEE TRULSON
Camila, go in and see if he'll talk to you.

INT. MARK'S BEDROOM - CONTINUOUS

Mark lies on the bed with his pillow over his head. Camila KNOCKS on the door.

            CAMILA (O.S.)
    Can I come in?

            MARK
    No.

            CAMILA (O.S.)
    You forgot to lock the door.

            MARK
    Stay away.

Camila PEEKS THROUGH the door.

            CAMILA
    I won't.

Camila walks in - sits on the bed next to Mark.

            MARK
    Lock the door.

Camila locks the door - comes back to the bed. She hesitates, then puts her hand on Mark's back. He abruptly pulls away. Camila persists. Slowly she begins to massage his back.

            MARK
    I'm not talking.

Camila lies down next to Mark, with her arm on his back. Mark pulls away. Camila pulls in closer.

                    CAMILA
          What are we going to do?

EXT. TRULSON HOME STREET - DAY - SUNRISE

A NEWSPAPER BOY on his bicycle throws a newspaper. MARK with backpack, RIDES OUT of the driveway onto the street - goes the opposite way.

EXT. CAMILA'S HOME - DAY

Mark rides into a driveway - jumps off his bike - walks the bike around to the back of the house. The LIGHT IS ON in the kitchen. He peeks through the kitchen window.

EXT/INT - CONTINUOUS

Camila is at the table writing a note. She sees Mark - puts her fingers to her lips. Mark waits. Camila picks up her backpack, turns off the kitchen light and EXITS. She opens the side door to the garage and TAKES OUT her bicycle.

EXT. GARAGE - CONTINUOUS

Mark WHISPERS.

                    MARK
          What did you put on the note?

                    CAMILA
          I told her we were going to your grand-
          parent's house on the river.

Mark SLAMS down his bicycle and walks away. Camila walks up to him.

> CAMILA

What's wrong?

> MARK

We'll never get there. They'll pick us up.

> CAMILA

Well, if I didn't tell mother, she'd call 911 when she gets up. This way she'll panic and run to your parents and they'll all try to find us.

> MARK

Go in and tear up that note. I'm going alone.

> CAMILA

No, you're not. Let's get creative. We'll have at least a two to three-hour start.

Mark jumps on his bike and TAKES OFF. Camila jumps on her bike and follows him.

EXT. STREET - CONTINUOUS

Mark stops a half block away - turns, sees CAMILA riding up.

> MARK

I don't want you along.

                    CAMILA
    Well, sucks for you, I'm coming.

They RIDE OFF.

EXT. GROCERY STORE - DAY - MONTAGE

Mark and Camila EXIT from a grocery store with backpacks on. They walk to their bicycles, get on, and ride off on a two lane highway.

EXT. ELEMENTARY SCHOOL - PLAY GROUND - DAY

They pull off at an elementary school ground at a play area where there is a table. They sit down - pull out food from their backpacks and eat. They go over and play on the swings. Some MOMS AND CHILDREN play close by.

END MONTAGE

                    CAMILA
    What time is it?

MARK checks his watch.

                    MARK
    Nine fifteen.

INT. CAMILA'S HOME KITCHEN - DAY

                    CAMILA (O.S.)
    Mom is up. She's crying. Give her ten
    minutes. She'll get her shit together
    enough to call your mom.

Drenched tissue lies on the kitchen table next to the note. Miranda calls on the phone - blows her nose.

INT. TRULSON HOME   KITCHEN - DAY

MONTAGE OF QUICK CUTS AS DESCRIBED IN DIALOGUE

Ben and Renee read the morning paper while Lindy plays with her breakfast cereal, banana and toast.

> MARK (O.S.)
>
> Mom will answer the phone... tell Dad to stop Lindy from making a mess and to stop feeding Boris her toast.
>
> Then mom will jump up and give Dad the phone. She'll run to my bedroom and knock. But I won't be there because I locked the door and went out the window.
>
> So she'll come running back to Dad, who has washed the food off Lindy, and they'll go running out to the backyard and check my bedroom window.
>
> MARK (O.S.)
>
> Then they'll run back inside and call your mother and tell her to get ready so they can come and find us.

INT. CAMILA'S HOME - BATHROOM - DAY

CAMILA (O.S.)

> That will take them a half hour, and then another half hour after they get to our house.
>
> Mom will have to shower, powder herself, change three times, go to the bathroom three times, spray herself with that stinky perfume, and decide how many drugs to take before she leaves, and then how much to take along.

INT. TRULSON HOME - KITCHEN - DAY

> MARK (O.S.)
> And then my dad will plot out where he'll think he'll find us. I figure we've got an hour and forty minutes and then we'll have to hide.

END MONTAGE

EXT. ELEMENTARY SCHOOL PLAYGROUND - DAY

Mark has the map out on the table.

> MARK
> Let's go. There's a back road that parallels the highway. It goes along Wolf Creek.

Mark and Camila clean up. Camila waves to the other children at the playground and they ride off.

EXT. PSYCHOLOGIST'S BUILDING - DAY

INT. DR. BECK'S OFFICE - DAY

Dr. Beck, Ben and Renee Trulson, and Miranda are in a heated discussion with Dr. Beck. Miranda is "unglued." Lindy is in the corner in a play area for children.

> MIRANDA
>
> Camila has never been away from me. She won't know what to do.

> BEN TRULSON
>
> Now, Miranda. We have two smart kids. Emotionally screwed up, yes, but....

> RENEE TRULSON
>
> I want to know what they had in mind. I think they planned to run away.
>
> (to Dr. Beck)
> Did he say anything to you?

Miranda interrupts.

> MIRANDA
>
> What makes our children want to turn against us? What did we do to them that makes them hate us so?

> BEN TRULSON
>
> They planned this.

Dr. Beck doesn't know whom to answer to first as the MULTIPLE CONVERSATIONS continue.

RENEE TRULSON

Camila said something about going back to my parent's house on the river this weekend. She said it to me in the kitchen last night. She said she and Mark were talking about it earlier.

BEN TRULSON

I want to hear from the Doctor here. Our son's been clammed up tighter than a can of sardines the last five years and then he uncorks his top.

RENEE TRULSON

(breaks into a smile)

Can of sardines?

DR. BECK

Miranda, these children don't hate you, they—

Ben is intense - gets LOUD.

BEN TRULSON

Doc, I want you to cut to the chase. Are our kids at risk?

DR. BECK

I haven't met Camila. I only saw her with Katy. I'm sorry, Mark, on the main street. Mark has been disconnected from his feelings. Now a transition is happening where he could be unpredictable.

BEN TRULSON

Unpredictable? Jesus Christ. Cut the psychobabble. Is he suicidal?

LINDY

Daddy, you said a swear word.

BEN TRULSON

(to Lindy)

I apologize.

(back to Dr. Beck)

Do you have children?

RENEE TRULSON

Ben! Ben. Calm down.

DR. BECK

I have children.

BEN TRULSON

Well, answer my question.

DR. BECK

Yes, I'm worried. But he has Camila.

Miranda swoons.

DR. BECK

Miranda, Camila is protecting Mark from something. Or the two are co-conspirators on some dark secret that has something to do with Katy.

BEN TRULSON

That makes no sense to me. Until the other day, those two kids hadn't seen each other for five years.

RENEE TRULSON

Would you slow down, Ben?

DR. BECK

Someone needs to calculate the degree of rage Mark has for himself. Camila may not be able to control that.

RENEE TRULSON

You're talking about whether he's suicidal or not.

DR. BECK

Has he done anything stupid in the past?

RENEE TRULSON

Nothing other than skipping school and running away a half dozen times or more. He says to us, if you call the police, I'll stay away longer. He's stubborn.

BEN TRULSON

And unrevealing.

RENEE TRULSON

Emotionally unrevealing.

DR. BECK

Until yesterday in my office. Don't you think you ought to call the police?

BEN TRULSON

That has never worked. He makes a hide and seek game of it. In the past, he'd call us and say he'd come home as long as the police aren't there.

DR. BECK

This is confusing. Where does he go?

RENEE TRULSON

He doesn't tell us. Food disappears.

DR. BECK

But that's not what is happening now. So what are you going to do?

BEN TRULSON

They're riding their bikes to the river.

DR. BECK

The place of Katy's drowning?

RENEE TRULSON

Yes.

DR. BECK

How far away?

RENEE TRULSON

Eighty miles. Ben, if Dr. Beck thinks Mark is suicidal, we need to get there first.

DR. BECK

This is your parents' cabin?

RENEE TRULSON

Yes. What shall we do?

DR. BECK

Well, it's getting to the scene of the accident before Mark and Camila get there.

Renee turns to Ben - grips his hand.

RENEE TRULSON

Ben, if we're not going to involve the police, I want Dr. Beck to be there with us.

Ben turns back to Dr. Beck.

BEN TRULSON

What do you think?

DR. BECK

Let's go. I'll get my weekend bicycle ride in. Maybe we can catch them before they get there.

EXT. CREEK'S EDGE - DAY

MONTAGE

Two bicycles are parked along the creek. Boulders and lush forest cover the creek's edge. Tennis shoes sit on a flat rock. Mark and Camila are bent over in shallow water.

They try to catch salamanders. Mark catches one. Mark gets Camila to hold it. Eventually she lets it go as he scouts for flat rocks to skip. He tries to teach her to skip rocks.

DISSOLVE TO

Mark and Camila are napping. Camila sleeps peacefully. Mark sleeps fitfully - eventually gets up - paces - stops - looks into the river.

END MONTAGE

FLASHBACK (FIVE YEARS EARLIER) – YOUNG MARK'S POV

EXT. ROGUE RIVER'S EDGE (3) – DAY

A distance away, Ben lifts drowned Katy out of the river. The rest of the family including Miranda, Camila, and Boris run towards Ben.

END FLASHBACK POV

EXT. STATION WAGON - DAY

MONTAGE

Ben et al travel to a number of locations along the two-lane highway. Ben inquires about the teens at gas stations, drive-ins - ends up driving by the grocery store. A bicycle rack with bicycle is on back of the car, with glimpses of Dr. Beck, riding in front and Renee, Miranda, Lindy, and Boris taking up the rear seats.

EXT. ELEMENTARY SCHOOL YARD - SUNSET

They stop at the empty elementary school playground. Lindy and Miranda are asleep.

END OF MONTAGE.

EXT. CREEK'S EDGE - SUNSET

Mark and Camila throw sticks in a campfire. They also play with burning sticks.

> CAMILA

It's getting cold.

> MARK
> (euphoric)

If we get up early, we can be there in a couple hours.

> CAMILA

I'm wondering what's happening to Mom.

> MARK

Nothing's happening to your mom.

> CAMILA

I gotta call her.

> MARK
>
> Forget it. They're already at the cabin unless they're looking for us. I know Dad. He'll be driving all over the place trying to find us.

EXT. COUNTRY STORE - EVENING

Dr. Beck (backpack on) EXITS from the country store - walks by a gas station pump. He climbs on his bicycle and rides towards a motel.

EXT. DRIVE-IN - EVENING

Ben, Renee, Miranda, Lindy eat at an outside table.

Dr. Beck RIDES UP on his bicycle. Lindy is feeding Boris the rest of her hamburger. She LAUGHS when Boris LAPS UP the water from her cup.

Dr. Beck goes and finds a container and gets Boris more water. Lindy plays with whatever is near that she can climb on. Dr. Beck sits down and pulls out health foods from his bicycle pack.

Throughout the drama, Lindy TALKS/HUMS to herself spontaneously. She periodically asks permission (IMPROVISATION) to do things, which gets either a nod or head shake.

Dr. Beck seats himself at the table.

> RENEE TRULSON
>
> So what do we do now?
>
> MIRANDA
>
> Can't we check more parks?

BEN TRULSON

It's getting late. Let's get to the cabin. How about you, Robert?

DR. BECK

I'm in training for Ride Oregon. You said forty more miles to the Cabin. I'll stay at a motel tonight and ride the rest of the way tomorrow morning. Who knows, I may catch up with them and we'll ride in together.

RENEE TRULSON

Are you sure you want to do this?

DR. BECK

Yes.

RENEE TRULSON

We want to take care of your motel bill and breakfast and—

DR. BECK

Until we find them, this is my own little adventure, but with a purpose. Now show me the map.

EXT. MOTEL - NIGHT

Dr. Beck rides over to a motel next to the country store. He padlocks his bicycle and ENTERS.

EXT. COUNTRY ROAD - NIGHT

Mark and Camila pushing bicycles, slowly negotiate along a country road in the dark. Now and then a pickup or car or DRIVES BY.

CAMILA

This sucks, Mark.

MARK

The highway is ahead. I saw a motel when we rode in.

CAMILA

Mom's going to be pissed if she finds out we're sleeping in a motel together. Did you bring protection?

MARK

Shut up!

CAMILA

Just kidding.

They walk/ride silently. A bright yard light is on with a farmhouse and barn next to the road.

MARK

Wait!

CAMILA

What?

> MARK
>
> Dad used to tell me stories about sleeping in a barn when he was little.
>
> CAMILA
>
> I'm not sleeping in a barn. I don't want my first sexual exper—
>
> MARK
>
> You've been watching too much T.V. Be quiet. I'm thinking. I hope they don't have dogs.
>
> CAMILA
>
> Your thinking stinks. I don't trust you.

Mark and Camila walk a short way up the driveway. Mark cuts into the trees, Camila following. He quietly padlocks the bicycles to a tree.

EXT. BARNYARD - NIGHT

They sneak towards the barn. They slip around the side of the barn. In the dark, Camila touches the SNOUT OF A COW. She CRIES OUT.

> CAMILA
>
> Oh my God, what was that?
>
> MARK
>
> Shhh!

A DOG BARKS. Then TWO DOGS BARK. Mark and Camila are frozen to the barn wall. The dogs don't stop BARKING.

FARMER (O.S.)
Shut up, Shadow. You, too, Slip.

The dogs keep BARKING. FOOTSTEPS APPROACH on the gravel. The footsteps become quiet as the farmer enters the barn. The dogs COME RUNNING AROUND the corner of the barn BARKING. Mark and Camila take off running. The dogs give chase.

EXT. FARM YARD - NIGHT

FARMER (O.S.)
Hey! This is private property. Shadow! Slip! Come here!

The DOGS PULL OFF and DISAPPEAR.

EXT. TREES - NIGHT

Mark and Camila run through the trees. They hunker down and wait.

EXT. MOTEL - NIGHT

INT. MOTEL ROOM - NIGHT

Dr. Beck, out of the shower, finishes toweling off - begins dressing. He has nuts, dried fruit, and a liquid concoction on the small table. He glances through the curtains at the country store - turns away - picks up the motel phone.

EXT. MOTEL - NIGHT

Mark and Camila ride/walk/stop outside the motel. They hesitate.

CAMILA

What if they won't let us stay? They'll want ID and find out we're not brother and sister? It's probably illegal anyway.

MARK

You want to go to the store first?

CAMILA

Yeah. I'm really thirsty. Hungry, too.

MARK

Let's go.

EXT. COUNTRY STORE - NIGHT

A PICKUP is at the gas pump. Mark and Camila walk over to the store - park and padlock their bicycles and ENTER.

INT. COUNTRY STORE - CONTINUOUS

The storekeeper, HANK, and an ELDERLY COUPLE, ED and MARTHA, are the only occupants. Ed and Martha are buying groceries and getting gas for the pickup.

ED

Well, Hank, this the best time of the year for diggin' for clams.

HANK

Forecast says seventy-five degrees at Brookings. A good time to go, alright.

Mark listens to the conversation as Camila picks out drinks and snacks.

ED

Fill 'er up. I can get the bugs off that windshield.

HANK

Nah, I'll get it.
>(looks at MARK and
>Camila)
You kids in a hurry?

Hank and Ed walk to exit.

MARK

No. How far is it to Merlin from here?

The two men WALK OUT. Mark FOLLOWS.

EXT. COUNTRY STORE - NIGHT

Hank fills the gas and cleans the windshield, while Ed looks under the hood. Mark watches.

ED

I saw you come up here on those bikes of yours... You're not going to ride there tonight are you?

MARK

Nah. We're staying here.

ED

Well, it's about another forty miles, wouldn't you say so, Hank? That's a far ride for you and that young girl in there.

Martha and Camila EXIT from the store. Mark stands next to Ed - looks under the hood.

> MARK
>
> We're fine.

> ED
>
> I don't mean to get in your business, but you two seem to be running to or running from someone.

Martha and Camila APPROACH.

> MARTHA
>
> Ed, you don't need to be prying now.

> HANK
>
> Well, here we go now. A feller came in on a bike about half an hour ago looking for you two. I thought you were with him. He's staying over there right in that there motel. You been catching up with him?

> MARTHA
>
> See there, Ed. You keep thinking they're up to mischief and here they are taking a bicycle trip with their father.

Camila looks at Mark who looks trapped - unable to respond.

> CAMILA
>
> We've never met that man. He's been trying to follow us all day. We just got

here. We hid from him hoping he'd ride on.

There's a pause as all look at Mark to add to Camila's contrived drama.

> MARK
>
> We were at a drive in—

> HANK
>
> Mack's drive in—

> MARK
>
> —back there a few miles and he kept looking at my sister. Before that we stopped at an elementary school yard...

> MARTHA
>
> Must have been Williams Elementary—

> CAMILA
>
> And he was hanging around there watching the kids.

> HANK
>
> I've heard about them kind of fellers. So then, where' you trying to go tonight?

Camila looks at Mark. Mark hesitates.

> CAMILA
>
> Our parents are waiting for us at a cabin on the Rogue River outside of Merlin.

MARTHA

They let you ride your bicycles?

MARK

We're in a bicycle club.

HANK

I've heard of them there clubs. They come by here about every day.

MARTHA

Ed, why don't we give these young ones...

CAMILA

I'm Camila.

Martha looks at Mark.

MARK

Mark.

MARTHA

Like I was saying, why don't we give Mark and Camila a ride down the road and help them find a place to stay for the night.

ED

Well, we've got extra room at our home. We can take you to Merlin after church in the morning.

Mark looks at Camila. No response. Ed looks at Martha.

                    ED

You go in and pay for the gas and this
boy and I will load up the bikes.

Camila looks at Mark. They hesitate. Ed signals to Mark
to help load the bicycles in the truck bed. Martha and
Camila ENTER the store with Hank following.

Hank stops - faces Mark.

                    HANK

You don't have to be afraid of Ed and
Martha here. They about brought me
and my family up.

Hank GOES IN the store. Ed checks the oil. Mark follows Ed - watches.

A beat.

Martha and Camila COME OUT of the store with Hank
FOLLOWING.

                    ED

Climb in here with Martha and me. It's
a couple miles.

                    CAMILA

Can we ride in back? I've never ridden
in the back of a truck.

                    ED

It's against the law, but no one around
here pays attention to that one. Climb
up there.

Camila slips trying to get in back. Looks at Mark to help. Mark is distracted. He watches Ed and Martha.

> CAMILA
> Are you going to help me or what?

Mark jumps into the back - helps Camila climb in.

INT. MOTEL ROOM - CONTINUOUS

Dr. Beck finishes on the phone. He gets up - walks to the curtains - looks out.

INT/EXT. COUNTRY STORE PICKUP - CONTINUOUS

Dr. Beck sees Mark and Camila sit down in the truck bed. Sees Ed and Martha get in the truck. The truck LEAVES.

INT. MOTEL ROOM - CONTINUOUS

Dr. Beck runs to the door, partially clad.

EXT. MOTEL/COUNTRY STORE - CONTINUOUS

Dr. Beck RUNS ACROSS the open area by the gas pumps to catch up to Hank before he enters the store.

> DR. BECK
> Sir, do you know where that pickup is going?

Hank eyes Dr. Beck suspiciously. He looks at Dr. Beck's unbuttoned shirt and unzipped fly on his trousers.

> HANK
> Nope. Never laid eyes on them before.

Dr. Beck turns and runs back to the motel.

EXT. ELDERLY COUPLE'S HOME - PICKUP - NIGHT

The pickup drives up to a small country house. All get out. Ed gestures that the bicycles are safe in the back of the pickup. Mark and Camila climb out with their backpacks.

EXT. ROGUE RIVER CABIN - SUV - NIGHT

Lindy is CARRIED IN by Renee. Miranda follows. Ben unloads the station wagon. He carries suitcases and bags into the cabin.

EXT. ELDERLY COUPLE'S HOME – DAY (MORNING)

A garden, compost containers, old farming implements and other lifelong utilitarian and home built physical structures show how close Ed and Martha are to the land and to their history.

INT. ELDERLY COUPLE'S HOME - BEDROOM - DAY

Mark walks around the room. Looks at pictures on the wall and dresser. Ed ENTERS - watches Mark.

          ED

    Breakfast is ready... That's my son Jason there. He died in Vietnam.

Mark wants to know more. He picks up another picture.

          ED

    That's one of my granddaughters. She lives down the road apiece.

Ed goes over to other photos - points.

> ED
>
> That's my son, John. You'll see him and his family at church today. We're going to have to be hopping along here and we're still going to be late. Come along now.

INT. ELDERLY COUPLE'S HOME - ANOTHER BEDROOM - DAY

Martha and Camila sit on the bed. Camila is looking at pictures of families. Large photos of family gatherings.

> CAMILA
>
> How many children did you and Ed have?

> MARTHA
>
> Five. Two are gone now.

> CAMILA
>
> Wow! You'd never be lonely with all that family.

> MARTHA
>
> There are eleven grandchildren and now six great grandchildren.
>
> Come, we have breakfast ready.

They EXIT.

INT. ELDERLY COUPLE'S HOME - KITCHEN - CONTINUOUS

Mark and Ed are at the table waiting on an old fashioned breakfast. Martha and Camila ENTER. They sit down and Ed offers a prayer. A CHURCH HYMN is HEARD: "In My Heart There Rings a Melody." (page 164, Melodies of Praise, Gospel Publishing House, Springfield, MO., 1957.)

                    ED
> God is great and God is good; let us thank him for this food. And bless Mark and Camila today on their travels back to their parents. Amen.

                    MARTHA
> Jesus, bless our new friends on their journey through all of life. Amen.

EXT. COUNTRY PENTECOSTAL CHURCH - DAY

SAME MUSIC

Ed and Martha's pickup drives up with everyone inside to a COUNTRY CHURCH parking lot.

INT. CHURCH WORSHIPERS - DAY

WORSHIPERS are standing. As they finish the SONG, Ed, Martha, Mark, and Camila ENTER and take seats.

                    PREACHER
> Praise the Lord.

                    SCATTERED WORSHIPERS
> Amen.

The congregation takes their seats after a FEW WORSHIPERS COME OVER and welcome Ed and Martha. A hand or two goes out to Mark and Camila.

> PREACHER
> One announcement. The potluck starts at four-thirty instead of five this afternoon. Don't forget to bring a friend.

The PREACHER bows his head.

> PREACHER
> Let us pray.
>
> Oh Lord, our savior and redeemer, help us in our daily...

EXT. COUNTRY MOTEL/COUNTRY STORE - DAY

Dr. Beck straddles his bicycle. He puts on his helmet - arranges his backpack. RIDES AWAY. A LARGE DIRTY WHITE VAN drives up to the gas pump. A MEAN LOOKING, UNKEMPT MALE DRIVER gets out of the van. Hank ENTERS.

The male driver waits impatiently. The back of the van opens. An EMACIATED, DISHEVELED MOTHER AND DIRTY 4-YEAR-OLD EXIT. TWO OTHER ROUGH LOOKING MEN STEP OUT OF THE VAN.

> THE WOMAN
> You got a bathroom?

Hank points to inside the store.

> MALE DRIVER
> Five dollars' worth.

                    HANK

    That won't get you far in that gas
    burner.

The male driver doesn't respond.

INT. COUNTRY PENTECOSTAL CHURCH - MORNING

The Preacher leans forward on the pulpit/lectern. Mark and Camila sit between Ed and Martha.

                    PREACHER

    The Bible says every one of us shall give
    account of himself to God.

    "For whatsoever a man soweth, that
    shall he also reap."

The church audience can be heard with proclamations of YES and AMEN.

                    PREACHER

    Listen to me, brothers and sisters. On
    earth you can try to escape, but God will
    find you out. Your sins will follow you.
    There is no hiding place. "For the wages
    of sin is death."... God is talking to you.

    God is angry with you. I say to you
    friends, Hell is real. And your first taste
    of Hell is here.

                    (MORE)

PREACHER (CONT'D)
(eyes burning with
conviction)

Hell is lust without love. Hell is selfishness and greed. Hell is hopelessness, and Hell is helplessness.

(Pauses, then continues
in a softer voice)

Do you want to be saved?

The preacher looks up towards heaven.

PREACHER

Thank you Jesus for coming to earth to be here today.

WORSHIPERS

He's here. He's here today.

PREACHER

DO YOU WANT TO BE SAVED? DO YOU WANT TO BE SAVED?

Mark and Camila are in a trance.

WORSHIPERS

Yes, Lord. Yes. Yes.

PREACHER

Believe in the Lord Jesus Christ and you will be saved.

WORSHIPERS

Hallelujah! Thank you Jesus. Praise the Lord.

The Preacher signals the pianist to play and the worshipers to stand. ("Almost Persuaded," page 325, same hymnal). The Worshipers SING AND SWAY to the music.

PREACHER

Can you receive him now? He loves you. He forgives you. Can you come to him now? Let his precious blood wash away your sins and your guilt.

The Preacher comes from the pulpit/lectern and walks among the worshipers - touching hands - shoulders - children's hair.

PREACHER

He is here today... I know. I can feel his spirit.

SCATTERED WORSHIPERS

Yes... Yes... He is here.

The worshipers sway and HUM the melody.

PREACHER

Those of you who are not right with Jesus, come forward now. Not tomorrow, not next Sunday. Now!

Scattered worshipers come forward.

                   PREACHER
    Let us pray for his spirit to move us.
    Brothers and sisters are coming for-
    ward. Will you kneel before me.

Camila, TEARS STREAMING down her cheeks stumbles forward. She kneels with the others (including other children) who have come forward.

                   PREACHER
    They tied Jesus to a post, stripped his
    clothes from his back, then beat him 'til
    blood poured from his flesh.

    Then they took him to the top of a hill
    and nailed his hands and feet to a cross
    and hung him there until he died.

Mark, agitated, can take it no longer. He RUNS OUT of the church. The Preacher puts his hands one by one on the heads to all who are kneeling. Camila is SOBBING. Others are CRYING.

                   PREACHER
    He died for you brother (sister).

    Your sins are forgiven. Go now and sin
    no more.

              SCATTERED WORSHIPERS
    Praise Jesus. Amen. Praise the Lord.

The Preacher gets to Camila, puts his hands around her tearful, wet cheeks.

> PREACHER
> What's your name?

> CAMILA
> Camila.

> PREACHER
> Camila, your sins are forgiven. Go now and sin no more.

Camila gets up - sees Mark has left - goes back to sit with Martha. Martha wipes her own tears away. Then Martha wipes Camila's tears away - squeezes her hand. Camila WHISPERS to Martha.

> CAMILA
> I'll go be with Mark.

Martha nods. Camila THREADS HER WAY through the worshipers. EXITS.

> PREACHER
> Let us sing Hymn 689.

("ONE DAY" from the Original Trinity Hymnal)

EXT. CHURCH GRAVEYARD - CONTINUOUS

Mark walks slowly among the gravestones. Camila APPROACHES. The REFRAIN from the gospel song comes through. They remain quiet as Camila watches Mark. He averts his eyes.

> MARK
> What's it with you?

There's a long pause.

> CAMILA
>
> Wow! I guess I went with the flow.

A beat.

> MARK
>
> You were crying. Do you believe all that Jesus stuff?

> CAMILA.
>
> I don't know. It's a great story.

They slowly walk together among the gravestones. They stop at a gravestone.

> MARK
>
> Look at this. Elizabeth Olness. She was nine years old.

Camila reads from the gravestone.

> CAMILA
>
> "Take her tenderly, Lift her with care. Fashioned so slenderly, young and so fair. Laid to rest 1937."

The hymn has stopped. An ORCHESTRAL RENDERING of the hymn continues. Other than the music, there is silence.

> CAMILA
>
> She was younger than Katy.

> (MORE)

CAMILA (CONT'D)
(a beat)
Why haven't we told our parents the truth?

MARK
About what?

CAMILA
About everything. Our lies about Katy falling into the river... and all the other lies. Letting her get away with climbing that old tree.

Where were you when she got up on top of the cliff?

MARK
Where were you?

Camila starts to CRY.

CAMILA
I never told you before. I was hiding... You were supposed to be with her.

MARK
I thought she was with you.

Ed and Martha APPROACH. Wave to Mark and Camila to come. Camila and Mark slowly LEAVE the graveyard. Camila stops - faces Mark.

CAMILA
I'm over it, Mark.

Mark looks at Camila a long time. Camila turns, walks to Ed and Martha. Mark looks back at the grave - slowly follows Camila.

EXT. CHURCH PARKING LOT - DAY

Cars and trucks DRIVE AWAY FROM THE CHURCH while other worshipers stay and visit. Ed and Martha's RELATIVES are gathered around them. Hugs - CHILDREN PLAY/CHASE each other - LAUGHTER.

Mark and Camila approach the gathering and are greeted like long lost friends. Eventually they get in the truck with Ed and Martha and DEPART as relatives and friends wave their good byes.

EXT. GRAVEL ROAD - PICKUP - DAY

The pickup comes to a stop along the side of the road. All get out. Ed and Mark retrieve the bicycles from the truck bed. Ed shakes Mark's hand and reaches to shake Camila's hand after Martha hugs Camila. Camila hugs Ed as Martha hugs Mark, who accepts the hug, but remains stiff.

The MUSIC FADES OUT as Ed and Martha DRIVE AWAY.

Mark and Camila hurry along on their bicycles. The large dirty white van seen earlier from the country store FOLLOWS at a distance.

> MARK
> There's a road following a creek that takes us to the bridge up ahead. You'll remember when we get close.

> CAMILA
> Slow down. I can't hear you.

Mark stops.

> MARK
> There's a short cut up ahead.

They ride on silently. They turn into a one-lane dirt road.

EXT. ONE LANE DIRT ROAD - DAY

The white van turns off behind them. Suddenly there's a POP. Camila's front tire has blown out.

> MARK
> What was that?

> CAMILA
> My tire blew out.

She tries to ride but it becomes labor intensive.

> CAMILA
> How far?

Mark looks back - gets off his bicycle.

> MARK
> It's still four, five miles. This was stupid not to have a repair kit or tube.

> CAMILA
> You were stupid. I don't know about those things.

MARK

Well, I didn't believe you were going to come along.

CAMILA

Are you sorry?

They walk together, wheeling their bikes.

MARK
(glancing back)
Why doesn't that van go by?

Camila turns around.

CAMILA

Let's hitch a ride.

They pull off the road and wave the van ahead. The van drives slowly up to them - stops. The Male Driver AND SHOTGUN RIDER peer out the driver's window.

MALE DRIVER

Flat tire, huh?

MARK

Yeah. We can walk to the bridge.

MALE DRIVER

What you going to do there?

MARK

Meet our parents.

MALE DRIVER
Hop in. I'll give you a ride.

MARK
(becoming cautious)
We're not going all the way.

CAMILA
We're not?

MALE DRIVER
What you looking for? Mushrooms?

MARK
Go ahead. We can walk.

MALE DRIVER
Your friend there looks beat. I'll drop you off where you want.

Camila silently pleads with Mark. The Male Driver gets out and opens the back. ANOTHER MAN and The Woman holding the 4-year-old sit on a floor of blankets, scattered clothing, dirty pillows, beer cans, and an assortment of junk.

All the van members (late 20s - early 30s) are long-time drug users with an emaciated, irritated physicality. In back the occupants push aside the junk to make room for the bicycles, Mark, and Camila.

Mark hesitates after the bicycles are in, but Camila has already crawled in. Mark follows. The MALE DRIVER SLAMS the van door behind Mark and Camila.

INT. VAN - CONTINUOUS

The driver gets in, looks back - drives on. Mark and Camila sit close together leaning back against their backpacks.

CAMILA
Hi, I'm Camila.

The two sitting on the floor nod their heads.

CAMILA
This is Mark.

They stare at Mark.

CAMILA
What's your boy's name?

THE WOMAN
Charlie.

A beat.

CAMILA
Gosh, it's kind of hot back here.

A beat.

CAMILA
I think I'll get a drink.

Camila opens her backpack - pulls out a water bottle - takes a long drink. She offers Mark a drink. He shakes his head. Camila offers the other two a drink.

Another Man takes the water bottle and drinks. He passes it on to The Woman. She drinks and hands it to the boy who drinks - gives it back to his mother who hands the water bottle back to Camila.

Camila puts the water bottle back in her backpack. Her wallet falls out. She hastily pushes the wallet back in.

Another Man reaches over and taps the driver. The van creeps to a stop.

> ANOTHER MAN
> What else do you have? Got anything to eat?

> CAMILA
> Yeah. We got some chips, candy bars - they've probably melted.

Camila turns to Mark.

> CAMILA
> You still have your jerky?

> MARK
> Looks like you stopped. We can get out here.

The Driver GETS OUT. Another Man eyeballs Camila.

> ANOTHER MAN
> Let's see what you have in your pack.

He reaches over - pulls the backpack towards him. Mark grabs it. There's a TUSSLE.

ANOTHER MAN
(menacing)
Don't do that.

Mark lets the backpack go. Another Man opens it - POURS the contents out. He tosses the wallet to The Woman. She quickly checks it for money. She flashes a couple of twenty-dollar bills to the Shot Gun Rider.

The back of the van OPENS UP. The Male Driver and Shot Gun Rider stand blocking the exit. Another Man reaches over to Mark.

ANOTHER MAN
Hand me yours.

Camila frightened, quickly hands Mark's backpack to the Woman. Mark grabs his backpack back and moves to exit. The Driver leans forward to block Mark. Another Man QUICKLY GRABS the backpack. Mark won't release it. Another Man PUSHES his hand in Mark's face. Mark FORCEFULLY PUSHES the hand away - clutches his backpack and LUNGES towards the back of the van.

MARK
C'mon, Camila.

Camila glances at The Woman, who has already emptied the contents of her backpack and is opening her wallet. Camila follows Mark. Mark gets caught by Another Man. Shot Gun Rider pushes Camila back. Another Man STRIKES Mark with his fist and Mark FIGHTS back. Mark is STRUCK AGAIN and backs off.

Another Man takes Mark's backpack and POURS the contents out on top of Camila's contents from her backpack. Scattered money, maps, and his hunting knife are spread out on the blanket. He hands the money to The Woman. He unsheathes the knife.

     ANOTHER MAN
  Were you going to try to use this on me?

He looks at Mark - then at Camila.

     ANOTHER MAN
  Let's see what the young lady has under
  that sweater.

The Woman pushes the boy aside - leaps forward and grabs the knife from Another Man. The boy begins to CRY.

     THE WOMAN
  You touch her, I'll cut your heart out.
  Throw them out.

Mark and Camila quickly JUMP OUT as The Male Driver and Shot Gun Rider step aside. Mark reaches back and tries to get his bicycle. He gets a FIERCE PUSH from the Driver.

     MALE DRIVER
  Rich kids' bikes.

The Male Driver SLAMS the back door and he and Shot Gun Rider ENTER the van. He quickly turns the van around, almost HITTING Mark and Camila. The van DRIVES OFF the opposite way. The back of the van opens. Backpacks, maps, and other materials are THROWN OUT of the back of the van.

Mark is BLEEDING. He's nursing a sore jaw. He picks up a rock and throws it at the van. Camila comes up behind Mark and puts her arms around him. The van's rear brake lights go on as the van SCREECHES to a halt.

Camila starts CRYING. The van BACKS up. Mark and Camila turn - RUN FOR THEIR LIVES. They run into the woods.

EXT. WOODS - CONTINUOUS

They stop after a few hundred yards and listen.

                MARK
              (winded)
       They've gone. They're too wasted to get out and chase us.

Camila is shaking. She reaches up to Mark - puts her arms around him.

              CAMILA
            (crying)
       I was really scared.

Mark ambivalent, allows Camila to hang on and CRY. He waits - looks around.

              MARK
       C'mon. This path.

They hustle on to the path through the trees. Camila periodically looks back.

EXT. HIGHWAY - DAY

Dr. Beck rides along the highway. The white van DRIVES BY from the opposite way. He drinks water as he rides. He turns on to the same dirt road.

EXT. ROGUE RIVER CABIN - DAY

Ben Trulson et al including Boris and Lindy EXIT the cabin. Renee and Miranda walk to the front yard with Lindy.

>   RENEE TRULSON
>   Nothing's changed. It's as beautiful as ever.

Miranda is emotional.

>   MIRANDA
>   I don't see them.

>   RENEE TRULSON
>   It's early yet, Miranda.

Boris WANDERS OFF.

>   RENEE TRULSON
>   Here, Boris! Boris! You remember, don't you.

>   BEN TRULSON
>   Don't we all.

EXT. FOREST PATH - DAY

MARK and Camila TROT UP the path. Camila stops.

CAMILA
            Here.

MARK trots ahead.

                         CAMILA
            Mark, stop.

MARK stops - turns around - walks back to Camila.

                         CAMILA
            The dead tree. Remember? I'm climbing
            up.

                         MARK
            I wanna to keep going.

                         CAMILA
            Go ahead. I'm gonna see what we left
            that summer.

Mark ambivalent, hesitates - starts walking/trotting as Camila climbs up the aged tree that leans against another pine tree. He stops - turns around - sees Camila halfway up the tree.

FLASHBACK (5 YEARS EARLIER) - MARK'S POV

EXT. WOODS - DEAD TREE - DAY

Camila is coming down off the tree. Katy jumps up and down.

                         KATY
            I want to do it.

                    YOUNG MARK (O.S.)
          You'll fall. I'm tired of getting in trouble
          because of you.

                         KATY
          It's not me, it's you... little bully. Camila,
          get me started.

                    YOUNG CAMILA
          I'm not going to get into your little
          fights.

Katy strikes at the unseen Mark. Katy searches - finds the base. She climbs - gets to the hollow end - reaches over the end - SQUEALS with delight.

                         KATY
             I feel it! I feel it!

FLASHBACK ENDS

EXT. WOODS - DEAD TREE - DAY

Camila gets to the hollow end - pulls out the lunch box.

She starts coming down - drops the lunch box. It breaks open and shells, rocks, homemade necklaces, and bones scatter.

Mark is HYPERVENTILATING - He runs up - stomps on the lunch box of shells, necklaces, bones ,and anything else that's breakable. He turns - breaks into a run on the path to the river. He SCREAMS/ROARS as he runs. Camila hustles down the tree - runs after him.

                        CAMILA
          Mark! I'm sorry. I'm sorry. Wait!

EXT. BOULDERS AND CLIFF - CONTINUOUS

Mark SCREAMING, approaches the boulders along the river at a full run. Camila in fast pursuit.

CAMILA
MARK! STOP!

Dr. Beck APPEARS on the path on his bicycle from the other direction.

DR. BECK
HEY! Mark!

Mark stops - ignores Dr. Beck. He veers off on another path. He TRIPS over a blackberry branch - gets up in a PRIMAL SCREAMING RAGE. Leaves the tangled tennis shoe.

He runs on through the familiar path and boulders. He climbs to the top of the cliff.

EXT. PATH - CONTINUOUS

Camila hesitates - stops - looks at Dr. Beck.

Dr. Beck DROPS his bicycle, pulls off his helmet.

DR. BECK
(SHOUTING)
Mark! Stop! Talk to me.

Boris races by Dr. Beck and Camila. Dr. Beck RACES AFTER Mark. Unseen, Mark has stopped screaming. Camila is SCREAMING:

CAMILA
MOM! MOM!

Miranda YELLS.

> MIRANDA (O.S.)
> Camila! We're coming.

Ben, Miranda, and Renee holding Lindy's hand come running on the path. Camila, CRYING, throws herself into Miranda's arms.

> CAMILA
> It was all my fault.

All hurry on the path through boulders. They climb to the cliff.

EXT. CLIFF - CONTINUOUS

Mark LOOMS above them at the cliff's edge. Boris runs around Mark, BARKING frantically.

EXT. CLIFF'S EDGE - RAGING RIVER - CONTINUOUS

Mark suddenly calm, stands at the cliff's edge. He turns.

MARK'S POV

He faces the SCREAMING PARENTS APPROACHING. He turns back - facing the RAGING RIVER below.

Dr. Beck, CLOSER, SCRAMBLES over the last boulder.

> DR. BECK
> Don't even think it. Your parents are—

END MARK'S POV

Mark whirls in a 360 over the cliff.

Ben ARRIVES - runs to the edge of the cliff. Boris, BARKING, runs by Ben and Dr. Beck.

> BEN TRULSON
> Oh, God!

Ben turns - looks at Dr. Beck.

> BEN TRULSON
> Too late.

Dr. Beck takes off his shoes and socks - steps to the cliff's edge.

> BEN TRULSON
> Doc, that's not smart.

Dr. Beck LEAPS.

> BEN TRULSON
> Oh, Jesus!

The rest of the family ARRIVES.

> BEN TRULSON
> Mark jumped.

Renee sees Dr. Beck's shoes.

> RENEE TRULSON
> Where's Dr. Beck?

Ben RACES OFF down river, SHOUTING:

> BEN TRULSON
> The idiot jumped too.

EXT. UNDERWATER SEQUENCE (3,2)- DAY

Red mixes in with the river water. Everything clouds over. The figure of Molly. Molly comes closer and a hand reaches out to grab Molly entangled in weeds. Everything fades from red to dark and then to a white light.

EXT. RIVER RAPIDS (2) - CONTINUOUS

Mark EXPLODES OUT OF THE RAPIDS GASPING for breath.

INTERCUT ACTION OF RIVERSIDE AND MARK

EXT. RIVER (3) - CONTINUOUS

Boris JUMPS in and out of the water. Mark goes under - comes up again. He hits a rock - his body turns. He grabs the rock - holds on. Then let's go. He goes under.

EXT. UNDERWATER SEQUENCE (2) MARK'S POV - CONTINUOUS

The unconscious, drowning Dr. Beck bumps Mark as he floats by.

END POV

Mark hangs on to the rock. Dr. Beck DISAPPEARS. Mark drops the rock - slowly swims - dives under.

EXT. RIVER'S EDGE (3)- CONTINUOUS

Ben runs along the river's edge - sees/hears Boris BARKING. Mark comes out of the rapids holding Dr. Beck.

> BEN TRULSON
> (SCREAMING)
>
> Renee! He's alive.

Ben races ahead of the raging river - gets ahead of MARK - wades out. Mark swims/wades towards Ben pulling the unconscious, bloody Dr. Beck. Ben reaches out. Mark lets Dr. Beck go. Ben grabs Dr. Beck and pulls him to shore.

Renee wades in to help Mark. Mark goes back into the current with self-destructive intentions.

> BEN TRULSON
> (shouting)
>
> Mark! Over here.

> MARK
>
> No.

Mark glances back at Renee and Lindy. Miranda and Camila ENTER running along the river's edge.

> BEN TRULSON
>
> Mark! For God's sake! Listen!

Ben starts CPR on Dr. Beck, who has a deep bloody gash on his forehead.

EXT. RIVER'S EDGE (3) RENEE - CONTINUOUS

Renee runs downstream after Mark. Boris and Lindy follow.

INTERCUT SCENE

EXT. RIVER'S EDGE (3) BEN - CONTINUOUS

Miranda and Camila RUN UP to Ben and Dr. Beck. Miranda stops to help Ben. Camila hesitates - runs after Renee, Lindy, and Boris.

EXT. RIVERS EDGE (3) RENEE - CONTINUOUS

Camila ARRIVES - grabs Lindy's hand as Renee runs to the edge. Renee wades into the rapids to intercept Mark, who just can't seem to drown himself. Renee SLIPS and FALLS - gets up - goes deeper into the rapids.

> MARK
>
> No!

> RENEE TRULSON
> (SCREAMING)
>
> You want to drown? I'll go with you.

Renee slips again - goes under. Mark swims towards Renee - helps her up. Renee grabs Mark by the shirt - JERKS him. Mark pushes Renee towards shore. They struggle.

When Renee gets her balance. Mark lets go and turns back into the rapids. Renee DIVES for him - gets a good hold of him - SHAKES him with all her might.

Renee SCREAMING - SOBBING - keeps SHAKING Mark.

> RENEE TRULSON
>
> Don't you get it? Katy's dead and we're not. It's over.

SOBBING, Renee wraps her arms around Mark - hugs - drags him to the edge. Camila wades in the water - wraps her arms around both. All SOB.

> LINDY
> Dad's going to be mad, Mark.

EXT. RIVER'S EDGE (3) - DAY

Lindy runs ahead with Boris. Renee, Camila, and Mark walk behind. Renee and Camila each hang on to his arm as they approach Ben, Miranda, and Dr. Beck.

Dr. Beck is sitting up. BEN PROPS HIM from behind. Dr. Beck reaches out his hand to Mark. Mark puts his hand out.

FREEZE FRAME

EPILOGUE WITH THE CREDITS

EXT. TRULSON HOME BACKYARD - SUNSET

Mark turns around to plant another shrub. Renee helps. Ben sits on the love seat reading the newspaper. Lindy in her pajamas, pushes a scooter. Boris rests.

> RENEE TRULSON
> You do good work.

Ben looks over the paper at Mark and Renee - watches.

> RENEE TRULSON
> Can you clean up?

Renee shows her dirty hands. Mark picks up the garden tools and supplies - CARRIES THEM to the garage. Lindy FOLLOWS. Boris FOLLOWS.

INT. GARAGE - CONTINUOUS

Mark puts the tools against a tool rack.

Ben ENTERS - brings a forgotten tool.

>BEN TRULSON
>You missed one.
>
>>(looks at the tool
>>rack)
>
>Is that the best you can do?

Mark does it right. Mark WALKS IN the house. Lindy drops the scooter - RUNS AFTER HIM. Boris FOLLOWS.

INT. KITCHEN - NIGHT

Mark washes his hands in the kitchen sink - slops water around. Renee WALKS BY.

>RENEE TRULSON
>Clean up after yourself.

Renee DISAPPEARS to the bathroom.

>RENEE TRULSON (O.S.)
>Can you put Lindy to bed? Her teeth are brushed.

>MARK
>I was gonna check out some tunes.

Mark wipes his hands - throws the towel on the counter. Looks at the towel. Hangs it up. Drinks a glass of water.

                LINDY
    Mark, read me a story.

Mark doesn't answer.

                LINDY
    You can pick the story.

                MARK
    No, you pick the story.

                LINDY
    Mark, it's your turn.

A beat.

Mark turns.

                MARK
    Mom, do we have any children's Bible
    stories around?

            RENEE TRULSON (O.S.)
    Yeah. On the bottom shelf - next to that
    group of Native American stories.

Lindy RUNS to her bedroom. Ben stands looking at Mark.

                MARK
    What are you lookin' at?

Ben smiles.

Ben opens the refrigerator. Lindy TROTS IN with a book of Bible stories. Lindy grabs Mark's hand and DRAGS HIM to the living room.

INT. LIVING ROOM - NIGHT

Lindy hops on the couch. Mark sits down beside his sister. Lindy hands Mark the book. Mark pages through it.

> MARK
> (loudly)
> Some of these stories ought to be R-rated for violence.

> LINDY
> Mark? Can I sit in your lap?

> MARK
> Yeah, I guess.

Lindy hops on Mark's lap.

Mark reads.

> MARK
> "How David became the king of Israel.
>
> "There was a shepherd boy named David."

> LINDY
> Move your hand. I can't see the picture.

>>> FADE OUT.

THE END

THE ORIGINS OF OTHER WORKS IN PROGRESS

Below are other projects currently in various stages of development. *Blood Atonement,* a low budgeted psychological horror drama has seed money to move forward to preproduction April 2019, and production in Southern Oregon in October/November 2019.

My next book, *Non-Official Cover (NOC) Confessions,* will be submitted for publication later this year.

But first, a little autobiographical history.

At twenty years of age, while in training as a Navy pilot in Corpus Christi, Texas, I decided there were two things I wanted to do professionally in my life. One was to teach psychology at a college while maintaining a small practice as a clinical psychologist.

The other was to become a filmmaker. Either way I hoped to live in Ashland, Oregon and raise a family.

I became a university teacher (Southern Oregon University) and clinical psychologist first. I retired as professor emeritus in 1997 and closed my clinical practice in 2009.

I attended USC Film School during the 1970s. Not wanting to leave southern Oregon, my only option to pursue filmmaking was to begin writing screenplays in my spare time.

My dream was also to become a director of film scripts I wrote that went into production.

My first movie as a writer/director is a feature length psychological drama: *Raspberry Heaven*.

Watch Raspberry Heaven (Amazon Instant Video) with your friends.

With *Raspberry Heaven* and my current projects, and products in various phases of development, I have recognized that I cannot escape my life as a psychologist. I have spent my life living in the midst of the conscious and unconscious contradictions of others and myself. I have observed and experienced how the verities of love, sex, friendship, and belonging get twisted by fears of intimacy, inadequacy, rejection, estrangement, and, finally, the loss of control over our own lives. Thus, there are autobiographical elements in *Raspberry Heaven.* If psychological realism and truthfulness in human actions are what you're looking for in a movie, you'll find it in all projects I'm currently working on.

BLOOD ATONEMENT

Genre: Psychological/horror drama, low budget independent production.

Logline: During a weekend retreat to Bad Medicine Lake, eight paranormal seers, seekers, and deniers challenge Dr. Manion, a research psychologist, on whether the power of faith and prophecy can defy reason and validate that we exist in a parallel universe.

Synopsis: Dr. Manion, a research psychologist has received a generous Foundation Grant to attempt to validate whether the five primary emotions of Happiness, Anger, Sadness, Apprehension, and Confusion can be transported over distance by mind alone. His associate, Lin Li, a parapsychology doctoral student from Edinburgh University, Scotland, is completing her research on Remote Viewing, the paranormal ability to perceive an emotion or event from a distance by mind alone. She assisted Dr. Manion in the selection and screening of the accepted applicants for the research to begin after a "getting to know you" retreat.

Clay, wall street broker; Azo, a Haitian healer; Max, a magician and ventriloquist; Chrystal, a survivor of a near-death experience; Ahmed, a student of Islamic faiths, ancestor worship, and Egyptian symbology; Sandy, an otherworld astrologist; and John, a reluctant participating son, with an identical brain-damaged twin, prepare after introductions, to bus with Dr. Manion and Lin Li to Bad Medicine Lake.

As a bonding experience at the retreat, Dr. Manion conducts a spiritual and ceremonial Fire Walk to demonstrate the power of mind as a transformative power over the physical universe. Ed Winston, ex-English professor/alcoholic dropout from academia and longtime property and caretaker, prepares the fire pit with the help of Miguel, cook and unauthorized illegal Latino immigrant. As bystanders, they contrast with the otherworld seekers with their own mythology.

The clash of competing beliefs unfolds with a turn of events that thwart escape from the unearthly demonic vibrations at the lake that shake each participant's will to survive.

Will the denouement of this story challenge you to look again at what creates meaning for your psychological survival in a world that has become twisted by so many alternate views of reality?

(Screenplay is registered with WGAW)

NON-OFFICIAL COVER (NOC) CONFESSIONS
BOOK 1

January 1, 1957. For a while, I followed my brother and became a Navy pilot. I loved flying. I was good at flying. Yet I committed one of my biggest acts of defiance, essentially telling Admiral Robert Goldthwaite (in his office), the Vice Admiral Chief of Naval Aviation Operations in Corpus Christi, Texas, to shove the Navy up his ass. I told him that I was refusing my wings and commission unless he changed my orders away from flying multiengine aircraft. I had been given the promise to fly the A-4D Skyhawk off carriers. They deliberately hid my orders, knowing I would resist what amounted to drawing names from a bowl of newly commissioned pilots to fly supplies to Lebanon. Next week was graduation to become an "Officer and Gentleman" with wings and commission. The Admiral said I couldn't run the Navy and wouldn't have the guts to give up the $100,000 plus training and the elitist recognition I would get as a Navy/Marine Corp pilot. I followed through and refused my wings and commission.

If I had taken my wings and commission in late 1958, I was required to serve as an officer and pilot for six more years. That would have brought me into the action in Vietnam as a pilot. Now I can relive what may have been a real experience by creating a fantasy story. To add to the fantasy, I spent time at Berkeley and on Haight Ashbury Street in San Francisco in the late 1960s and early 1970s. I also discovered McNamara's secret CIA war in Laos.

Rather, than go back to school to major in psychology; I fooled around with going into the CIA. Using my desire to survive in life, I took the safe academic route.

That gave me freedom to plunge into research and into my fantasy life as a CIA agent and pilot in Vietnam and Laos (Book 1), and later, (Book 2) in South and Central America.

———————————————————

Acknowledgements

My thanks to Luminare Press staff, from manuscript and book cover assistance to final book publication; Z.S. Liang, book cover images; Eugene Field: Wynken, Blynken and Nod; and the composers and publishers of heartwarming Christian hymns cited in the screenplays.

Support filmmaking in southern Oregon. Help make these screenplays a movie reality.

 David Oas
Retired Professor emeritus Southern Oregon University 1997
Retired Clinical psychologist 2009
Research: Aging and mild cognitive impairment (MCI) and Dementia and Alzheimer's disease.
www.screeningformemoryloss.com

Film: University of Southern California Film School 1970s: *Raspberry Heaven.*
Amazon Instant Video Writer/producer/director
www.raspberry-heaven.com
www.roguefilmsandbooks.com

Contact information
davidoas@mind.net
www.raspberry-heaven.com
www.roguefilm/bookproductions.com
Facebook and Twitter

www.ingramcontent.com/pod-product-compliance
Lightning Source LLC
LaVergne TN
LVHW011926070526
838202LV00054B/4512